Continuity Slip

Till Noever

FIRST EDITION

ISBN: 1-4116-5676-8

Copyright © 2005 by Till Noever

All rights reserved. Reproduction or utilization of this work in any form, by any means now known or hereafter invented, including xerography, photocopying and recording, and in any known storage and retrieval system, is forbidden without written permission from the copyright holder.

Cover design and art: Till Noever

Continuity Slip is a work of fiction. Any resemblance between the characters depicted herein and any persons living or dead would be coincidental.

www.owlglass.com

*To my wife and daughters,
for everything, as always...*

Friday

1.

The world reclaimed Ray's full and undivided attention with a drawn-out, high-pitched screech of tires that descended the scale and suddenly broke off. Ray glanced into the rear-vision mirror, at an angry face, and a middle finger jabbing upward sharply.

He made an apologetic gesture. The driver behind him shook his head. The mouth moved. Ray's imagination supplied the uncomplimentary subtext. The car pulled into the lane next to him and accelerated away.

Damn!

Where'd that car come from? How could he possibly have missed it on such a straight piece of road?

He'd looked! He *always* did. Distracted or not. Checking for traffic when pulling out of the business park was an automatic action, requiring no conscious control or effort.

"Bullshit". He could almost *hear* Debbie say it. "You just weren't paying attention!" Something along those lines. Ray was pathetically grateful that she wasn't with him right now. She was getting very impatient with his current state of mind—or what, according to her, was left of it.

Case in point: the reason why he was leaving work so early today.

Dinner at the Jackson's. On a Friday, for goodness' sake! They hadn't gone out on a Friday for years!

He'd be damned if he could remember anything about it!

"I told you last week."

She might have.

"Do you actually listen to anything I say?"

"Of course, I do!"

"Nothing 'of course' about it!" Followed by a list of recent and no-so-recent failures-to-pay-attention.

Ray sighed and changed lanes, threading the car into the stream of vehicles heading for the I-285. This time he looked twice before he made his move. Maybe Debbie was right. Maybe he *was* stressed out of his mind. But the next release of *Wild Worlds* was due out at the end of the month, and there was still a shitload of work. Ray, like most software developers, took his work with him wherever he went; if not always in a physical sense, then at least in spirit; constantly distracting thoughts bouncing forth and back somewhere in his mind; interfering with the smooth running of his social interactions—including those involving his wife of eleven years.

Again—and this thought had been on his mind a lot over the last few weeks and months—he was grateful that there weren't any children in the marriage. It simply wouldn't have worked. It was hard enough to make it function as it was. With kids to add to the demands, it probably would have self-nuked some time ago.

Tiredly he rubbed his free hand over his scalp; feeling the stubble left behind by his recent visit to the hairdresser. Premature hair loss disguised not-so-cunningly by clear-felling. Quite embarrassing, really, how he was losing it even faster than his father—who at the age of sixty-eight still had twice as much hair on his head than his son had at forty one.

Rays father had died in a car crash.

Remember that!

As he approached the on-ramp to the I-285, Ray slowed down; disoriented by something he couldn't define, disrupting the familiar patterns of his life. Another anomaly in this day of subtly alienating snags.

Then he figured it out—and he almost lost control over the car.

Two lanes?

What?!

It jerked him into the present.

Easy, man!

Had he day-dreamed himself past his usual turn?

Couldn't be. The landmarks told him that he was exactly where he thought he was. Halcyon Business Park to his left; just as it should be. Except that, at least as far as he remembered it—from using it for a mere four-odd years—this ramp only had *one* lane!

Unless they'd done the work of months in one night!

Yeah, right.

You could always tell a new piece of road from an old one. This one had become grimy and shiny with the passage and wear of uncounted vehicles. And the sign he'd just passed under: stained by exhaust gases and bird-shit and punctured by a dozen or so small-caliber bullet holes, especially around the 'O's. The boys doing target practice with .22 caliber rifles at night, when the cops were busy in the inner city.

Ray swallowed hard and took a couple of deep breaths to calm himself. He managed to keep enough of his attention on the traffic to file onto the ramp and merge, at its bottom, with the steel-plastic-and-rubber avalanche flowing along the I-285 at a treacly thirty-something miles per hour. There wasn't that much traffic, but what there was progressed with tired viscosity.

Must be the heat.

Ray looked at his hands, clamped vise-like around the steering-wheel. He willed himself to relax them, took the right hand off the wheel and held it horizontally before his eyes.

It shook; jerking to the tune of uncontrollably firing nerves.

Debbie *was* right. Time to lay off the late nights, stale coffee and endless staring at computer screens and simulated critters. When he got to the stage that he was freaked out by his non-existent memory of double lanes, which had probably been there forever, and...

They had been, hadn't they?

Of course.

Ray shook his head.

Of course!

Except that...

Don't go there!

Except, he had to. Because it wasn't just an isolated memory of a single-lane on-ramp, but a whole context of stuff supporting it. Cars piling up in long queues between the lights at the intersection and the ramp. More than once he'd *wished* there'd be another lane, of course...but there never was...

Or had he been dreaming that?

Which part?

It looked like something was telling him to get his act together. Crisis-situation time.

John wasn't going to like it, of course: not now, just before an already-late beta-release. Still, it wasn't going to do anybody any good if Ray blew a fuse. He'd talk to Debbie tonight; after the agony of meeting the Jacksons had abated.

The traffic again reclaimed Ray's full attention. A bright-red convertible Japanese two-seater nudged into the two or three car-lengths he'd left between himself and the Pontiac in front of him. Ray shook his head. Lots of pain without much gain. In this treacle nobody was going anywhere in a hurry.

The driver of the sporty Jap was a woman. Her short, dark hair fluttered in the slipstream. Ray thought that she might have turned her head briefly to look into the mirror. Just checking that the guy whose space she'd just invaded wasn't too pissed off about it. Or maybe hoping that he was. After all, the territorial instinct wasn't a male preserve. And what was he to her but another competitor for freeway space? A pain in he ass. Surplus humanity.

Despite this Ray allowed himself a brief bout of daydreaming, where the world wasn't like it was at all, and the woman ahead of him had actually seen him as more than just a face in another car.

He caught her looking in the mirror again. Or maybe it just appeared that way. Hard to tell with the wraparound shades she was wearing. Another bit of the daydream. Suppose she *had* looked... Not that she'd be interested; not that she *should* be. He was, after all, married, unavailable and certainly not in the market for flings, no matter how tempting. Besides, the likelihood that she'd even *think* of being interested was so vanishingly small as to turn even the daydream into his own private embarrassment.

Ray cringed inwardly and told himself to stop being such a pathetic loser and get a life. Of course, thoughts and daydreams were free, but this was the kind of juvenile crap one should've left behind with one's teens. But the stress at work during the last few months, the general boredom everywhere else in his life: it all combined to put him into a curiously inside-out state of mind. Maybe that's why he was forgetting things he should remember, and remembering things which, according to Debbie, simply hadn't happened.

Ray tried to force his morbid reflections into other channels and eased up on the accelerator to widen the gap between him and the woman to a safe size. He wasn't in the mood for freeway games.

A flicker of motion in his peripheral vision.

His foot slid off the accelerator and onto the brake.

Just in time. The metallic blue Ford was just...*there*. Bang! Out of nowhere. Like it had materialized out of thin air.

The vehicle careened into Ray's lane ahead of him and impacted on the red convertible. The collision threw the woman's car against the concrete center partition. The Ford bounced back from the impact, out of control. Its tires squealed as it spun around. It bounced off another car a couple of lanes to the right and came Ray's way again. The convertible rebounded from its impact with the concrete wall. The two vehicles crunched into each other again. Around and behind Ray a cacophony of brakes being slammed on and tires squealing on the hot asphalt.

The Ford bounced back into the adjacent lane, and caused havoc on that side. The convertible crashed into the barrier again, spun around once more and came to rest. Ray, seeing that there was no way he was going to stop in time, instinctively swerved around the red car. Somehow, miraculously, he missed the car right next to him, felt the Toyota swerve, caught it, regained his lane just on the other side of the convertible. Ahead of him, the cars unaffected by the disaster were drawing away from the scene. His way was free. He just had to put his foot down, and it would be as if the whole thing had never happened. A brief shock, soon forgotten.

Talk about lucky escapes! *And* he would be home on time. Those poor bastards behind him were going to be there for a long time.

Ray hit the brakes: hard. The Toyota came to a screeching halt. Ray jerked the automatic's control stick into 'R' and, with the gearbox howling under the strain, reversed all the way back along the now-empty lane to the scene of the crash. A few seconds later he slammed on the brakes again, jammed the stick into 'P', turned off the engine and got out of the car.

What am I doing?

He surveyed the scene of the collision. The red convertible blocked the lane, crunched up on all sides. Considering the battering it had taken it didn't look too bad. A write-off, but not the wreck Ray had expected. The woman hung limply in her seat belt. The blue Ford, equally mangled, blocked the other two lanes; surrounded by the cars it had taken with it to an early retirement. Ray couldn't see the driver.

The crash had propagated along the lines of now-stopped cars like a shockwave. There would be hundreds of insurance claims. A few of the other drivers, still dazed from the suddenness of it all, were also getting out of their cars. For some the shock was mingling with anger. Ray could hear their voices, complaining about the inconvenience of it all.

He looked back at the woman, suspended in her seat-belt. She'd been lucky: if her car had flipped over she would have been crushed.

His nostrils registered an acrid smell.

Gas!

He looked down, saw a wetness pooling underneath the convertible and seeping across the road surface, spreading quickly and with ominous inevitability. The stench became overpowering. Ray crossed the distance to the convertible and, seeing that the door was twisted and jammed, vaulted into it. He reached down and unbuckled her belt. With nothing to hold her up the woman slumped sideways. Ray placed his hands under her armpits and heaved. She moaned weakly.

The reek of gas was getting stronger. The fluid was rapidly spreading across the hot asphalt, vaporizing almost as quickly as it leaked out of the tank.

Ray heaved again. Then he realized that she was stuck. He bent down and saw one foot jammed under the brake pedal. Its angle told him that the ankle was either sprained or broken. He released the body and she slumped back. Ray bent forward to reach down along her legs to free her foot. When he touched it she moaned again; louder this time. Ray ignored it and manipulated the foot out from underneath the brake pedal. He straightened and pulled under her arms again.

A soft cry. He looked into her face and saw that her eyes were open; glazed over with pain, but apparently conscious.

"You've got to get out of here!" he said urgently. "Now!"

He pulled again. Her inert body was heavy and unwieldy.

"Help me!" he snapped.

She moaned again.

"Do you want to die? Help me!"

Somehow, through the haze of pain, she must have understood his urgency. Her arms ceased to hang limp. She reached up and wrapped them around his neck. Ray leaned back and gave another heave. She was a tall. It took a lot to get those legs out from under the dashboard.

Then she was free. He bent down, picked her up under her arms and legs and lifted her up, holding her across his chest. Her weight and the precarious footing on the carseat almost made his lose his balance, but somehow he didn't. He turned, stepped on the side of the car, felt it rock underneath him, and, with her holding onto him tightly, jumped onto the road surface—and straight into the spreading gas stain. Ray didn't wait to contemplate the situation too closely. He just ran, as fast as he could with the additional weight in his arms bouncing up and down. Somewhere in the back of his mind he congratulated himself for his twice-weekly workouts in the gym.

Finally, at what seemed like a safe distance, he stopped and turned around. The Atlanta afternoon summer sun beat down mercilessly. The blood was singing in his ears. Perspiration was pouring down his forehead, his back and just plain everywhere. His breath came in gasps. The body in his arms weighed a ton. But he couldn't put her down: not yet anyway.

He saw people standing around the scene—staring at him standing there, gaping with morbid fascination.

Idiots! Didn't they realize that they were far too close? Even here the reek of gas was strong, the hot freeway air an explosive mix of fumes.

He backed off even further and opened his mouth to shout a warning.

Too late.

A dull hiss. A muffled *THUD*.

The air was fire.

Instinctively, Ray put his face down, close to her, to shield himself from the worst. He felt her arms tighten around him and her face bury itself against his neck. The heat wave washed over them and nearly made him lose his balance again. He could almost feel the hairs on his head, his face, the back of his hands and arms, being singed away in that one brief moment. Instinctively, he refrained from inhaling.

But mercifully the light breeze was blowing the highest concentrations of the gas away from them and into the faces of the gawkers on the other side. The screams from over there told him that they hadn't been so lucky.

There was nothing he could do but to back off even further. He'd taken only a few steps when the red convertible's gas tank blew up.

Another explosion: the blue Ford.

The screams and wails from behind the wall of flame redoubled, became a cacophony of agony and suffering. Ray tightened his grip on the woman and did his best to bring more distance between himself and the disaster scene. When he thought it was safe he stopped.

She lifted her face from his shoulder. For the first time they looked at each other closely. Her dark brown eyes were wild, desperate, questioning. Her eyelashes and eyebrows had been singed into withered curled-up stumps. The ends of the hair on her head had shriveled and curled into tiny spirals at the end; like the sprouts of ferns.

It stank!

But she was alive—as was he.

Behind him yet another explosion. He looked around. It was his own car, now enveloped in flames; adding to the pall of thick, black smoke rising high into the clear sky. Instinctively Ray backed off even further.

He saw her staring at the scene.

"Did *I* do that?" she whispered.

"No," he said. "You had nothing to do with it."

She looked at him, her eyes searching and troubled. "How do you know?"

"I was right behind you," he told her.

"That was *you*?" She exhaled and relaxed minutely. "Thank you," she said softly. "Thank you for my life."

Ray shrugged; suddenly embarrassed and acutely aware that he was holding a woman in his arms; in an awkward position, to be sure, and there were good reasons for doing what he was doing. But it was still a woman, and a beautiful one at that.

And she wasn't his wife.

Which reminded him that he was going to be late after all!

"I don't want to put you down," he said to her. "Not with that ankle. But..."

"I'll be fine."

"Sure?"

She tried to smile, but it was more of a grimace. She winced. "No; but I'll try."

He let her down. She made a small sound of pain as her foot shifted. He leaned her against the concrete barrier, supporting her on one side; then unbuttoned his left shirt pocket and took out a slim cellphone, hoping that it hadn't been damaged.

He looked up at the wall of flame. The screams grated on his senses. Someone would surely have dialed 911 by now. Ray hesitated for a moment, then pressed the speed-dial code for his home.

He got his own answering machine. Debbie was probably in the shower, getting ready to go out. He left a message detailing his plight and broke the connection.

"I'm Alyssa."

"Ray."

"Good to meet you, Ray."

"Same here," he said and held up the phone. "Need to call anybody?"

She nodded. "Thanks." She took the phone and dialed. From what she said it sounded like a call to her office. A meeting would have to be missed. She finished the call and gave the phone back to him.

"Thanks."

She winced softly. Her breath came in short, painful bursts. Ray kicked away a few bits of debris thrown against the barrier: Coke cans; a crumbled cigarette pack; bits of glass and concrete. He helped her to sit down and did the same himself. He leaned his back against the concrete. This side was turned away from the afternoon sun and had cooled down already. It felt good. Sitting down like this also got them out of the sun, which did wonders for his exposed skin, which felt like it was on fire. Gingerly he touched his face—and took them away immediately.

Alyssa leaned over and looked at him. "You all right?"

He nodded. "Singed."

She touched a light finger to his cheeks, and surprisingly it didn't feel half a bad as it had when he'd touched it himself. "I'm sorry you got hurt. I really don't know how to thank you."

He shook his head. "Don't."

She hesitated, searching for words. "Why?" she asked.

"Why what?"

"Why did you stop?"

He tried to grin, but found that it hurt; so he didn't.

"I don't know," he answered truthfully. He took a couple of deep breaths. "You ever have that feeling…like that everything kind-of just holds together, and that, no matter what you want or think or feel, there's only one thing you actually can *do*?" He wasn't too sure he understood it himself. "Well, it was a bit like that. I was going to just go on. If I had, I'd be most of the way home by now." He shrugged. "But… Oh, I don't know."

Alyssa said nothing and they sat in silence for a few moments. From their right the hissing sounds of the fire and the shouts and screams beyond it. Ray thought guiltily that he should be doing *something* to help; but when he looked at the solid wall of fire and black smoke he realized that he couldn't have even if he'd wanted to.

"Ray?"

"Yes?"

His cellphone beeped.

"Excuse me." He held it to his ear. "Hello?"

"Are you all right?" Debbie, sounding anxious.

"I'm fine. A bit crisp around the edges. The car's a write-off. Otherwise nothing to worry about."

"Are you hurt?"

"I'm now *completely* bald, but so what?"

"What happened?"

He gave her a stripped-down summary. "I'll call you from the hospital," he finished. "Once I know where they're taking me."

An afterthought: "I guess you'd better tell the Jacksons."

There was a minute pause at the other end. "Why?"

"Tell them I'm sorry. Higher force and all that."

"What have the Jacksons got to do with it?"

"We're going to be late."

"What are you talking about?"

Suddenly Ray felt even worse than he had.

"We're seeing them tonight. Right?"

"Not the Jacksons! We're having dinner with Michelle and Bob!"

Shit!

Ray swallowed hard. "Sorry," he said into the phone. "I'm just…confused, I guess."

"You sure you're all right?" she said dubiously.

"Yeah," he said soothingly. "It's been a long day—and now this shit. Anyway, tell them I'm sorry about the delay."

"Do you feel like doing this at all?"

Of course not!

"Yeah, sure. I told you: I'm not hurt. Just had my hair singed off. I probably look like some terminal chemo-case right now."

He glanced at Alyssa, who was tactfully pretending that she wasn't listening to the conversation. She saw his look and understood the silent question in his eyes. Her inspection was wry, but sympathetic.

Yeah, chemo-case.

"Well," came Debbie's voice, "if you're sure…"

"I'm sure. I'll call you as soon as I know where they'll be taking me."

"Be careful."

"Of course. Talk to you soon."

He disconnected and put the phone down.

"Everything all right?" Alyssa asked him.

Again he tried to smile, but stopped himself when the sensitive skin on his face screamed in pain.

"I guess so. Unless you consider the possibility that I may be losing my mind, of course."

"What makes you think that?"

"Oh, I don't know. Lots of things. Today especially. Maybe it's premature aging. Alzheimer's at forty three. I suppose it happens."

She studied him carefully. "You're joking. Right?"

He shrugged. "I don't know." He shook his head firmly to discourage her from saying anything that couldn't have been any more meaningful than what anybody could possibly have said. Alyssa, to his relief, picked up on his mood. She nodded and leaned back against the concrete.

Ray closed his eyes and did the same. From somewhere off to his left, coming from the direction of the empty freeway, a far-off symphony of sirens; from somewhere else, the characteristic clatter of a helicopter or two.

2.

They were taken to Crawford Long Hospital. There was a shortage of ambulances, so they had to double up. Ray managed to catch a ride in the ambulance carrying Alyssa and another victim of the accident. Like most of the other victims, this one had been caught unawares when the gas-soaked air had ignited around him. The inferno had peeled the skin off his face and melted the synthetic fabric of his shirt into the skin of his torso. The reek of burned flesh and plastic in the ambulance was overpowering. The victim was hooked up to an IV. A thick layer of jelly covered his face and exposed body. On top of that a layer of a thin, transparent film, wrapping the poor bastard up like a giant Christmas ham, cooked and ready to eat. A ventilator mask perched on the blotchy face, covering nose and mouth. A bunch of wires attached to pads on the guy's gooey chest led to a monitor above the stretcher. A paramedic watched patient and monitor with a skeptical expression. He clearly didn't expect the victim to survive the trip to the hospital.

Ray averted his eyes from the pre-cooked lump of humanity and concentrated on holding Alyssa's hand. He knew what she was thinking. They'd been the lucky ones. What he didn't know was why he was holding her hand. Mutual reassurance maybe.

At the hospital he and Alyssa were separated. Ray squeezed her hand one last time as they wheeled her away.

"Take care," he said.

"And you."

A doctor examined him and told him that he'd been lucky. He could have lost his eyes. His skin, the doctor told him, would be raw for some time to come. But it was just short of a serious burn and there was no need to keep him here.

The doctor left. A nurse came and applied a layer of jelly to Ray's face and head. "This'll help your skin retains its moisture and speed up the healing process. It'll also stop infections. You'll be glistening for a while, but that's all. Come in again in three or four days and we'll check it out."

She gave him a tube of the stuff. "Here. Keep your skin moist. That's really important, you understand?"

Ray thanked her, then finally got around to calling Debbie. She asked him again if he was sure about tonight. He told her he was. She sounded relieved. He guessed that his insistence on proceeding with their plans indicated to her that he was all right. Beside—as she had pointed out earlier in the day—she'd been planning this visit for a long time.

Ray was still mulling that one over. How could she have planning this visit for so long—if they'd seen Bob and Michelle only a couple of weeks ago?

Never mind.

"See you in half an hour," Debbie said.

"All right."

He broke the connection and called the police; explained who he was. They wanted to know if he had been involved in the crash. He told them 'no', but he'd been as close as could be.

Less than ten minutes later a couple of officers appeared in the waiting room to take his statement. He gave them a complete description of what he'd seen, which they recorded on a small hand-held tape-deck. One of them also scribbled brief notes on a small pad.

Did he know the name of the woman he'd pulled out of the car?

Ray shook his head. Actually, he didn't. They'd never gotten past first names. But she was here somewhere having her ankle attended to.

The officers thanked him and told him that he might be needed for a more formal testimony. As they left, Debbie came in. She took one look at him and paled.

He smiled thinly. "*That* bad?"

She sat down beside him and hugged him gingerly, taking care not to touch his jellyfied surfaces. Debbie was always fastidious about things like that; especially when she wore clothes she cared about. She stood back and subjected his glistening face and head to the intense scrutiny usually reserved for icky creepy-crawlies. She was trying to hide it, but he knew her too well.

"Poor darling!" she said compassionately.

Feeling like some injured pet, Ray shrugged. "I'm fine. Honestly. You should have seen the others."

She looked at the door. "What did the police want?"

"I was very close to the accident. Saw it all. Well—just about."

"Will you have to go to court?" Debbie had a proclivity toward the practical. Courts would mean extra inconvenience that she could really do without, thank you very much.

"Don't know," he said. "Whatever..."

He got up, debating with himself whether to check on Alyssa. Something in him really wanted to, but wisdom dictated otherwise. He had an inkling that Debbie would not be amused.

"Let's go," he said

"You sure you're OK to see Michelle and Bob like...this?"

"As long as *they* don't mind."

Debbie looked at him dubiously. "You look... strange."

Ray shook his head. "Never mind. Let's go home. I need a shower. After that... well, I don't think I'll have to put on this stuff quite a thick as the nurse did." He chuckled. "Besides, it'll give us something to talk about tonight. Fill in the gaps of the conversation."

She hesitated. Her mouth worked, as if to say something. Then she shrugged and nodded.

An orderly came in and wheeled him out through the front entrance. Ray was glad when he was out of the place. He got out of the wheelchair, thanked the orderly, and followed Debbie across the road to the parking lot where she'd left her car. As he followed her in the hot late Atlanta afternoon, he again wondered how Alyssa was doing. He also knew that he would do nothing to find out and that it would be prudent to play down this particular aspect of today's events.

When he saw Debbie's car he suddenly remembered his own. It was probably burned to a revolting black mess of steel, paint, and plastic. He'd better report it to his insurance company, if he wanted them to cough up the thousands of dollars they owed him now.

There goes my no-claim bonus!

3.

Alyssa saw her savior's figure stand motionlessly as they wheeled her out of his sight. She gave him a small wave which he returned. Then a pair of swinging doors closed on him and that was that. She stopped straining and relaxed; allowed her gaze to roam across the ceiling sliding past over her as they wheeled her into a small treatment room. A masked face leaned over her. Two blue eyes considered her carefully. Presently a hand, encased in a smooth surgical glove, reached out and carefully touched her right cheek. The touch was painful and she flinched. The head nodded. The mouth moved behind the mask, lending it the appearance of some surreal talking fish.

"It'll be sore for a few days; but you should be fine. We'd better look at that ankle though."

The face moved away. Somebody prodded at the bruised and swollen ankle.

Fish-face reappeared.

"We're going to take some X-rays—and then we'll see what needs to be done. I think you may have been lucky. No fracture—just a sprain. Still, we have to make sure."

Three hours later, after several tests and procedures, sporting a removable ankle-brace and with good prospects for a speedy recovery, her friend, colleague, and apartment-sharer, Susan, helped Alyssa out of Crawford Long and into a sticky Atlanta evening.

"Lean on me. I'm a strong girl. You can practice with those crutches later."

Alyssa grinned painfully. Despite the gel on her face, any contortion was pain.

"Home?" Susan asked her.

"Definitely," Alyssa told her. "I want a long shower. And then I want to go out and have an expensive dinner. My treat."

Susan, a petite brunette with an attractive dash of Latin ancestry, laughed. There was more than just a touch of relief in the sound.

"I agree," she said. "We'll celebrate until we drop. Want me to call the gang?" The 'gang' being their little clique of friends: the ones they hung out with when nothing more interesting was up. Which it usually wasn't.

Alyssa shook her head. "You haven't told them, have you?"

"You said not to."

Alyssa craned her neck to look at her friend. "When did you start paying attention to what I say?"

Susan chuckled. "This time you sounded like you meant it."

Alyssa nodded thoughtfully. She had. Strange that. But it was true: she didn't want a lot of company tonight. Just Susan was fine. Just one person to talk to. Go and quietly celebrate of the fact that she was alive and comparatively healthy, when she should have been a fried corpse—or, even if she had survived the inferno, mutilated for life.

And the only thing that had stood between her and either of those possibilities—'certainties' was more like it!—had been Ray. A nobody. A faceless entity in a car. Someone whom, had she laid eyes on him anywhere in a crowd, she would have dismissed without a second glance. Hell, she wouldn't even have noticed he was there. Like one didn't notice the vast majority of people. Like nobody really noticed anybody but those who, for some reason or other, attracted one's closer attention.

Well, Ray certainly had attracted hers. He'd emerged from the anonymity of the masses to become, for just a few short moments, the single most important person in her life. And then he had disappeared again; just like that; without leaving so much as his last name.

"What's the matter, Lys?"

Alyssa looked at her friend. "I don't know. Aftershocks?"

Susan nodded sympathetically. "It's all right. You don't have to come into work on Monday. I've already talked to Horrie."

"It's not *that*."

"Close encounters with death?" Susan suggested.

They had stopped in front of her car. Susan unlocked the door.

"I suppose so."

Alyssa lowered herself into the passenger seat. Susan tucked the crutches into the backseat.

"Mid-life crisis coming a decade early?" Susan plonked herself into the driver's seat and started the engine.

Alyssa gave her a nudge with her elbow. "I wouldn't put it quite that way!"

Susan shrugged. "That's what it is, my friend. Some people have to wait into middle age until fate delivers its shakabuku. You had the privilege of getting it at thirty two."

Alyssa shook her head. "I don't think so. It's not the death thing, really. Actually, it may be just the opposite."

She fell silent, and all of her friend's attempts to coax a conversation out of her remained futile. In their apartment she stood herself under the shower, making sure the water didn't hit her face; for when it did it was like someone was dragging sharp pins across her skin. Still, some of it was unavoidable, and she braved it until the pain faded to a dull background and she had washed every single tangle and bit of the sick smell of fire out of her hair. She dried herself very gingerly and, when she was dressed, applied the gel the hospital had given her: just enough so that it covered her, but not so much that she looked like a sideshow freak. The way her skin had reddened from its usual, delicately pale, tone was bad enough. No need to go out there with a mass of jelly plastered across her. She applied a sedately colored lipstick, but wisely refrained from applying makeup.

Susan was suitably impressed with Alyssa's effort and made the appropriate noises.

Alyssa chuckled dryly. "Let's find somewhere murky. I don't fancy dining out in the glare of fluorescents."

4.

To his surprise, Ray found that he was much better at telling the story the 'right' way than he had expected. Not even Debbie seemed to see through his doctored version, in which his lunatic feat of brinkmanship was transformed into an act one might have expected from any ordinary, sensible guy. Still, Ray knew that it wasn't so, and that his escape had been the result of dumb luck. He *still* didn't quite understand that.

He wondered why he didn't feel like a hero. After all, he *had* saved a human life. That was probably the greatest deed of his existence so far. Maybe the greatest thing he was ever likely to do.

It had also been the most stupid.

Maybe heroes have to be stupid. If they thought about what they did they probably wouldn't.

If that was the case, then being a hero was vastly overrated and probably should not be bragged about.

He looked around *El Gitano*, a Latin-themed restaurant in Decatur, where the two couples—apparently!—had arranged to meet for dinner. Around him a sane kind of normality, which he might have accepted even yesterday, but which he now knew to be a delusion. Too much had happened today to still make him believe in this pleasant fantasy.

His memory lapses. The accident. This inane conversation he was having right now. An air of unreality adhered to it all; as is if it could just slip out of his grasp at any time and become something else. Something unexpected—possibly unpleasant.

What am I doing here? Wasting his precious life in the company of a couple of people he didn't even *like*; talking about things that held no meaning for him; laughing at jokes that weren't funny; nodding at statements he disagreed with; being a good boy for the sake of…what?

Michelle interrupted his ruminations and asked him about the fate of the woman he'd pulled out of her car. He shrugged. "She had a broken ankle. I suppose she's still in the hospital. The cops wanted to talk to her."

"Why?"

Ray was about to tell them, when he remembered that the truth wouldn't fit his story without adjustments.

"Same reason they wanted to talk to me, I suppose. Several people died at that accident. They'll want to interview every witness they can get hold of."

"You probably saved her life," Michelle said. Ray thought that she could benefit from the application of less makeup. Without the heavy shading her eyes might have been fascinating. As it was, they lent her face a skull-like appearance. Mentally, he compared her to Debbie; who also spent far too much time compensating for the imaginary blemishes in her face, but who at least didn't end up looking like a primitive tribesman on the warpath.

Ray shrugged carelessly. "Maybe. Maybe not. If I hadn't done it, someone else would have."

Yeah, sure…

"You did get hurt in the process," Michelle insisted.

He wished she'd stop going on about it. If she pushed the point too far there would be hell to pay later on. Debbie might just realize what had really happened, and she wouldn't be pleased. The very notion that he might have risked his life for somebody who meant nothing to her would upset her, to say the least. She'd go straight past the hero-stuff and to the heart of the matter: stupidity.

"I got hurt because I stopped running too soon. Too close to the scene. Gas is fiendish stuff. Diffuses like…"

He saw Debbie's look and stopped.

Once a physics geek, always a physics geek.

It drove Debbie nuts. ("Why do you always have to be so *precise*? Just let things *be* sometimes!")

He chuckled. "Sorry!"

Why was he always apologizing for things like that?

"Anyway," he concluded, "my mistake. Luckily I just got singed. I wished others had been so fortunate."

Bob, a dark-haired, taciturn individual whose lack of volubility sometimes verged on the offensive, and whose passions—golf and baseball—meant that he and Ray had literally *nothing* interesting to say to each other, finally chose to make a pronouncement.

"I think you're selling yourself short," he said.

Screw you, Bob!

What was this? A conspiracy or something?

"What do you mean?" Michelle asked her husband.

"Ray's being modest. Before we left home I heard it on the news. Some guy telling a reporter how a man dragged that woman out of her car. Picked her up and ran away—just before everything blew sky-high." He looked at Ray. "Sounded like a pretty close call."

Why can't you just die?

Ray could have strangled the asshole. Was he out to get him, or something? But, when he looked at Bob he saw nothing but…what? Respect? Maybe even admiration?

Not now, you prick!

"Vastly exaggerated," Ray said, but he sounded unconvincing, even to himself. He didn't look at Debbie, but he knew that her full attention was now upon him.

He gave a false laugh. "Hey guys—I'd love to be a hero, but fact is I'm not. OK? You know the media. They need their sensations. Seems like they found one here."

His attention was distracted. Above Michelle's head, near the entrance to *El Gitano*, he saw two new customers enter the restaurant.

Ray stared.

Oh, shit!

5.

Alyssa spotted Ray a few moments after entering *El Gitano*. He was sitting with a group of three others around a table in the far corner of the restaurant. She saw that he'd noticed her, too—but, after a brief mutual meeting of the eyes, he lowered them again and then, very deliberately, moved his head from side to side.

She felt her momentary elation at the unexpected encounter give way to an irrational feeling of rejection and hurt. He glanced up again and, even across the distance, she could see a plea in his face. Then he looked away again and addressed the man to his right.

"What's the matter?" Susan's voice came from beside her. "Don't you like it?" She chuckled. "Too bright?"

Alyssa shook her head. "No, it's fine. Great actually."

She snuck another peek at Ray's table; remembered what he had said to her in the ambulance. "I hope Debbie never finds out what really happened back there. There'd be hell to pay."

Debbie must be one of the two women at the table. Probably the one with her hand on Ray's arm and saying something to the others. Hard to see from this distance what she was like; but to Alyssa's, admittedly biased, perception, there was a air of control-freak about her. She decided there and then that she didn't like Debbie; and immediately admitted to herself that she had no reason whatever to do so—but ignored that and decided to dislike Debbie anyway.

She also told herself that she *owed* Ray; and that the very least she could do was not to intrude upon his life when he obviously didn't want her to.

A waitress took them to their table. Alyssa's heart sank when she realized that it was the one next to Ray's party.

Hey, fate! What're you up to?

But fate was being deliberately inscrutable today.

Or maybe…

Why was it making her end up sitting in such a way that Ray was right in her line of sight? She wondered how to get out of this gracefully, but soon decided that there was just no way; not without making a fuss that would surely get noticed by Debbie's watchful eyes, and which might cause her and everybody else even more embarrassment.

She saw that the significance of the configuration hadn't escaped Ray either. Boy, this was going to be an *interesting* dinner! The situation had all the ingredients and plot-twists of a bad soap opera. Somewhat guiltily she caught herself secretly enjoying it. Poor Ray definitely wasn't though! Maybe they should...

She was about to turn to Susan and suggest a change of venue, when a waitress placed a carafe of water on their table, recited her *spiel* about the specials of the day, and handed them a menu each.

Alyssa sighed and surrendered to the inevitable.

The waitress departed. Susan studied the menu, but Alyssa saw that she was really scanning the other patrons. Susan always did that; and at some length. "You wouldn't believe what I could tell you about these people," she was fond of asserting. Followed, often enough, by character analyses of people Susan had never met and most likely never would—all based on no more evidence than a few moments of furtive study.

Susan leaned over to Alyssa. "See that guy at the table next to us?" she whispered.

She meant Ray, of course. Had to. This close up, his sadly depilated head and face, together with the glistening shine of the same gel she wore herself, provided a definite focus of attention for anybody like Susan. Again, Alyssa caught herself thinking that under normal circumstances she herself wouldn't have paid Ray anything but the most cursory attention. Maybe a passing, probably dismissive, thought; tinged, possibly, with a hint of pity; maybe even compassion. He *did* look like someone on chemo. A hint of freakishness, especially when contrasted with the other people at the table.

Now that she was close enough she had a better opportunity to study Debbie. Quite pretty, with big eyes that might have been soft, but Alyssa thought them just a trifle too alert and harsh. A shock of carefully-unruly dark-brown hair. Under a pert nose a lively mouth that never seemed to rest, but even in silence constantly twitched and moved.

The other couple were subtly mismatched with Ray and his wife. It was hard to define why, but it was there anyway. Maybe it was just the body language: the couples on opposite sides of the table; Debbie with a distinctly artificial air about her; Ray definitely ill at ease.

Shit! I'm turning into Susan!

"Do you see him?" Susan repeated.

"What about him?"

"He looks just like...you know, like you described the guy who pulled you from the car," Susan whispered conspiratorially.

Ah, what the heck!

"That's probably because it *is* him," she told her friend.

"What?" Susan's voice rose just a tad as she stared at Alyssa. Enough to attract the attention of Ray's wife, who cast a quick, hooded glance at the two women; only to avert it just as quickly.

Alyssa gave Susan a look that should have struck her dead on the spot.

"Could you be a little less discreet?" she hissed.

Susan's eyes caught hers above the menu. "Are you serious?" she breathed, just loud enough for Alyssa to hear. "Why don't you say hello?"

Alyssa leaned over to her friend. "Because he doesn't want me to."

"How do you know?"

"I've known since we came in here."

"You telepathic now?"

Alyssa's look shut Susan up. She returned her attention to the menu; but, just as Alyssa knew she would, leaned closer a moment later. "What kind of a freak is he anyway? Why wouldn't he want to talk to you?"

The derogatory term got Alyssa's hackles up. "Nothing 'freak' about it," she hissed softly. "He told me his wife wouldn't appreciate the full details of the situation. I respect that, all right? I certainly wouldn't do anything to make his life more difficult than it already is."

Susan considered her for a heartbeat or two, then nodded. "I guess," she said slowly. She gave the neighboring table another furtive scan. "You're right. He looks uncomfortable enough." She leaned back again and proceeded to study her menu.

Alyssa put hers down and got up. "Red wine for me."

"Where are you going?"

"Where do you think?"

Susan rolled up her eyes. Alyssa got up and left.

The bathrooms were in the back of the restaurant. A swinging door led into a small hallway, at the end of which were two doors. Alyssa headed for the one marked with a cutesy lady-in-skirt symbol and the label *Señoras*. She was relieved to realize that she was alone. She didn't really have to go to the toilet. She wanted to be alone. Alone, so she could think.

Alyssa Weaver stared back at her from the wide mirror above the basins. Alyssa Weaver with the pink face, the now-somewhat-messed-up hair. She stepped closer to inspect herself and gently touched her face with a probing finger. It was tender and the spot where she'd touched herself retained the sensation long after she'd removed the finger. Despite the doctor's assurances she had a vision of her face in blisters for weeks. Showing up at the office that way and facing her clients—some of which were corporate bigwigs with the minds of roaches and the lecherous dispositions of rutting stags—wasn't a prospect to enchant her.

What do you think? she asked her silent reflection—but, like fate, it wasn't exactly forthcoming with answers.

Alyssa shook her head and took out her lipstick. She didn't really need it, but there was something comforting about running it over her tender lips. She took a tissue out of the dispenser, daubed off the excess, and dropped the lipstick back into her purse. Again she looked at her reflection. How did this face compare with Debbie's?

What did it matter? What's in a face anyway?

And yet, as she stared at herself, she knew that everything was in a face. And she wondered what was in hers.

In the small hallway someone was waiting for her.

"Hi," he said softly.

How had she known that he would be there?

"Hi."

"Look," he began awkwardly, "I'm sorry about…you know…"

"That's all right," she said.

"I mean, it's weird, isn't it?" he continued. "Running into each other again. Consider the number of restaurants in Atlanta. What's the probability of this happening? Like one in a thousand? Maybe less?"

She stepped closer to him and he pushed himself off the wall. She noted—for the first time consciously—that he was maybe and inch or two shorter than herself. Which was no wonder: at five foot eleven she was a tall girl.

"It's good to see you again," she said. "Sorry about the table; but I had no control over that, you know."

He chuckled, but kept a straight face.

"Hurts to smile?"

He looked at her shrewdly. "I guess you know."

"Yep."

"Don't worry about the table," he said. "I got a bit...flustered. But now I think I'm going to enjoy this." He paused. "Maybe we both should: enjoy our private little joke."

"Looks like the joke's on us," she pointed out.

"Yeah, well. Let's make the best of it. Our personal little sitcom." The lights along the walls reflected as pinpoints in his eyes.

She nodded. She could see the humor. So, it seemed, did he.

Alyssa took a deep breath. "There's just one thing," she said.

"What?"

"Unfinished business."

"Like what?"

"Something I've wanted to do since...you know. But I couldn't. Someone was always looking."

One of his now-hairless brows went up. His lips crinkled into the merest of smiles. But his eyes weren't laughing.

"You know Murphy's law, right?" he said. "When it's most inconvenient, someone's going to come in that door."

She was unsurprised that he knew.

"But you're going to let me do it anyway, aren't you?"

He made a wry face. "Do Vulcans have pointy ears? I know shouldn't, of course—but, to tell you the truth, right now I don't care."

Do it now, girl! Before you change your mind. Before he *changes* his!

She bridged the final step between them.

"Thanks for saving my life," she whispered—and kissed him.

It was supposed to be just a friendly thank-you-for-everything. A kind of closure to the whole thing. Telling the guy who saved her life that she really, really appreciated what he'd done for her.

That's what it was meant to be.

Really.

Really?

Yeah, right...

Then why was it more like opening Pandora's Box, braving the whirlwind of pheromones that came out of it like a shockwave?

She knew that she was making small sounds, but she couldn't help it...
...felt his brief resistance...
...his yielding...
...as her hands slipped around his neck and pulled him closer.
Her lips hurt like hell, but who gave a shit? Not if it also felt so good.
Footsteps: discordant and heavy.
They jerked apart, looking at each other with a mix of surprise and guilt.
Damn!
His eyes pleaded with her. She let out the breath she hadn't known she was holding, turned away from him, and started toward the door. It opened inward as the unwelcome intruder pushed his way in.
A man. Just as well. He wouldn't notice. Men were so dense.
Without daring to look back at Ray, Alyssa returned to her table, ignoring Susan's curious look as she sat down. Behind her she felt, rather than heard, Ray make his own way back to his table.
When Alyssa was seated Susan leaned across to her. "Tell me more," she whispered.
Alyssa attempted to fake a look of puzzled indifference. "More of what?"
Susan's lips twitched. "What happened back there?" she asked, clearly amused at Alyssa's discomfiture. "Tell me that *something* happened!"
Alyssa shrugged.
Susan prodded her under the table. "Come on, damn you!"
"We...talked."
Susan grinned. "I bet!" she chuckled. "He got up as soon as you were out of sight. Trying to be casual about it; but, boy, was he wound up!"
"We said goodbye," Alyssa told her.
Susan considered her friend for a few moments.
"Right."

6.

Ray sat down at the table and took a sip of his wine to cover his confusion. Michelle was telling a story: something lurid, about her office; a veritable breeding grounds for scandals, if she could be believed. Ray wasn't listening. He took another sip of the tart red wine. That was about all he was capable of at this point. The rest was a muddle: total and complete chaos.
All he'd wanted was to apologize to Alyssa for his churlish behavior; his dismissal of her; the total lack of backbone he'd exhibited throughout this whole affair; which he had exacerbated to the point where he had become the prisoner of his own deception. Amazing how easily something like that could happen. How simple caution, and what he thought was tact, could give rise to such a confused mess.
And then...
You should have known, you prick!
Like how?
Liar!
Of course he should have known! The whole damn thing had been leading to this from the moment he'd followed one of the most irrational impulses of his life and

stopped at that accident scene.

On the other hand, things would never have gone this far if she hadn't shown up here...

Do the words 'marital fidelity' mean anything to you?

"What do you think?"

"What? Sorry..."

Bob was talking to him. He had probably heard enough of Michelle's office-scandal stories to last him for a lifetime, and was now vectoring in on his favorite subject: golf. The only thing that could make him talk with animation and an unflagging enthusiasm which Ray found strangely unnerving—especially if one considered that he had not a shred of interest in golf—or most other sports for that matter—and couldn't give a shit how Bob was working himself toward par for his course—or, for that matter, which course they were talking about!

If he focused his gaze just past Bob's head, Ray looked straight into Alyssa's face. Which he did now, though Bob couldn't know that, of course. But Alyssa would. No doubt about it. She looked just as bewildered as he felt, and the secret of that dizzy moment in the hallway was like a string that linked them together and wouldn't be broken.

Alyssa's friend, a petite brunette whose eyes seemed to be all over the restaurant, was in on the secret. Her quick, knowing glances, gave her away. Maybe she didn't know exactly what was going on, but she knew who he was—and she'd obviously done the numbers and come to a pretty accurate result.

Man!

The rest of the evening passed in an odd trance-like state. It was like he was halfway here and halfway somewhere else. The social interaction with Bob and the two women ran along on autopilot. The rest of him was trying to figure out what the hell was going on—and watching Alyssa and catching her glance every few seconds.

Somehow he knew that her thoughts were running along similar lines and that she was a puzzled as he. Maybe more so, because she seemed like a woman who normally had herself under fairly strict control; and this situation must surely have her quite worked up.

Somehow he managed to hold in there. The strange evening drew to a close. His party left when Alyssa and her friend were still picking at their dessert. As they departed he managed to look around casually to catch a last glimpse of her—only to find her staring after him with an intensity that was almost a physical touch, reaching right across the tables. He smiled, though it hurt his face, and turned away to follow the others out the door. And as it closed behind him and they walked to the car he became aware that, for the second time, he had parted from Alyssa without ever finding out her last name, or where she worked, or who she was.

Which, he told himself, was probably the best way. Because any other way led to scenarios that were too troublesome to contemplate—thought he also found himself wondering...

7.

"So—what was *that* all about?" Debbie asked him almost the moment they had departed the Bob and Michelle's house, after a brief sojourn for a coffee and another bit of ineffable boredom.

"What was *what* about?"

The question was valid. He really didn't know what particularly had attracted Debbie's attention and been singled out for post-mortem analysis on this particular occasion. There was always a post-mortem. It was a ritual with Debbie, after every evening with just about anybody. Therefore her question wasn't exactly unexpected, even though Ray dreaded what exactly she might have come up with this time. After all, there was something that he'd really rather not discuss.

Instead of answering him, Debbie performed a sudden conversational U-turn. "I'm worried about you."

Ray took his eye off the road for a second to glance at his wife's profile, outlined and brought into occasional relief by street-lights and the beams from passing cars.

"I'll be all right. It's just a singe."

She sighed. "That's not what I mean." A pause. "Or maybe it is. Oh, I don't know…"

From his peripheral vision he saw her face turn in his direction. "Why did you get involved this afternoon?"

He shrugged, feigning puzzlement. "Involved? In what?"

"You *know*!" she said accusingly. "You risked your life! I *know* you did! What you told me—that wasn't true. You pulled that woman out of that car and you *knew* you were risking your life."

He shrugged again. "Maybe. And what if I did?"

"If you don't know that…"

"No, I don't. Maybe you could tell me. What should I have done? Leave her stuck there, with gas leaking all over the road—to become human toast, just like those others? Is that what you wanted me to have done?"

"No, but…"

"But *what*, Debbie? It was this or that—with nothing in between. No time to think. Just enough time to *do*." He took a deep breath. "And I did tell you the truth—because I wouldn't have been singed like this if I'd just kept running for a few more seconds. It was my stupid fault that I underestimated the range of the fire-ball. The problem wasn't that I pulled out that woman, but that I didn't think properly afterwards!"

"You should have told me."

"And what? Have the same discussion we're having right now? That's exactly what I wanted to avoid—and if that asshole hadn't opened his big mouth we *would* have avoided it."

"That what got you so upset in the restaurant?"

"I wasn't upset."

"Yes, you were. You're usually rude when you get upset. That's how I can tell."

"Rude? Who? Me? When? To whom?"

"You mean you don't remember?"

"Remember what?"

"That you told Michelle you thought certain things shouldn't be spread around."

"When did I say that?" He didn't remember, but he wasn't surprised that he might have. Michelle was prone to spreading lurid gossip.

"When she told us that Marty suffered from incontinence."

"When did she tell us that? And who's Marty?"

"Stop this! You know what I'm talking about!"

"I wish I did!"

"Stop it—damn you!"

The whole damn thing was rapidly getting out of hand. Ray took a couple of deep breaths of the rapidly congealing air inside the car. This was even worse than what he had been dreading. He had thought that maybe Debbie had picked up on Alyssa and the strange goings on surrounding whatever happened back there. But it didn't look like it. Instead there was another issue which was much, much closer to the bone—because he really didn't remember anything even remotely connected to what Debbie was talking about.

Mentally, he went back through his own memories of whatever had happened at the table. What been said and done. But there was nothing—nothing! that corresponded to what Debbie had just referred to.

"Look," he began, but she cut him short.

"Stop it!" she snapped. "Just *stop* it! Why do you always do this to me?"

"Well, I don't remember!" he shouted at her. "Get it? I—do—not—remember. Period. There is nothing in my memory about Michelle talking about her incontinent friend Marty. Believe me, if I'd been told something like that—something as bizarre as that!—I *would* remember. Or at least I *think* I would! That's quite a piece of work; even coming from Michelle!"

"How could you not?" she shouted back.

"I don't know," he said, quieter. He took a deep breath. Maybe that was a lie. Maybe he did know. But he couldn't tell her that. Not this.

"I'm going to see a doctor."

Her head snapped around. He glanced at her and saw that her expression had softened just a tad.

"I think you should," she said.

"I know."

"It's just stress." She laid a hand on his arm and squeezed it. The touch felt soothing; and yet odd, coming so close as it did after one of their post-mortem flare-ups. One of the reasons why he'd recently begun to hate socializing.

"I hope so," he said darkly.

"Of course it is," she insisted. "There's nothing wrong with you. You do all the right things. You have a physical once a year. You don't take drugs, you hardly drink, you don't smoke, you exercise. You're just working too hard."

"You spend more time at work than I do," he pointed out. "You certainly have in the last few months."

"My work isn't quite as intense as yours," she retorted, oddly defensive.

"That's not what you told me a couple of days ago."

"And you keep telling me how much 'mind-space' your work occupies. That's what's doing it, you know. I think you forget the real world with being immersed in all these imaginary ones."

There was a grain of truth in that.

He hoped that's all it was: a grain.

8.

"All right, he's gone. Calming down? Gonna tell me now?"

"Tell you what?"

"What really happened back there. What did you say to him? What did *he* say?"

"I told you: we said goodbye. Closure. You know…"

Susan snorted. "Yeah. I can see that." She shook her head in an exasperated kind of way. "Hello there! Remember me? Your friend for more years than I care to admit to?"

Alyssa let out a pent-up breath. The caramel flan had ceased to appeal to her. She put the spoon down and looked at her friend.

"That's what we did," she said. "We said goodbye."

That was the intention.

Susan's eyes didn't leave her face, and finally Alyssa felt compelled to elaborate. "I kissed him."

"Ah, now we're getting somewhere!" Susan grinned. Alyssa saw the predatory glint in her eyes and knew that she'd said too much.

"You *kissed* him!"

Alyssa sighed. "Yes!"

"And…" Susan prompted.

"And nothing. I kissed him—and that was that. You know—showing my appreciation for what he did for me. Somehow 'thanks' just didn't seem to cut it."

"No," Susan agreed wryly. "I guess not." She eyed Alyssa intently, as if waiting for something.

When nothing came… "*And?*"

"And nothing. I told you!"

"Why not?"

"What do you mean?"

"You know what I mean!"

Alyssa shrugged. "Somebody came in."

"I see."

"Yeah."

But Susan wasn't finished yet. "*And?*"

Alyssa shrugged. "He…responded." She made a small gesture. "Of course he did. Men do, on the whole, react favorably to that kind of thing."

Susan smile wryly. "Even married ones."

"Especially married ones."

Now, why had she said that? What did she know about it? She'd never had a fling with a married man.

Susan chuckled. "That's if they're not scared shitless of us." She narrowed her eyes. "You're trying to veer off the subject."

Alyssa made a wry face. "Would I dare? With you?"

"Yeah. Like now." Susan pursed her lips and gave her friend a knowing look. "And his tongue didn't exactly stay in his mouth, eh?"

Alyssa grimaced.

"And neither did yours."

"No," Alyssa admitted.

"I see." Susan leaned back. "What're you going to do?"

"Do?"

"Yeah."

"Nothing."

"Nothing? Hey, kiddo, you've just impulse-french-kissed a guy who obviously pushed all the right buttons without so much as trying very hard—and you're gonna tell me you're going to do *nothing*?"

"That's right. As you've noticed he's married."

"Since when does that have anything to do with it?" Susan looked genuinely surprised. "Anyway," she declared, "that marriage is on the rocks. It doesn't need a shrink to figure that one out."

"That's hardly for me to judge," Alyssa pointed out. "Or to take advantage of. Damn it, Susan, this guy saved my life! What am I going to do? Wreck his marriage in turn, thereby demonstrating my undying gratitude?"

"It was *you* who kissed him!"

"That was an impulse. I wasn't thinking."

"Oh, yes, you were! You know what? Sleep on it. In the morning you might see this much more clearly."

Alyssa shook her head. "No."

"Don't be so sure."

"But I am. You see, I don't know the first thing about him. Just that he's Ray I don't even know his last name—and he doesn't know mine either. Unless we run into each other again like tonight we're never likely to set eyes on each other again."

Which was how it was going to be.

Saturday

1.

A good night's sleep provided an experiential separation from the previous day, and by now Ray was already re-considering last night's hasty promise to Debbie. Maybe seeing a doctor—even seeing a shrink—was taking things a bit too far. No doubt that he was under some serious stress right now—but easing that just a notch or two might well do the trick. The effort, expense, and everything else that came with seeing a neurologist—batteries of tests and interminable dumb-ass questions—might not be worth it after all.

He wasn't going to take drugs anyway. Matter of principle: he didn't believe in drugs; not unless there was a clear-cut case for them. Antibiotics in serious cases of infection. The odd Aspirin for headaches. And that was about it. But if he started to put himself through the medical system and if they found anything at all, drugs—probably psychotropic ones—would surely enter the picture, sooner, rather than later.

But he couldn't tell Debbie that. Not now; not here; certainly not today. She was worried sick about him, and when she reached that stage she was just ready to flip over into fits of anger, that sent shrapnel all through their relationship. Loss of control was Debbie's worst nightmare. She needed at least the illusion of it. That was why she had freaked out when she realized what he'd done yesterday. The very notion that he might be doing something over which she had no say whatsoever scared the shits out of her. It was bad enough that the world at large proceeded along its path in blissful ignorance of Debbie Shannon's wishes and aspirations. That her husband should do the same was intolerable.

No—he couldn't tell her. There were things he could never tell her: things he wished he could share with her, but which she just couldn't handle. It was a simple and sad as that.

He leaned back and tried to ignore the fact that Debbie was driving.

Control-freak yourself.

True, of course. Who wasn't scared of losing it? Funny thing: nobody really had it to begin with. The grand delusion...

Debbie pulled over to the right and onto the off-ramp. Ray used the opportunity to look across the I-285 to the other side; where he'd gotten on yesterday and found himself faced with the severely disturbing fact of a re-arranged universe.

Maybe he *should* see a doctor.

He froze, his mouth agape. The car wound its way up the ramp. Debbie indicated right and prepared to cross the over-bridge.

Ray, careful not to let his dismay show, turned to her. "Stay in the right lane, will you? I'll get out at the lights."

"Why?"

"I'll walk the last bit."

She looked at him as if he were out of his mind. "Walk?" Like that was the silliest thing she'd ever heard from him.

"It's just across the road! Besides, that way you can get straight back onto the interstate. You're late as it is."

She pursed her lips dubiously, but stayed in the right lane. He grabbed the soft case with the portable from the back seat and, when she stopped at the red light, blew her a kiss and jumped out.

"Don't forget to call me."

"I won't. As soon as I have a free moment."

He slammed the door and managed to gain the curb just as the lights turned green. He caught Debbie's look as she drove off and turned right and right again and onto the ramp that only had *one* lane, and merged into the stream of cars on the I-285.

Ray stared at the ramp. He *would* see a doctor. As soon as he could.

He stood there, breathing heavily, and feeling just a little dizzy. He leaned on the bridge railing and considered the cars winding themselves down the ramp. He had a whole set of memories—*clear* memories: images as crisp and definite as any he had of yesterday!—which involved him driving onto a *two*-lane ramp on his way home. Added to that were memories of him doubting his sanity, because as far as he knew, there'd been only one lane the last time he looked.

And so on, and so on. A whole context of things, supporting and reinforcing each other. A totally coherent framework of events that led into the accident and meeting Alyssa, and the hospital, and…

And now there was only *one* lane—again! Ray felt a sickness spread through him such as he had never known before. A mental thing that fed back into his body and made him want to retch and vomit his breakfast across the cars passing below him. He'd never had a migraine before, but he'd heard about the symptoms, and it seemed like they were suddenly all there. The world dissolving into a blur of wavy lines; and a pressure on the side of his head, as if someone was slowly tightening a vise.

He took a few deep breaths and found that even sucking in air was an effort. Panic seized him as he realized just how helpless he was, here and now; and despite the people all around him in their cars going places.

Ray shook his head violently, occasioning another brief and intense bout of nausea and an almost irresistible urge to heave up the entire contents of his stomach and intestines. He could feel the heave come, and…

Then it was gone. Just like that.

And it was still a one-lane ramp.

Yes, he would see definitely a doctor. Hell, he'd even see a *shrink* if he had to. This was going too far!

Still shaking, he crossed the road and ambled along the green verge of Halcyon Business Park until he came to the next intersection. Beyond it, on the corner, hidden behind firs and bushes, the offices of *Jitterbug Software*, developers of recreational software for PCs and Macs; producers of *Wild Worlds*, one of the hottest games going in a very competitive and volatile marketplace. And he, Ray, was responsible for much of what made it so hot: the apparent sentience of the creatures populating *Wild Worlds'* cyberverse. Fancy graphics were an old hat, and everybody had them these days. Nowadays 'Contextual Complexity' was 'in'. 'Behavioral authenticity'. The buzz-phrases *du jour*.

Ray crossed the road and walked up the drive; checked the cars in the parking lot. It was Saturday, and yet just about everybody was here; as they would be here tomorrow. Nobody at 'JS' really cared much about what ordinary folk knew as 'office hours'. The work needed to be done, and the Protestant work-ethic dictated that you did what it took to get it done. Ask not what your company can do for you, but what you can do for your company. The stuff that made America great.

Yeah, well...

Saturdays and Sundays: *that* would just have to change; for him anyway.

Ray stopped. It looked like Pete had a new car. A white Japanese job. He went across to get a better look. A brand new Honda. Interesting change from his crapped-out ten-year-old Chevy.

Funny he'd never mentioned anything. Pete wasn't prone to impulse-buying. Not cars anyway.

Well, we're all entitled to a bit of craziness. Who am I to judge?

Still, it was odd that Pete had never...

The entrance door slid aside as he stepped up to it. Beyond it was Heidi, guarding the front-desk. A discordant note around the place. Not negatively so; more like 'interesting', but definitely out-of-tune; if for no other reason that, while the name invoked images of a cutesy, possibly buxomly, blonde with bimbo potential—something just falling short of someone called 'Barbie' maybe—the real Heidi was middle-aged, very dignified, and extremely competent. She oversaw the administrative day-to-day operations with unflagging efficiency, and an accompanying unflappability that must have lesser secretaries green with envy. At the same time she also insisted on being the company's receptionist: the guardian past whom everybody passing into the halls of *Jitterbug Software* had to make it.

Ray nodded at Heidi. The lady, too, worked Saturdays—but drew the line at Sundays. Certain things were sacred. 'On the seventh day' and all that...

"Good morning, Ray."

"Morning, Heidi."

"Looks like another scorcher."

"Yep. Already shaping up that way."

He turned left and proceeded along the hallway with the *Wild Worlds* team's offices, all of which were arranged along the periphery of the building so that each had at least one window facing the greenery beyond.

Ray stopped at Pete's door and poked in his head.

"Nice..."

The words stuck in his throat. His left hand grabbed for the doorjamb.

"...car," he completed.

But he wasn't saying it to Pete. Because it wasn't Pete who looked up at him from his screen. And it was not Pete's office. Not *this* thing.

Not an item out of place here. Everything so neatly arranged that it looked like the centerpiece of an office showroom. Nothing like Pete's 'cave'. Pete lived for chaos—and consequently created it around himself; because that was the only way he could possibly have it. Bits of hand-drawings scattered like someone had run through the place opening drawers at random and throwing papers up in the air with wild abandon.

A minefield that had to be trodden through with the greatest of circumspections. Walls plastered with blue-tacked drawings of screen, scene, and creature designs, next to a couple of posters with maniacal wizards atop fire-breathing dragons...

"Ray?" the strange man said. "You all right?"

Ray steadied himself. "Yeah," he said vaguely, "I'm fine." He turned to glance at the sign on the open door. 'Jack Duvane'.

"I'm all right...Jack..."

"You look like you've seen a ghost. And what the hell happened to your face?"

Ray grinned weakly. "Long story—believe me..." He let go of the doorjamb and nodded at...'Jack'. "Anyway: nice car."

"You only notice that *now*?" the stranger laughed. "I've only had it for like a year!"

Ray shrugged. "Yeah, well—better late than never, huh?" He took another quick look around the obscenely tidy office. "I better go and finish those interfaces."

With a last nod at a very puzzled Jack he stepped out of view and headed for his own office, only a couple of doors down. If that still was his office, of course. He was willing to doubt just about *anything* right now.

The sign on the door said 'Ray Shannon', so he guessed it still was his. Unless, he thought with a gallows humor that surprised him, there was another 'Ray' inside—in which case he *really* was in trouble.

He pushed the door open.

Relief. No other Ray in sight. And it was his office. Sort of. Not quite, but close. It looked right and it felt almost right. A few things in places where he wouldn't have put them. On one wall a picture he'd never seen. At least he didn't remember that he had.

Ray placed the portable on his desk, walked around it and stared out at the lawn and the trees beyond.

Shit!

He thought he'd handled the situation in 'Jack's' office with a truly amazing presence of mind. Talked himself out of all the corners and never let on what really going on.

I'm getting used *to this crap*!

What a marvelously adaptable thing the human mind. Even when it was going around the twist, it still found ways and means to cope. And going around the twist it was in this instance.

Jesus! Only yesterday he wouldn't have reacted like this! Probably would have made a fuss and a half, and a fool of himself in front of everybody. And today? Today he just took it in his stride. What was another...

Yeah, what was he going to call it? These bugs in the fabric of his reality.

Or maybe 'bugs' wasn't the right term. It was more like 'anomalies'. And not necessarily in 'reality' either. More, it seemed, in his own perception of things.

Sorry, Jack. You're not supposed to be here. You're supposed to be Pete—a guy I've known for almost six years. Sort of a buddy of mine. Overweight, like so many programmers, but not too badly so. Likes Tequila and RPG's. You have a phobia of pretty girls—which isn't a problem, since they overall ignore you anyway. A sad character really, like so many programmers. Not quite 'here', if you know what I mean. You relate better to your computer than people. Stereotypical, really. Just what like you'd expect from a geek. Still, you're a nice guy. Probably could be a real human being if you hadn't been so screwed up by your elder brother, who brought you up and taught you absolutely nothing of what you know—mainly because he didn't give a shit.

That Pete. That was the guy Jack was supposed to be. Not some alien from the planet of tidiness freaks.

What're you doing in Pete's office?
What're you doing in my life?

Ray leaned his forehead against the glass, feeling it cool against the hot skin on his forehead. He lifted his head and considered at the greasy smear it had left behind; took a tissue from a box on his desk and tried to wipe it away. It yielded only reluctantly. He took another tissue, breathed on the glass and wiped off the last traces of skin-grease and burn-gel. He dropped the used tissue into the wastepaper basket and slumped into his chair. Yesterday— only yesterday!—he would have freaked out if something like this had happened. Today he was taking it like he'd *expected* it!

Let's run through this 'Pete' thing again! Pete Klein. Programmer. Thirty-something. Untidy, curly, dark hair. Overweight. Loves Tequila. Margaritas. Fond of sick jokes. Like the one about the one-eyed chicken. And boob-jokes. Yep. Especially boob-jokes. But nothing ethnic. Ethnic was *out*. No jokes about handicaps either.

Debbie disliked Pete. She'd met him once and that was that. His eating manners did it—as well as just about everything else. Meaning that, after that first time, when he went out with Pete, it was on their own. Come to think about it, he was probably the only one at the office (maybe the only one—period!) who did go out with Pete to anywhere. Unless it was office party kind of stuff, of course.

Debbie...

Ray picked up the phone and speed-dialed her cellphone. She answered almost immediately.

"Hi."

"Hi. What's up?"

"You're at the shop yet?"

"Traffic's been heavy. Big snag on Peachtree. How are you?"

"All right. Just thought I'd let you know I got to the office. You didn't seem too sure that I could manage."

She laughed. It relieved some of his anxiety, because it meant that she was reasonably relaxed.

Now all he had to do was to make this sound innocuous.

"Guess what I found out?" he asked.

"What?"

"We lost Pete." That was *one* way of putting it.

More like 'I lost Pete'.

"Pete Who?"

Ahh, yes...

"I guess you don't remember him," he said lightly. "He was working in graphics module design. Short guy. Total geek."

"Did he ever come to office parties?"

"No. I guess that's why you never met him."

"So—he's gone, is he? Why. They're not downsizing, are they?"

"No. Nothing like it. He just left. Went West. To bigger and better things in California, I suppose. Surf and sun."

"Plenty of sun around here," she said. "I've got the aircon full-on."

"Yeah, well," he said , "just take care of yourself. Call me when you get a break, huh?"

"All right."

"Bye."

He hung up and leaned back.

That was it! He was now officially insane. Nobody but he knew about it, of course, but he was anyway.

Funny, he thought, how that suddenly and inexplicably didn't bother him. Which probably meant that he was actually *seriously* insane. The kind of lunatic who passes himself off as normal, even though he's as wacko as they come. Hell, he couldn't even agree with the rest of the world as to who was real and who wasn't!

His detachment amused him. He knew that it probably wouldn't last forever, and that, sooner or later, something would give and he'd be in real deep shit. But, for the moment at least, he didn't really care. For the moment this was something akin to a game, and he almost felt like a player with the option to quit any time it pleased him.

Of course, this game was serious, but basically not much different from the kind of stuff he did every day in the cyberworld inside his PC.

As long as his 'buggy' personal reality didn't crash the system, as it were, maybe he could try to deal with it; just like his cyber-characters dealt with the anomalies of 'their' worlds.

Yeah right. How *did* he keep the despair—which must surely be lurking somewhere, waiting to leap out at him—at bay? Maybe, he thought, it was because it had been building up for so long to this that it didn't seem all that extraordinary.

How long for? A month? A year? More? It was hard to tell when an innocuous quirk had turned into something that wasn't quite as ordinary as it should have been.

The discrepancies had, of course, always been there. They were a part of just about everybody's daily life; whether they knew it or not. Nobody ever remembered what 'really' happened. Heinlein's 'fair witnesses' were a pleasant fiction. Memory was a mélange of imprinted, recallable experiences, most of which were *not* of whatever constituted 'reality', but of internal states and processes—mixed in with a good deal of imagination and confabulation. Just how much it corresponded to verifiable reality was a matter of dispute—and probably depended on the individual.

Every marriage suffered from divergent memories. This was a fact of life. Some suffered more than others. Ray's and Debbie's had been afflicted with possibly more than its fair share of such discrepancies. Initially it had been small things: the kind every couple is likely to run across. What was said and what wasn't. *Whether* something was said or not. Did we really decide to do this? But I told you so. No you didn't. I never agreed to that. But...

Stuff like that.

Life.

Then, some time, maybe halfway through their marriage, there had been more important matters. Like that constant—still ongoing—disagreement as to whether they had met Bob and Michelle, albeit fleetingly, when they still lived in North Carolina. At a college party, to be exact.

That was an odd one, not just because it lingered, but also because, when Debbie thought to resolve the issue one day by actually *asking* Michelle about her view of things, Michelle concurred that this may well have happened. That *she* also had a memory of being introduced to them. Bob, on the other hand was noncommittal. He didn't even seem to understand the issue. Quite in line with everything else Ray knew and learned about him.

Debbie had dismissed the whole matter. After all, everybody knew that women simply have a better memory for such things than men. Just like they can listen to three conversations at once; a feat a man had yet to emulate with any degree of success.

But Ray hadn't been in any doubt about the 'facts'. He was certain, beyond a shadow of doubt, that when the Shannons and the Grummonds met at a party in Atlanta, this was the very first time he'd ever laid eyes on each other. How did he know? He just *did*! There wasn't even the slightest trace of deja vu, of any kind of familiarity. Their names, their faces, their mannerisms, their predilections... *everything* was new. He remembered his perplexity at Debbie's 'recognition'. Worse even was the fact that she remembered their first names!

Maybe she'd met them at a different occasion. Maybe on her own—without Ray present at the time?

Whatever, the matter remained a sore point between them. Ray had long since given up arguing it and had admitted, on several occasions that he might have been mistaken. But Debbie knew that he didn't mean it, and she wanted more than his mere agreement to disagree. Which he simply couldn't provide.

Then there were other things. Details of living that shouldn't have been vexatious but which became that way, because Debbie had decided that, since her memory for the small facts of life was so much more accurate than Ray's, in most of these matters he was mistaken and she wasn't. Equally certain of the integrity of his own world-image, Ray had learned to avoid confrontation involving such matters.

He knew that this wasn't necessarily the healthiest way of handling things, but he knew no other way of protecting himself, Debbie and their relationship. He simply didn't want to fight over what he considered to be essentially trivial matters; especially if it involved Debbie finding new evidence to support her personal psycho-myth about Ray's memory.

Over the last couple of years the number of issues where he'd had to shut up and dissimulate had proliferated alarmingly. To the point where now it wasn't just Debbie who disagreed with him, but, so it seemed 'reality' itself. Another step on the road to...what?

Insanity?

Was that where he was heading? Had he been sliding down a gentle slope to a place of no return?

Maybe.

But why didn't *he* think so?

Was that, too, a part of his 'problem'?

First things first!

Priority one: retain whatever sanity he was capable of holding onto.

Which brought him to...

Doctors!

Of course, he would have to see one. A 'physical' doctor. Someone who did real tests on real things. Shrinks were a last resort.

He owed himself that much: to make sure that there was nothing wrong with the physical components of the entity that was 'Ray'. Whatever happened in his mind... well, that was a different issue. He'd tackle that if and when it was inevitable. Until then...

But, whatever happened, he had no intention—not a shred of it—of telling *anybody* about the full extent of his problems. To do so was unthinkable. He'd be committed instantly. Lose his job. Become the object of pity and, no doubt, a certain amount of mockery. Behind his back, of course; but it would be there.

Pete, where have you gone? I remember you! Your face. Your voice. Your office. Your jokes. The way you sometimes bored me to tears. The way I sensed that you were not just a geek.

Where the hell have you gone? And what's that freak, Jack, doing here, taking up your space in the office and my life?

Good question!

Ray got up and went back to Jack's office. He stuck his head in the door. "Got a moment?"

"Sure." Jack looked up and swung around in his chair. "What's up?"

"How're you getting along?" He had to feel himself into this carefully and judiciously; avoiding the obvious traps and pitfalls.

Jack nodded. "Fine."

"Ready to integrate?"

Jack shrugged. "A week maybe. How about you?"

"Sounds about right," Ray agreed. He nodded at the screen. "Can you show me a bit of the current interface? And I need the latest spec for the controls and A.I. links."

Jack nodded agreeably. "Sure." He leaned forward, clicked keys, moved the mouse. Computer stuff. Utterly normal—and yet wrong.

How can it be 'wrong'?

"Apart from a few snags," Jack said, "this is it."

Ray spent the best part of half an hour looking over Jack's shoulder as the stranger ran the graphics module through its paces. It was, he reflected, still pretty much what he remembered. As were the internal hooks for his own modules. So far, it appeared, his personal dysfunctions hadn't fed into his work yet; not into the nuts and bolts aspects anyway.

But that didn't mean that things were exactly the same. As he watched Jack, Ray noted subtle changes in the graphics: texture mappings; colors; the shapes of monsters and player-characters alike. The kind of change one would expect when one switched the design from the hands of the geeky, disorganized, flatulent, messy, but extremely creative and imaginative, genius Pete had been—'was'? if so, then 'where'?—to the care of one super-organized tidiness freak.

The world on the screen had lost an indefinable something; an element of creative chaos and believable disorder; a worldliness that added a touch of the fractal nature and unsystematic context of the 'real' world to that of the cyberverse.

'Real'?

Ha! What did he know about 'real'?

He left 'Jack', returned to his own office, and switched on his computer, which so far had been untouched. As the machine booted itself he stared at the screen, seeing nothing.

My world is falling apart. Bit by bit.

And what was he doing about it?

He shook his head. He went through the logon procedure on his computer and then just sat there.

There was no way he could do *any* sensible work today!

He checked his email.

Nothing. Not even junk mail.

He started up the web-browser, opened up the *Atlanta Journal-Constitution* website and scanned the local news pages for reports of yesterday's accident on the I-285. He found it and scanned through it. Well, here at least most things seems to correlate with what he knew and had seen and read. Well, he didn't recall reading about only three fatalities. It was more like a dozen or more last time *he'd* heard about it. Plus more than forty injured. That had shrunk to eight. Still—everything else seemed to hang together. What's a few details of the body-count?

Ray printed out the page and considered the hard-copy from the printer. Here at least, was something solid. His memory and reality in synch. As far as he knew.

Unbidden, something else pushed to the forefront of his mind.

Alyssa. Last night. *El Gitano*. That was *very* real to him indeed. Especially you-know-what.

Magic. And a major guilt-trip thing with it. He wasn't supposed to enjoy being kissed by anybody but Debbie quite that much.

He sighed. Not to put too fine a point on it, sore lips or not, he couldn't remember *ever* having been kissed like that. Or maybe his first one—back in the wasted days of his mid-teens.

Jane.

Maybe then. That absolutely devastatingly delicious feeling when, for the first time in his life, he'd suddenly realized that the girl *was* actually looking at *him* with that certain expression. He'd never thought it would happen—but then it did, and it was…

Words? There'd never been the words to describe it.

But nothing after that could compare. Until last night.

Philandering jerk-off!

Why? Because a woman kissed you and you enjoyed it?

Exactly!

He pushed images of Alyssa aside, but they wouldn't yield that easily, but they returned with increased tenacity the more he tried. He told himself that it was pointless. He knew nothing about her.

He tried to focus on matters of more pressing and consequential concern. Like for how long he could he possibly survive and remain functional? If his memory was really going to the dogs at the drastic pace it had exhibited over the last day or two—

When was he going to reach a stage where he had forgotten or 'remembered' something that *really* tripped him up. It was on the cards; and when he thought about it, despite his attempt to keep the situation at an emotional distance, he felt a hollow pit in his stomach, and he felt himself drawn back into a nausea not unlike the one he'd experienced earlier on the bridge.

Damn—he was *scared*! And the worst thing was that he had this feeling—no: this *certainty*!—that there wasn't a doctor in the world who could help him.

Ray shook his head and went to the Atlanta phone directory web-page. He typed in 'Gitano' and obtained the number of the restaurant. He picked up the phone and dialed. A female voice answered.

Ray didn't really have any idea where to go from there. He enquired as to the opening times. Yes, they would be open for lunch.

He thanked the woman and hung up. He sat still for a few moments, thinking.

He needed a car! He found the Hertz number in the directory and reserved himself a compact for the weekend. Yes, for an extra charge they would deliver the car to his business address within the hour. He gave them his VISA number and hung up.

All right! What now?

He got up and went along the hallway to John's office; stuck his head in the door.

"Got a minute?"

"Sure!" John waved him in and swiveled around. "What's up? How're you getting along?"

"It'll be ready when Jack's ready."

John nodded. "Good." He looked at Ray expectantly.

"Look," Ray began, "I had an accident yesterday. In that pile-up on 285."

John's eyes widened. "Shit! Are you all right?"

"Fine. Still a bit shook up though," Ray told him. "I think I'll take today off. I'm not going to get anything sensible done."

John made a dismissive gesture. "Sure!"

"I'll take some code home," Ray said. "Maybe, if I feel up to it later today—or tomorrow."

John shook his head. "Nahh. Don't worry. Just get back into shape."

"Thanks," Ray said, grateful for the complete lack of objections. "I'll see you Monday."

He returned to his office to wait for the delivery of his rental.

2.

He's hitting on me!

It happened—occasionally; unavoidably so. Some men just couldn't help it. They saw an attractive female and it was like a green light! Floor that accelerator and go for it!

Never mind that they were her clients and she was their prospective litigation attorney. And it certainly didn't matter that she wore a simple, thin band on the ring finger of her left hand: an innocent-enough stratagem for avoiding just such situations; and it worked in most cases, but not here. Jeff Samuel was determined to play the game his way.

Power-play, sexual inadequacy, or simple horniness? It was hard to tell. The fact that Samuel was in his late forties to early fifties didn't provide any answers. The absence of a wedding ring on his hand was equally inconclusive. Men didn't wear wedding rings for all sorts of reasons. For all she knew he might have it hanging on that thin gold-chain around his neck, only part of which she could see.

The meeting had been arranged by her boss, Horrie, yesterday—before the accident. Samuel's company was a potential major account and Horrie had demonstrated a significant degree of faith in her when he placed it into her hands. Not the kind of thing you pass on, just because it was Saturday, she suffered from some minor cosmetic flaws, had a sprained ankle, or because she had almost been burned to a crisp the day before.

And not forgetting the kiss, of course. Especially that. She had a hard time forgetting *that*, and it was very distracting indeed. Now if it had been Ray sitting there...

Get a grip!

The meeting was informal. Following the strange tradition which dictates that what you can only discuss wearing a suit during weekdays you must discuss wearing leisure clothing on a weekend. Funny world we live in.

Still, as always she had taken pains to ensure that even her 'leisure' outfits were carefully chosen for optimum effect, and with 'impression' in mind. Which was good policy for business purposes, but in this instance also seemed to have the less desirable side-effect of getting Mr. Samuel turned on to her.

She controlled a knee-jerk reaction that urged her to lean back and bring some more distance between herself and Jeff Samuel. They had met in a stylish cafe in the precincts of Northlake Mall. Keeping in the tone of the informality of the meeting, Samuel had steered her to one of the small tables along the side, which were suitable for single patrons, or maybe couples, who wanted the small size in order to have an excuse to entangle their legs—or maybe lean forward across the table into each others' proximity.

Alyssa's long legs, clad in sandy-colored loose linen pants which covered much of the cast around her ankle, weren't made to fold under tables like that. Her knees would at the very least have ended up uncomfortably close to Jeff Samuel's crotch. Not a prospect she relished.

She wondered if he had foreseen all this; if it was part of a design, executed with practiced deliberation. Looking at him, without being too obvious about it, she wouldn't have put it past him. On the contrary; this guy wouldn't be stopped by bagatelles like a game leg. Probably turned him on. Anything for a thrill.

Or was she being too hasty in her judgment? Susan rubbing off maybe?

Sure...

Anyway, Jeff Samuel was doomed to suffer disappointment, as he would find out in due course. Alyssa positioned herself strategically at an angle to the table, being ostentatious about it and using her injury as a license. Her legs never even got close to him. He was careful to conceal whatever reaction he might have had; but his other signals were just short of blatant—and his manner told her that he intended to succeed. Alyssa decided that he was the kind of guy who, if disappointed, might well take his business elsewhere from sheer spite.

Horrie would not be happy! Meaning that she had to play the game, no matter how revolting.

She gave Samuel a beaming smile to emphasize her last point: using his predilections against him; giving him an idea that maybe, even if it wasn't going to be today, there were definite possibilities in the future.

Something in his body-language told him that she'd achieved precisely the desired effect.

Good.

Bastard!

The prospect of having to work with this piece of human slime didn't enchant her, but maybe she could unload some of the Jeff Samuel's business onto Jean or Mike. Including most of the face-to-face stuff.

God, sometimes she *hated* this job. If only it weren't so lucrative and, often enough, just sheer adrenaline thrills...

"Ten o'clock then?" Samuel asked. "In your office?"

She nodded. "Yes. We'll need Horace and Mike to finalize our contract. There's some things I cannot negotiate on my own."

And I certainly don't want to be alone with you behind any closed door.

"Fair enough."

He looked prepared to linger; but she wasn't. She got up and stretched out a slim-fingered hand. "You'll have to excuse me. I have some...weekend business to attend to." She smiled. "You know, private life and all that."

He took her hand. She made it into a firm handshake, which preempted anything he might have made out of the touch.

"Nice to meet you." The way he said it made her want to puke.

"And you."

"Would you like me to help you to your car?" he said solicitously.

She shook her head. "No, thanks," she said firmly. "I'm fine." Her tone left no doubt that she meant it. She was *not* going to have him follow her through the mall as he had on the way here! She'd rather go at her own pace.

"See you Monday," she said. She picked up the crutch and limped out of the cafe, feeling his eyes on her back as she did so.

Fact was that she *did* have a very private matter to attend to. So private in fact that she hadn't even told Susan about it. It wasn't the kind of thing she wanted to spread beyond the confines of her own skull. If the truth be told, she wasn't too sure she wanted to know about it herself—and when she scrutinized her own reasons for doing what she was about to do she came up against a disconcerting blank. But it was like a compulsion, and, as she steered the rental Buick down Ponce de Leon toward Decatur through the thick Saturday morning traffic, she admitted to herself the complete irrationality of the whole thing.

3.

El Gitano looked different in daytime; but then, these places always did. Take away the night and the lighting and everything changes. The place looked smaller somehow, dwarfed by its position between a miraculously as-yet-unrazed, leftover of native Georgia woodland on one side and a small local shopping complex on the other. The multi-colored neon sign depicting a stylized gypsy head blinked feebly in the glare of the midday sun.

Alyssa left the car in the shopping complex parking lot and, leaning on her crutch, made her way through the heat to the restaurant. In her head she ran over what she was going to say. How she was going to get...

What? His name? A phone number?

How was she going to persuade these people to give out personal details of their patrons? They could be—justifiably!—reluctant to do anything of the sort.

Alyssa squared her shoulders and pushed open the door. Inside, the air conditioner was going full-blast, chilling her down almost instantly. She shivered and glanced around. A few occupied tables. Early lunchtime crowd. Mostly folks with definite Latin heritage in their blood. The spicy reek of fried onions, garlic, and a whole host of unidentifiables wafted up her nose. Somehow even *that* was different from the way she remembered it from last night.

A waitress approached her with a menu under her arm.

"Table for one?" She cast a quick glance at the crutch.

Alyssa shook her head. "No, thanks. Not today. I came here because…" She paused. "Were you working here last night?"

The woman looked at her quizzically and shook her head. "No. I work Saturdays only. Noon till midnight. Why?"

How was she going to handle this? Maybe the truth would do the job. Or some of it anyway…

"My name's Weaver. Alyssa Weaver. I was here last night," she said to the woman. "With a friend. For dinner. Sitting over"—she pointed—"there. At the table beside us was a party of four. Among them was a man. During the evening we talked briefly." She gave the waitress a tentative smile, and noted that she had the woman's full attention. She probably smelled some item of gossip value.

"Anyway, we didn't get a chance to say too much—but he *did* give me his phone number." Alyssa sighed. "Which I lost."

A grin spread across the waitress' face. "Ahh…"

Alyssa tried to look as pitiful and helpless as she could manage. The crutches no doubt helped to reinforce the image. "I was wondering… I know this isn't done—but you must have a number." She gave a helpless shrug. "I just don't know what else to do."

"You don't know his name?"

Alyssa shook her head. "Just his first name. And that phone number. Which…"

"…you lost," the woman completed. She shook her head. "It must have been some conversation," she said conspiratorially. "Short but interesting, eh?"

Alyssa nodded. "Something like that."

The woman cast a furtive glance toward the till. "You know, we're not supposed to…"

Alyssa nodded. "I know—but I don't know what else to do."

The waitress nodded. "The boss would flay me alive." She looked at Alyssa and back at the till. "What table was he at?"

Alyssa pointed discreetly. "That one. Over to the left."

"Sixteen. I see. About what time?"

"They left at about midnight."

"Party of four, you say?"

Alyssa nodded.

"Wait here."

The woman, with a furtive air that was almost ludicrous, sidled up to the register and busied herself with a book beside it. She picked up a piece of paper and wrote something on it. A waiter came up behind her and said something. She pointed in the direction of one of the tables. He nodded and disappeared into the kitchen.

The woman came back to Alyssa. "The table was booked in the name of 'Shannon'. Here's the contact phone." She slipped the paper into Alyssa's hand and grinned. "Good luck."

Alyssa gave her a big smile and pressed a twenty-dollar bill into the woman's hand. "Thanks so much."

"You don't have to."

"Neither do you," Alyssa reminded her. "But you did, so I owe you…"

"Maria. And you're very welcome. I hope it works out."

"So do I." Alyssa smiled at Maria, turned, hobbled toward the door and pushed out into the wave of heat blasting in her face.

And stopped dead when she recognized the figure striding toward her.

4.

He stared at her.

"You?" he said, disbelieving.

Alyssa, just as stunned, still managed a soft laugh.

"Great minds think alike."

"You!" He still didn't know what to say.

"Ray Shannon?"

"That's me."

"Alyssa Weaver." She held out a hand.

He laughed and took it, held it in a firm grip.

"Took us three meetings to get to this!"

"Indeed."

They fell silent; suddenly embarrassed and unable to continue. And then, when it got too much, it also became funny, and they laughed.

"What're we going to do *now*?" she asked.

"Now that we're on full-name basis?" he grinned. "Heck, I don't know. I suppose we should get out of this heat. Cooks the brain, it does. Hard to think clearly."

"There's a Haagen Dasz over there." She motioned at the shopping center.

"Ice-cream? Excellent idea."

She indicated her crutch. "If you'll help me I'll leave that in the car."

"Sure."

He took the crutch, and, with her arm around his shoulder for support, she hobbled back to her car. Since she was taller than him it was a very comfortable way of doing things. Under his T-shirt she felt the smooth play of well-toned muscles. Despite the heat and the wet patches under his armpits she also noted that, unlike many men, he didn't reek either; not any more than herself at any rate.

They deposited the crutch in her car and proceeded to the Haagen Dasz, where she slumped into a chair at the one and only free table, and he went off to get them both a frozen yogurt.

They busied themselves for a little while with the ice-cream. A companionable kind of activity. There was a need to talk, but, for some reason or other, there seemed to be no hurry about it. Not now.

He dropped the plastic spoon into his empty cup and looked at her. "This is going to sound strange," he began, "but I'll have to ask you anyway. All right?"

She grinned. "Everything about this...thing...is strange."

"Yeah, right... Well, I want to ask you something—about yesterday..."

About the kiss, I bet.

What else? It was what *she* would have asked—if she had the courage to do so.

"About the accident."

Oh?

"There are some details I need to get clear."

"Details?"

He considered her quietly for a few moments; with an unnerving kind of intensity that would have been scary from anyone else—but which, coming from him, was strangely exciting.

He sighed. "Do you mind?" he said; almost pleading with her.

"Of course not. Go ahead."

He went over the events step by step, detailing what he said was *his* recollection of things and asking her to confirm that it corresponded to what *she* remembered had happened. So far as she could discern, his memory was flawless. When he was done running through the sequence, without her having corrected him in any significant aspect, he looked inexplicably relieved. He exhaled slowly and deeply and leaned back.

"Good," he said softly. "Very good."

She took the little plastic spoon out of her mouth and pointed it at him. "All right, Ray. Your turn. Why all these questions?"

He looked at her thoughtfully. "I needed to confirm that my recollection of events was correct."

"Why? Is this a police thing or something?"

He shook his head. "Nothing to do with them. Or with my insurance company, or anything."

"Then why?"

He gazed right through her and said nothing. She was about to get irritated when he seemed to snap out of it.

He made a grimace of doubt and regret. "I'm sorry. I'm being very rude. But there are reasons..." His voice trailed off again.

He took another breath and released it.

"Do you really want to know?"

She nodded. "Definitely."

"You may not like the answers."

"Try me." For some reason at this very instant she thought of the kiss. It was a cliché, of course, but her heart was definitely beating faster.

Down girl!

"Thing is," he said, "I'm slowly losing my mind. Or, to be more exact, my memories of things. It's been a progressive kind of thing—which came to a head yesterday...not long before we...met."

"What are you talking about?"

He shrugged. "I wish I knew." He took his lower lip between his teeth. "Look, I'm sorry. It's not really something I want to bother you with. Honestly."

His blue eyes gazed at her from under the stubble of his singed-off eyebrows. "Tell you what," he said. "Can we forget about this? Please! As my wife points out, it's probably just a stress-thing, and I'm attributing far too much importance to it."

You don't believe a word of that.

"Bullshit!"

For a moment she didn't actually believe she'd said it. It was *not* the kind of thing she was wont to come out with in social contexts requiring a certain amount of decorum. Still, it was out there now!

He eyed her with a curious expression, not at all taken aback by her outburst.

"Listen," she added, encouraged by his reaction. "You're here. I'm here. And why? Because we both went back to that restaurant." She shook her head. "I don't know *what* is going on—but you and I... Look, we've been thrown together by some freakish coincidence *three* times in less than a day. That's got to count for something, right?"

He smiled thinly. "Some interesting coincidences," he admitted.

"I'd say! Look: you pulled me out of that car; you saved my life! Maybe I can do something in return? Even if it's just to listen to whatever it is that's bothering you. Because I have the feeling that want to talk to *somebody* about it. So—why not me?"

He nodded slowly. "Why not?" He sighed. "How much time have you got?"

"All day. I have no plans." That was a lie, but if it was necessary everything else could and would have to wait.

Ray looked at his watch. "I've got about four hours before Debbie gets off work." He glanced around the parlor. "Shall we go somewhere else?"

She shrugged. "Sure."

He got up and offered her a hand. "Where to"

She took the hand and pulled herself up. Then she placed her arm around his shoulder again and started to hobble out of the parlor. "There's a nice park near Emory. Lots of shade. I'm sure we'll find a quiet spot."

He nodded. "Sounds good."

5.

When he finished talking she said nothing for a while, but sat there, staring into the distance. For which he was pathetically grateful, because he didn't think that anybody could possibly say anything sensible. And he didn't want false reassurances either. Not from her. Just a sympathetic ear and no judgment.

She looked at him. He shrugged helplessly. "More than just 'stress', huh?"

"Sounds like it." She shook her head. "Shit..."

"My sentiments exactly."

"You're incredible."

"Eh?"

She nodded emphatically. "I don't know if *I* could handle this. I'd go nuts."

He chuckled grimly and she realized what she'd said. She put a hand over her mouth. "I'm sorry... Ray, please... I'm *so* sorry..."

He reached out and took her hand away from her face; held onto it for another couple of seconds before letting go. He managed a grin. "It's all right," he said softly. "Got to admit it was funny!"

"That's what I meant!' she exclaimed. "I don't know if I could even laugh about something like that. I just can't believe how you handle this!"

"Gallows humor," he said, "Besides, it snuck up on me slowly. I guess I got used to it. Now it's just...big."

"What're you going to do?"

He was prevented from answering by the beeping of his cellphone.

It was Debbie.

"Ray? Where are you? I tried to call you at work."

"Sorry. I decided to call it a day. Just couldn't focus."

"Where are you?"

"Sitting in a park, trying to relax."

"Are you all right?"

"Yes. I am, actually... Better than I've been for quite a while."

"How did you get there?"

"I rented a car for the weekend."

"You didn't have to! The police called. They said you could have yours back!"

"The police...*what?*" He stared at Alyssa and held his hand over the mouthpiece. "My car," he hissed. "It was burned, yes?"

Alyssa looked at him, puzzled.

"Ray?" Debbie's voice sounded in his ear. He took his hand from the mouthpiece. "Hold on. Just a moment." He covered it up again.

"My car!"

"Yes," Alyssa said, still looking puzzled and bewildered, "Of course it was burned. It blew up!"

Ray gaped at her for a few seconds.

"I see," he whispered and took the hand off the mouthpiece again.

"Debbie?"

"Ray, are you all right?"

"Yeah, sure. Just someone asking for directions. What exactly did the cops say?"

"They said they've finished their forensics or whatever, and that you can have the car back. They're satisfied that it wasn't involved in the accident."

Ray took a couple of deep breaths, keeping his eyes on Alyssa's curious face, and his attention focused on Debbie's voice.

"Pick it up? Where?"

"North Fulton County something or other. In Roswell Road. Sandy Springs or somewhere near there."

"Yeah, I know the place. Did they say until what time they'd be open?"

"Four, I think."

"All right, Debs. Tell you what I'll do. I'll call Hertz and tell them they can have the rental back. I'll just leave it at the station when I pick up the car. All right?"

"You're going home then?"

"Yes. I'll see you when you get back."

"Are you all right?"

"You keep asking that! I'm fine. Honestly. I just needed a break. Doing what you told me."

She laughed nervously. "It's not like you—that's all."

He chuckled. "Don't worry about a thing," he said. "Bye."

He pressed 'clear' and put the phone down. He took his eyes off Alyssa and gazed around the park; tried to take in the whole scene, the trees, grass, the people, the road beyond, the wind blowing across his face—and back to Alyssa, who was staring at him.

"Alyssa?" he said slowly.

"My friends call me 'Lys'," she said softly.

"Lys."

"Wanna tell me about that phone call? You look like you've seen a ghost."

He sighed. "I have another one of those questions: about yesterday."

"Yes?"

"About last night actually. In the restaurant. Did we…"

"Did I kiss you in the hallway?"

"Yeah."

"I did."

"I see. And it was…quite a thing, huh?"

She nodded. Her eyes had acquired a certain dreamy look.

"Quite."

"Would you mind if I did something quite…well, shall we say, 'odd'?"

She smiled. "It's not going to embarrass me in public, is it?"

"I hope not."

"Could I touch your face?"

She was puzzled again. "Sure."

He reached out and touched his right hand to the side of her face, which was still redder than it should have been, but not as bad as it might have.

She didn't flinch as his fingertips touched her cheek and ran along it. He discontinued the touch and moved his hand to her hair and ran it over her short almost-black locks. She closed her eyes as he did so, a tiny smile playing around her mouth.

Ray took his hand back. If he was going insane he was doing it thoroughly.

Alyssa opened her eyes again. "Satisfied?"

"You feel as real as can be."

Don't do this!

"Look, I don't want to push my luck—and I just hope you can believe that there's a good reason for me asking this…"

"Wanna kiss me again?"

He felt his face get hot.

"Yes."

She smiled. "I'm game. We were rudely interrupted…"

She didn't close her eyes as he leaned across, but saw him in all the way.

Zap!

Just like last night. More so, if anything.

They eased away from each other.

"I lied," he whispered.

"I know. What about?"
"About the reason I wanted to kiss you."
"Really?"
"Really. I told myself it was just because I wanted to know if you were real."
"Oh?"
"But that was only a small part of it."
"What was the rest?"
"I don't want to think about it."
She considered him for a moment. "I think we both have to think about it."
"I know."
Her lips twitched. "What's the verdict?"
"You're real."
Which brought him back to...
"Look," he said, "tell me about my car again. You saw it burn—right?"
She nodded. "Are you going to tell me why you keep on asking that?"
He shook his head. "There's probably a mistake—" He hesitated. "You said you had some time on your hands?"
"How much do you need?"
"I want you to come with me to Sandy Springs. We've got to look at something. I need you to be there. Just in case it's..." He didn't dare complete the sentence. It was too preposterous. Everything was just so damn fucking preposterous!
Her eyes widened. He could see that she was getting a whiff of what was coming up.
"Your car?"
"I'm sure it's a mistake," he said. "It's got to be."
"Shit!"
"There are a gazillion possible explanations: all of them perfectly logical, I bet. Just like my...condition...can be explained."
Her expression changed from puzzlement to compassion. "I'm real," she said gently. "You've got to believe that. Don't let this take you down *that* road." She reached out and touched his face, just like he had touched hers a little while ago. He felt her fingers on his cheek, gently gliding toward his jaw line and to his mouth.
How do you know reality?
By sensation? By observation? By feeling? Contextual consistency?
Were any of those things reliable? How could anybody *know*?
He reached up and touched her hand; held it to his face and felt the warmth and solidity of her.
"Definitely," he said. "If you're not real, I don't know what is."
He kept her hand in his as they rose.
"Let's take my car," he said. "I'll take you back here afterwards."

6.

As he drove them to Sandy Springs, Ray reflected, with a considerable measure of dismay, that he had turned into an adulterer. A philandering husband. One of those pathetic creatures he'd always looked down upon.

Well, he hadn't *quite*, of course. Technically, kissing another woman wasn't exactly adulterous. More like straying from the straight and narrow. After all, what was a kiss? Or two?

A damn lot, if those two kisses were anything to go by. Adultery was an act of the mind and at that level he was guilty, clear and simple. All he could do now was to try and salvage what could be salvaged. But whatever *that* was, he had no idea.

Lys was quiet, looking thoughtful and maybe a bit subdued. Probably pondering the ramifications of what they might find. He glanced fleetingly at her every now and then. The proud profile. Lips compressed and determined. The chin sticking out with just a touch of pugnacity. Determined to face whatever came her way.

And what was coming her way? And his?

Ray found himself hoping and dreading what they would find. Dreading either alternative. Indeed, the explanation which involved his own loss of sanity was strangely attractive when he considered the consequences of the *other* option. At least it was something he could get his mind around, no matter how grim the consequences for him might be. But if that was his car…

But it wouldn't be.

Couldn't, actually.

No way.

They pulled into the car park on Roswell Road. Quite a few cars here still. There was a drivers' testing center here and Saturday was usually busy. Ray knew. He'd been here several times.

He pulled into a free space and stopped.

"Coming?"

Lys nodded. Her face was tight.

"Don't worry," he said lightly. "You know that it *can't* be my car."

She shook her head as if to dislodge a pesky insect. "I don't know that."

"Lys…"

She opened her door. "Let's just go, all right? Get this over and done with."

She was right.

In more ways than one.

Because it was his car.

7.

Lys stared at the Toyota. Ray felt sick. Really sick. Especially since, just beside his own car, stood another: a red convertible.

He saw Lys sway and grabbed her arm. She shook it off with a jerky twist. The cop—a middle-aged guy with a limp, consigned to a desk-job for the rest of his working days—who had accompanied them, eyed them curiously, but said nothing.

"That's her car," Ray told him.

"Oh, good," said the cop. "Ms. Weaver, is it? We've been trying to get hold of you all morning. Your friend gave us your cellphone number but there was no answer."

Lys looked at the cop. Her face was a carefully composed mask. "I turned it off."

The cop shrugged. "Well, you're here now. Your vehicle's been released. It's all yours again."

Then his eyes traveled down her right leg. "On the other hand... we could keep it here until Monday. But then it'll *have* to be claimed."

"I'll arrange something," she said tonelessly.

The cop glanced at Ray and handed him a clip-board. "If you could sign here."

Ray nodded and affixed his signature to confirm that he had picked up his car. The cop gave him a key that should have been on his key ring, but for some odd reason wasn't. Then he nodded at them and left. Lys stood like a statue.

"Come on," Ray said to her. He reached out a hand to support her, but she stepped back. The look she gave him was one reserved for a complete stranger. Maybe even something worse.

Ray stood his ground. "Listen to me," he said softly. "Please!"

"What?" she snapped.

He lifted up his hands to chest level and pointed his thumbs back at himself.

"See me? Ray Shannon? You do? Well, *I'm* the guy who completely—and I mean like totally, utterly and fully—understands what you're going through right now. All right?

"Just don't forget that! I may not know what the hell is going on here, but I *do* understand! So, please, Lys—*please* don't block me out, huh? Because I have this feeling that if you do... Well, we're *both* screwed. And I mean *really* screwed. For good and forever."

She held her breath for a few moments—then exhaled sharply. "Why?"

He shrugged helplessly. "I don't know. Hell, how *could* I? I don't even know 'what'?"

"I mean, why *me*?"

"I don't *know*! Period..."

The silence grew into a monstrosity. Ray finally had enough of it. He took a couple of steps in Lys's direction and, as she backed away, grabbed her arms and, against her resistance, pulled her to him. It wasn't the kind of thing he usually did: when people backed off, so did he. Usually. But this here was different.

She fought him for a few brief moments. But he slipped his arms around her back and didn't let go—until she finally gave up the fight. He loosened his grip, half-expecting her to jerk away again. But she didn't. Instead she leaned against him, wrapped her arms around his neck, and pressed her face against his cheek. Despite the sensitivity of his skin, despite the brief surge of pain and a mutual stiffening, the touch was... comforting. They relaxed against each other. The pain went away. Or maybe it didn't, but neither noticed nor cared.

"Are we *both* going crazy?" she whispered.

"I don't think so," he said. "Unless there's a contagious disease around that makes people hallucinate in the most peculiar ways..."

"What if there is?"

"I doubt it," he said firmly.

She pulled back and looked at him. For the first time he became conscious of tiny freckles across her nose and cheeks.

"What are you looking at?"

He smiled. "Your freckles."

"What?"

"They're...very attractive."

"You're crazy!"

His smile broadened. "Actually...I don't think so."

"You sound...relieved."

He sighed. She was right. Of course, she was right! He *was* relieved. And he realized that he had been lying to himself on the drive here. What he had really dreaded, was being proven insane. That hadn't happened. Quite the opposite. And, whatever else it was that held him and Lys in its grasp, it simply couldn't be worse than the prospect of losing his mind.

Whatever it was...

"Guilty." He pulled her close, and it seemed the most natural of things to do.

"Do you know what it means to *know* that you're not insane after all?"

There was a sharp little blast of air in his ear. And another. Her body shook. Her abdomen jerked in erratic little twitches. Concerned, he loosened his arms around her; but she clung to him as her body convulsed in small spasms.

Then she pulled her head back and he saw that she was laughing. Laughing, and maybe crying a bit, too.

Smiling now. "Do you know how crazy that sounds?" she whispered.

"What?"

"What you just said—about how great it is to know that you're not insane—when what's happening to us is the most insane thing you possibly ever imagine!"

She took a deep breath and calmed herself. Her arms stayed around his neck.

"What are we going to do?" she said, her face only inches from, and her eyes slightly above, his.

Tall girl.

"I have no idea," he said truthfully. "Not even a trace of an idea. I thought I was going insane—so that was at least an acceptable hypothesis. A pretty grim one, but it had...parallels...

"Now that it looks like we're either both nuts...or that it's something that got nothing to do with the insides of our heads...now I find myself kind-of hoping that maybe it's...well, temporary. Know what I mean? That it'll just go away if we just wait it out—and if we survive it!"

"You think it's a natural phenomenon of some kind?"

"Is there *anything* 'un-natural'?" he asked her.

"I don't know," she said thoughtfully. "But if it isn't natural then we'd have presume intent."

He chuckled, despite everything. "You sound like a lawyer."

"I *am* a lawyer."

"Oh, shit."

"What?! You got something against lawyers?"

"Not any more." He held up his hands in a pacifying gesture. "Anyway, intent or not, I'm not too hopeful that we're ever going to understand any of this."

"It *is* odd though," she said, "how we got thrown together—again and again."

"Yeah."

"Some people would call that 'fate', you know? Implying some form of intent."

"Hidden variables," he said.

"What?"

"Physicist jargon for the same thing. The notion that there are no random events; that 'coincidence' is just a term describing our ignorance of all the variables involved in configuring a given physical situation."

"You into that kind of thing?"

"Used to be."

"Wow," she said with just a touch of sarcasm. "Looks like I picked the right guy to get crazy with."

He sighed. "Lys, I owe you my life; you know that?"

She cocked her head sideways. The way her hair hung over her face...

He was charmed.

"I thought it was the other way around."

"You know what I mean!"

Her mouth twitched. "I guess..."

"I'm sorry I dragged you into this."

"Who says you 'dragged'? You think there's anything you could have *done* about it?"

He rubbed his tired eyes. The salt from his sweat irritated the sensitive surface of his skin. He'd have to put on some more of that gel.

"I don't know, Lys. I have this feeling, you know. Like I infected you."

She started to say something, but he made a quick gesture. "No! Not a virus or anything like that. But there's got to be something...

"You see, until...when?...yesterday, I suppose...until yesterday my 'problem' was completely my own. In a way it was even ordinary. You know, just your average mildly-to-severely-dysfunctional, stressed-out, games-programmer with mild to severe memory lapses, withdrawal syndrome, a functioning but not exactly thrilling marriage, working six to seven days a week for somebody else, with nothing but a nice house to show for it.

"Muddling along at the brink. Not knowing it, and probably better off for it—because this whole existential *angst* crap isn't really my scene and would probably have freaked me out if I'd thought about it too much. And if I'd spent too much time thinking about how more than half of my life's already behind me...

"But that was it. Nothing out of the ordinary. There are a gazillion guys like me. Society only works as it does because there are. Until yesterday. When there were two lanes instead of one..."

He paused. Lys, her face still just a couple of handbreadths from his own, looked at him attentively.

"What is it?"

Maybe there was a way to test this. Bring some method into this madness.

Reluctantly he took his arms from around her waist. She released his neck and stood back.

"I have an idea," he said. "Let's talk about it while I drive you back."

"All right," she agreed. "You know I still don't believe *any* of this? I should wake up any moment now, right?"

"That would be nice, I suppose."

"Except that you'd go '*poof!*' with the dream."

"That mightn't be such a loss. If it gets your life back into some semblance of order."

"Order isn't everything."

"Isn't it? Right now I'm not so sure."

Ray got into his car and Alyssa maneuvered herself into the passenger seat. Ray called Hertz from his cellphone and told them where they could pick up their vehicle, and to charge the weekend's rental to his VISA card.

As they drove out of the parking lot, Ray reflected that his world had changed yet again.

"Lys? Before we go our separate ways today...I want to know as much about you as I can. Anything that would allow me to trace you, in case..."

"In case something happens?"

"Yeah. Like if the world goes crazy again. I want to know your phone numbers; every one of them. Where you live. Where you work. Who your friends are. Anything that'll allow me to work my way back to you if I have to."

"Same here."

"Of course."

"You know what I'm *really* afraid of?"

"I know *exactly* what you're afraid of. It scares the shits out of me as well. That we'll lose sight of each other. That the other will suddenly be gone. And sanity with it."

"Something like that."

"We'll have to keep in touch. Regularly."

"You mean like phone each other?"

"Might be better if I phoned you. I don't think Debbie would understand."

Debbie.

What was he going to do about Debbie?

"Shit!"

"What is it?"

He hadn't realized that he'd said it aloud.

He shook his head. "Never mind. *My* problems."

"Are you sure?"

"Yes. I think so."

"Then think again. Looks to me like *mi problema es su problema*."

"I'll keep that in mind."

"What were you going to talk to me about?"

"Oh, that. Well, about yesterday. The accident. Did you watch any news yesterday? Or maybe today? Read a paper?"

"TV last night—as I was getting ready to go out with Susan."

"So tell me: what's *your* recollection of the statistics?"

"Statistics?"

"Yeah. You know: number of people killed and injured. Cars involved. Stuff like that."

"It was awful! Over a dozen dead. Forty of fifty injured—which included us, I suppose."

"I see."

"Why?"

"Let's get ourselves a paper, shall we?" He pulled into a nearby shopping center on

Peachtree and found a Journal-Constitution dispenser. He brought the Saturday issue back to the car and folded open the front page.

"Here. 'Pileup on 285'. Four dead. Six injured."

He looked at her. "I know what you're thinking. I thought the same thing—at first. Media exaggeration, subsequently adjusted to fit the facts."

"But you don't think so."

"That *is* my car we're in. And that *is* your car at the police station."

"What's your point?"

"Well, I have this...hypothesis. Something we can probably test with some degree of confidence in the results.

"The theory is this: that your memories of things *prior* to our...encounter...on the 285 will agree closely with what other people think happened—'other people' meaning everybody but you and I. But I bet you that anything after that moment won't necessarily..."

She stared at him. "What are you trying to say? That our meeting *started* this?"

"For you, yes. For me, it's been going on for a while. Don't know how long, but it must have been for months. Maybe years."

She shook her head. "You're just trying to find a reason to blame yourself for this."

Was he? Maybe—but...

"No. I'm just trying to find something to work with. Any theory, any *system* in this madness is better than just a total blank. Whether it helps or not doesn't matter. But I need something to make me believe that there's not just chaos out there!"

She laid a hand on his arm. "All right," she said softly. "But no guilt. Please!"

"No guilt."

She smiled, then grew pensive. "I'll do what I can to find out if you're right."

"What can you do?"

"Talk to people. I'm a lawyer, remember? We have ways of finding out things."

"What kind of a lawyer?"

"Corporate litigation."

"What drew you to that?"

"The prospect of screwing some real power-players."

He looked at her—trying to keep a straight face, but she knew anyway. She gave him a dirty look, but her mouth twitched.

"In a strictly legal sense."

"Of course."

"Though they sometimes come on more than legally," she added.

"I bet."

"Just the usual dysfunctional alpha-male shit."

"Hmm. Speaking of alpha-males—who's the president of the US?"

"Trent. Why? You worried that..." She didn't finish.

He nodded. "Right now I'm taking nothing for granted. We'll have to get together again soon. I need to know everything you think *you* 'know' about the world. Maybe we should tape each other—just so we have a record."

"What for?"

"Don't know yet. But I've got to do *something*."

8.

She'd never felt so alone. He'd dropped her off and waited until she was safely in her car. Then he'd waved at her and drove off.

She looked at the piece of paper in her hand. A name, an address, four phone numbers.

It didn't comfort her at all. She was probably making a total fool of herself, but...

She picked up her cellphone and turned the power back on. She was about to dial when it beeped.

"Hello?"

"Just making sure," his voice came back to her.

She could have cried.

"I was just going to do the same."

"Beat you to it."

"You know, I'm freaked out of my skull."

"I know the feeling. Well, just...oh, I don't know what. Just hang in there, all right?"

"Just remember to call."

"Once an hour," he agreed. "But don't worry if I don't. A million things could interfere."

"As long as they're unimportant things."

"Lys?"

"Yeah?"

"We'll make it through this."

She sighed. "I'm scared."

"Yeah—so am I."

"Talk to you soon."

"Hey, you don't have to hang up! We've got a little while yet."

"All right." She held onto the phone as if it was a life-line. Which it was.

He made her talk about herself some more. Her childhood. Parents, School. College. People she'd met. Guys she'd dated.

When they got that far time was up.

"I'm just about home," he told her. "I'll call you back as soon as I can."

"Be careful."

"And you."

She pressed 'clear' and dropped the phone on the seat beside her.

Concentrate, girl! Things had to be done.

Susan was in a cleaning mood. She got that way every now and then. Alyssa had tried to discern a pattern behind the bouts of cleaning and rearranging furniture, but had found herself thwarted. If there was a system behind the madness it proved elusive.

Not that Alyssa complained. Despite the occasional disorientation caused by furniture that wasn't any more where it had been only hours ago, Susan's attacks had the virtue of leaving behind a meticulously cleaned apartment. Which, Alyssa told herself guiltily, she contributed little to. Her cleaning confined itself to small daily chores, like dishes and sweeping the rear balcony.

The apartment, Alyssa saw as she came in, was back in a state similar to that it had been in a few months ago, give or take a few rearrangements. There was only so much one could do with a limited number of pieces, and sooner or later configurations would repeat themselves. This one here was one that Alyssa had actually liked.

Susan breezed into the room. She wore a old bikini that she wouldn't have dared to exhibit outside and had a band tied around her curly hair to hold it up. Despite the sparse clothing her skin was filmed with perspiration. No wonder. She must have been doing some heaving. Susan, Alyssa suspected, sometimes treated housework like it was a workout. Might as well have spent an hour at the gym.

Susan swept her hand around the lounge. "Like it?"

Alyssa nodded and smiled. "We've been here before."

"Of course," her friend agreed. "But not quite the same way."

Alyssa deposited the cellphone on the counter between kitchen and lounge.

"How did it go?" Susan asked her. She went to the refrigerator and got out a can of Coors, which she opened and guzzled with gusto. When Susan felt like it, she could do it better than any guy.

"How did what go?" But then she remembered. The 'informal' meeting in the cafe had almost slipped her mind. "Mr. Samuel's a dickhead."

"Is he going to come to us?"

"Maybe. If he thinks he can get to fuck me as a bonus."

Susan took another swig. "One of those, huh?"

"Yep. All the way. "

"So, you left him dangling? With a tantalizing hint of possibilities that shall never materialize?"

"Something like that."

"They'll love you for it. His software company is worth at least five million."

"Hmm."

"You're not impressed?"

"I wonder how much of that money is real? Looks to me like this guy's operating by sweet-talking his investors, and feeding them promises galore. He hasn't even got a finished product on the market. So how he has the gall to claim that another company is infringing on his copyright is beyond me."

Susan leaned on the counter and laughed. "I'm sure *he* knows."

"Yeah," Alyssa said darkly.

Susan straightened. "Anyway, you talked to him for a long time!"

Alyssa shook her head. "I got out of there as fast as I could."

"Where have you been? It's almost five!"

Alyssa shrugged. "Driving around. Sitting in parks watching pigeons. Thinking. Planning. Trying to ignore the world."

"The police called."

"Yeah, I know. I went to see them."

"And?"

"Could do me a really bog favor and pick up my car on Monday? I can't really drive a manual right now."

"Sure."

Susan took another swig.

"Susan?"

"Uh-huh?"

"How long have we known each other?"

"Oh, I don't know. Got to be more than ten years. Why?"

"As I said, I've just been thinking."

"About what?" Susan plonked herself on the couch. "Life?"

"That, too. All sorts of things."

"Still in that near-death mode?"

"I suppose."

"It wasn't *that* close!"

"It felt pretty close to *me*!"

"Yeah, but you weren't the girl that got jammed in the car and killed."

Alyssa froze and stared at her friend. "No," she said slowly, "I suppose not."

"Of course, if you had been closer to the explosion…"

"Yeah. Lucky me."

"You shouldn't have stopped at all. If you hadn't, and you hadn't gotten out of your car, you wouldn't have slipped and sprained your ankle. For that matter, the cops wouldn't have wanted your car for 'forensics'. Hell, I don't even know why they ever wanted it. There was no way you could have been involved in the pileup. I mean, you were out front, right?"

"Right."

"You all right?" Susan raised her head to look at Alyssa. "What's the matter?"

Alyssa shook her head. "Nothing. Just headache. Hot day."

Susan sighed. "Well, I'd better finish this shit off." She heaved herself up. Her generous breasts protested against being confined into the constrictions of the bikini top.

"Susan?"

"Hmm?"

"What was the name of that restaurant we went to last night?"

"*El Gitano*. Why? I got the impression you didn't like the food."

"It wasn't bad. But I wasn't thinking of the food. Just the people at the table next to us?"

"The two geriatrics? Why?"

"Oh, I don't know. Just wondering what they were doing there. They looked kind of out-of-place—don't you think?"

Susan eyed her critically. "I thought *I* was the body-language specialist here! What's it with you? You weren't interested in them last night."

"I don't know," Alyssa said slowly. "They just popped into my mind today."

Susan laughed. A tinkly kind of sound, indicating that she was truly and highly amused. She ruffled Alyssa's hair as she walked past.

"Gotta finish the job."

Alyssa leaned back in her armchair. "I'll be with you in a moment."

"You can do the dishes."

"That, too."

The noises of Susan's activity echoed across from the spare bedroom. Alyssa stared at the wall and pondered what she'd just heard.

About an hour later her cellphone beeped.

"Hello?"

"How's things?"

"Hold on a tick." Alyssa took the phone off her ear. She heard the shower running and Susan's unmelodious voice chanting a distorted rendition of some pop-song.

"Ray?"

"Yes."

"According to Susan you were never in the restaurant last night."

There was a moment's silence. "That's interesting," he said finally. "Anything else?"

"Everything else is…normal… How's things with you?"

"We're going to a party that I didn't know was on. Some kind of gallery opening. It's got to do with Debbie's job. Apparently I've known about this for over a month. Which, needless to say, is news to me."

"Oh no."

He laughed. "Oh, this is nothing! Small fry. Dare I say 'normality'? The kind of stuff I've been living with for years." There was a pause. "I have to go," he said urgently. "I'll call you back later."

Alyssa stared at the silent telephone and slowly put it on the counter again. She was still standing there, cogitating, when Susan came out of the bathroom.

"I forgot to ask you—doing anything tonight?"

Alyssa shook her head. "I don't really feel up to much of anything. Besides, my ankle needs a rest."

Susan made a disappointed face. "Pity. I hoped I wouldn't have to go alone. Strength in company and all that…"

"Where you going?"

"Oh, this client of ours, Mitch Cage—art wheeler-dealer—gave me a couple of invitations yesterday. Apparently there's this new gallery. *Tantrevalles*. Official opening tonight. The governor himself. Big thing, looks like."

Alyssa's head snapped up. "A gallery?"

Susan gave her hair a vigorous rub with the towel. Apart from that she was stark naked.

"Look," she said, "it's no problem. I understand…"

Alyssa shook her head. "No. I changed my mind. I'm coming!"

Susan grinned. "Great! You sure you'll be OK with that ankle?"

"Sure. I won't even need a crutch."

Susan laughed. "Bring it! Men are funny. I wouldn't be surprised if they fell all over themselves in their eagerness to please you."

"Yeah, well, if it's like anything with that creep Samuel today—no thanks!"

9.

Ray managed to put the phone down before Debbie came into the room. He looked at his wife and wondered what in the world he was going to do. With their relationship.

With himself. With Lys. With everything. The whole damn world!

What a piece of chaotic shit had he gotten himself into?

Think, man!

It had always been an article of faith with him that the universe was a structure that made a basic kind of *sense*. Maybe humans weren't always capable of figuring out what the connections were—hell, they weren't even close!—but that didn't really matter. Somewhere, somehow, the whole crap hung together. Hidden variables. There was no 'chance'. No 'accident'. 'Randomness' was a meaningless term. And if it *did* mean something, then that also was the way it just *had* to be. Things were the way they were because they couldn't be any other way. And if there were no hidden variables, and it was chance, then that had to make sense, too. It was just that nobody had figured out why. Yet. Or maybe they had but they weren't talking.

"We'll have to leave at seven," Debbie told him. She was wearing a new dress. A really new one. Not just one he'd merely 'forgotten' she had. That much he had verified a few minutes ago. This one was the real thing. A black and navy affair with a tight blouse that accentuated her perfectly-shaped upper torso and a mini that did the same to her legs. Especially since they served to emphasize her knees—which were among the best-looking knees he'd ever seen.

Anybody with a knee-fetish would zoom in on Debbie like a blowfly on rotten meat. Such people did exist. Ray had seen it happen. A look at Debbie's knee and their eyes would go wide for just a moment; then maybe a licking of lips and some elevated breathing levels, followed by some kind of attempt to chat her up. The world was a weird enough place—even without the current complications.

Debbie pivoted on one foot. "Like it?"

He nodded. "I'm impressed."

"What're you going to wear?"

He shrugged. "Something suitably unimaginative."

Debbie rolled up her eyes. "Ray…"

"All right!" he exclaimed. "I'll try something suitable for the occasion. Arty and farty."

"Please!"

"*You* pick it out."

"You'll just complain."

"I'll try not to."

"Promise?"

"I promise to try."

"I knew it!"

"Give me a chance."

She shook her head and made a vexed sound before sweeping out of the room. Ray gazed after her. He made bets with himself about what she was going to choose.

"I'm going to have a shower!" he called out after her, but there was no reply.

When he had dried himself he went into their bedroom and inspected the clothes she'd placed on their bed. With some dismay he realized that he couldn't recall *any* of the garments. Neither the black, collar-less shirt nor the light-brown linen trousers. He recognized the shoes. Oddly enough, a pair which *he'd* bought, rather than Debbie.

He looked from the clothes to his wife, who was sitting in front of her dressing table, putting on war-paint with the deft practice of many years. Debbie had a thing about being immaculately made up. He had to admit that she was good at it. With Debbie you actually didn't see the makeup. Just like it should be.

As it was, and not considering the bothersome fact that he didn't remember ever possessing either the shirt or the trousers, he didn't really mind her selection, and proceeded to dress. By the time he was done it was just about time to call Alyssa again.

Did he really have to? Maybe every hour *was* overdoing it a bit. Paranoia taken to some extreme.

But a promise was a promise. It was more for her benefit than anything. She must be feeling totally bewildered; more than he ever had. The whole affair had been sprung on her with the suddenness of a personal catastrophe. And he still had the feeling—despite all attempts to tell himself otherwise—that, in some unknown way, it was *him* who was responsible for her predicament. If he hadn't meddled in her life…

And she might be dead now!

Maybe…

Debbie didn't look as if she was going to finish soon; so he went back into his study and called from the cellphone. It was safer.

"Hello."

"Me again."

"Hey, you." She sounded relieved. "I have news."

"Something that'll help?"

"Don't know. This place you're going to tonight. It wouldn't happen to be 'Tantrevalles Gallery'."

"That's the one."

"I thought so."

"Why?"

"Because guess where I'm going to go with Susan tonight?"

His heart missed a beat. "No shit?"

"No."

"That's number four."

"Yep."

"Wow!"

"That's what I thought, too."

"Well, I suppose I'll see you there."

"Definitely. Seems like we just can't get away from each other."

"It does."

"There's something else. I called *El Gitano*."

"Yes?"

"Pretended to be you. Told them I might have lost my wallet at their place. Gave them your name. Whoever was on the phone claimed that they have no record of anybody occupying a table booked under that name last night."

"Why am I not surprised?"

"You know, I'm heading that way, too. Amazing really, that I manage to retain any trace of sanity! Especially when one considers that only a few hours ago a waitress at the same place gave me a slip of paper with your name and phone number on it."

Ray froze. "You still got that slip?" he asked her.

"Sure."

"Bring it with you tonight."

"All right. It should be in my purse."

"Good. Look, I've got to go. I'll see you there."

"Take care."

"I intend to."

He broke the connection. If she really had that slip of paper...if his name was on it...

He shook his head. She wasn't going to find it. It was 'lost' somewhere. She'd probably think that it must have slipped out of her fingers. Something like that. But there would be no slip of paper. That he was certain of. Whatever it was that was happening to them: it wouldn't leave behind incompatible physical evidence.

10.

Tantrevalles Gallery, a project financed in no small measure—like so many things in Atlanta—by the estate of the late Robert Woodruff, was housed in a quirky looking three story complex placed into a nook that used to be populated by another one of those tiny oases of native forest still scattered throughout Atlanta, but which had fallen victim to the relentless desire of real estate developers to make a profit out of every square yard of usable land. Its establishment must have cost a few million. Or maybe more.

As Ray, with Debbie on his right arm, walked through the foyer and up a gentle sloping ramp to the upper part of the split-level first floor, he thought that somebody had really stuck out his neck here; expecting either some huge profit to materialize out of somewhere, or else needing a really big tax write-off! Or maybe both.

The first-floor exhibition hall, with its willful split-level arrangement, provided ample room for the guests to the opening to roam about and admire the, surprisingly conservative, offering of art on display. Paintings, mostly. Realistic and abstract, large and small. Occasionally disturbing. Sometimes enchanting. Ray thought to detect a common theme. The fantastic, possibly. Mental landscapes, even in the most 'realistic' of representations. Populated by creatures that might have come from a child's daydreams—or maybe its nightmares. In the center of the lower level, on a pedestal over six foot long, crouched the figure of a dragon, cast in gray polyester, and sculpted into its final form and meticulous detail with the tools of masons, then painted in stunning shades of red, ochre, brown, and yellow. A creature of fearsome power, gathering its energy to launch itself into the air, the eyes with the vertical irises ablaze with a fierce life-force that hypnotized anybody who dared gaze into them for too long. As he regarded it from a distance, avoiding those eyes, he felt the touch of a haunting familiarity. He groped for its roots but found only vague inklings of memories.

Debbie detached herself from his arm. "I have to help Ron."

He nodded. "See you later."

She disappeared in the crowd. Ray was left to his own devices.

He descended one of the three ramps to the lower level and looked over the exhibits, all the time keeping an unobtrusive eye out for Alyssa—but without success. On several occasions circulating waiters offered him nibbles drinks from silver trays. Ray confined himself to orange juice. He would be driving the car and he never drank in such instances. Debbie couldn't really afford to be too choosy about her drink. She was here at least partially on business. According to her the clients felt themselves at a disadvantage when confronted with a dealer who refused to imbibe alcohol. It was, Ray admitted to himself, not an entirely unfounded phobia.

When he was done he wandered back up the ramp to get a better view of the crowd in the lower part.

Debbie came up behind him, a young man in tow. "This is my husband," she said. "Ray, this is Marcus Hayek."

Ray, who hadn't the slightest idea who Marcus Hayek was, but, sensing that it would not be politic to let on, smiled at the man and shook his hand. A limp grip greeted his. He released the hand and resisted the urge to wipe the clammy sensation off on his trousers.

Debbie beamed at Hayek. "Ray is a software developer. Games."

She said that as positively as she could. Ray had to give her credit for that. Given how she felt about computer games… But it brought in the bucks and that's what mattered.

Hayek grinned inanely at Ray. "What kind of games?"

"I do the A.I. for *Wild Worlds*."

"Wow! *You* do that? *Wild Worlds* is cool!"

Ray saw that Debbie was pleased. Glowing, actually. It seemed like his bread and butter shit was appreciated by at least one person of consequence—whoever Marcus Hayek was…

Ray nodded. "We're close to releasing a beta of version three. You'll find some amazing stuff in there."

Debbie excused herself and left Marcus in Ray's care. Ray wasn't exactly thrilled, but yielded to the inevitable. He answered Marcus' queries about the game and the business in general, and, to his surprise, found the young man more interesting than he had expected. Eventually Marcus admitted, almost shamefacedly, that *Wild Worlds* had actually inspired him on several occasions. Especially when it came to the dragon…

Of course. That's why there had been that touch of *deja vu*. He'd seen it before. Many times. In Pete's Office. Sketches. Designs.

Darktooth. One of Pete's inspired creations—in both appearance and character; a character which he, Ray, was giving a cybernetic substance with his A.I. components. Jack, that sterile twerp in his super-tidy office, could never have produced anything even remotely resembling Darktooth. It was a Pete-thing—a creature out of Pete's psyche.

And now he remembered seeing the name on the plaque at the base of the statue. 'Marcus Hayek'.

"So you see," the artist told Ray, "I owe you quite a debt. Actually I just like totally admire you people. I *dream* of doing that kind of thing."

"Why don't you?" Ray asked him.

Marcus shrugged. "Because I function best in sculpture. That's how I can express things. Computers…well, I just can't *do* anything with them. You know…*make* things. There's a barrier…" His face had a wistful air. Ray, looking from the crouching dragon on the pedestal to the artist who had created it, felt the touch of awe.

"It's quite wonderful," he said. "Pete would be proud of you."

"Who's Pete?"

"The creator of Darktooth."

"I'd like to meet Pete," the artist said lowly.

"That would be difficult," Ray said dryly. "Pete's no longer with the company."

Marcus Hayek gave him an odd look. "That's a great loss."

"I thought so, too."

"Where's he gone?"

"Don't know. He didn't say."

Marcus nodded, as if confirming something he'd suspected for some time. "Thank you," he said to Ray.

"For what?"

"Nobody's ever called it that," Marcus said wistfully, considering his creation. "They all rave and use all the right buzzwords—but nobody's ever called it 'wonderful'. Thanks for saying that—especially since you sounded as if you meant it."

"I do."

"I know." The artist nodded. Suddenly he seemed distracted. "I...I'll talk to you later."

"Yeah, sure." Ray looked after him as he disappeared into the crowd. He passed by a group of five men, who stood around something that Ray couldn't see. But then one of them moved and he saw what it was. Or, to be more precise, *who* it was.

He smiled ruefully. Alyssa was quite a gal. It looked like he wasn't the only one to notice it.

He stood indecisively for a moment, wondering what he should do. Then he squared his shoulders and walked over to the group. He peered at her through the gap between two of her admirers. Alyssa, leaning against the wall, her crutch beside her, smiled when she saw him. She turned to the man who was explaining some of the finer points of whatever.

"If you'll excuse me. I have to see somebody."

He looked crestfallen. "Do you need a hand?" he inquired solicitously.

She smiled sweetly. "No thanks. I have two."

The guy took a couple of seconds to register the brush-off. By that time Alyssa had hooked the crutch under her armpit and started to hobble in Ray's direction. He backed off and walked away slowly as the group parted and the dogs looked sadly after her. Ray sneaked a look over his shoulder and saw then standing there, trying to hide their embarrassment with knowing grins and winks; and he reflected just how pathetic men could be, and how little had changed since the cave days. He ducked around a corner into the elevator lobby and waited for her to catch up with him.

She came around the corner. The way her face lit up when she saw him was a tonic on his tense nerves.

Her lips twitched. "Still real, I see," she said softly.

He grinned. "And intending to stay that way. Nice to see you, too."

"What's going on, Ray?"

"You keep asking me that—and I keep telling you that I have no idea."

She leaned against the wall and reached into the purse that hung from her shoulder; came out with a baby-blue square of paper.

"Well, maybe this'll make a difference..."

Ray gaped at her. He took the chit as if it was a million-dollar bill. 'Shannon'. Underneath his home phone number; written in a flowing kind of style. The lettering had just a touch of the unusual. Someone who hadn't learned to write cursive in the US.

"I don't believe this," he whispered.

"Believe it," she said triumphantly.

He looked at her.

"You didn't expect this, did you?" she asked.

"No."

She nodded thoughtfully.

"You think you could get away from here for a few minutes?"

"Why?"

"Because *El Gitano* is only a few minutes' drive from here. The woman who gave me this slip, Maria, she should be there now. I really think we ought to pay the place a visit, don't you?"

"Just sneak out without telling anyone?"

She grinned impishly. "Why not? Who'll miss us? I noticed your wife's busy; and Susan zeroed in on some hunk the moment she came in. Ditched me with a wink and smile. Leaving me to those..."

"...flies?" he suggested.

Alyssa laughed. "On a piece of rotten meat? I'm not sure the metaphor is flattering; but it's not inappropriate."

"Bees on honey then. How's that?"

"You're a charmer."

"Yeah. Once I get my foot out of my mouth!"

She grinned and held out a hand. "Come on. Let me lean on you. You're much nicer than the crutch."

"Thanks."

"You're welcome."

"Let's take the elevator. That way we won't have to push through the crowds."

They managed to get themselves out into the street and to her car, a rental automatic, without running into anybody who seemed aware of who they were. Which was just as well. Ray really didn't fancy running into Debbie right now—or Ron, her boss, for that matter. Just in case they did, he'd contrived a hasty story to cover the situation—but it still was infinitely preferable not to have to use it.

"You drive." She gave him the keys. They pulled away and into the late evening traffic.

The trip to *El Gitano* took less than ten minutes. The place was packed. A girl behind the reception counter informed them that without bookings they had not a chance.

"Actually we're looking for Maria."

"Maria?"

Alyssa nodded. "Yeah. I spoke to her this afternoon. She said she worked here Saturdays—until midnight."

The young woman shook her head. "I don't know any Maria. And I've been here since two. I really don't know who you talked to!"

Ray saw where this was going. Alyssa glanced at him and he nodded.

"Sorry," he said to the woman behind the counter. "Must have gotten our wires crossed." He smiled at her. "Thanks for your help."

"You're welcome." As they threaded their way out of the restaurant they could feel her eyes on their backs.

They made their way back to the car, which they'd left in the shopping center's parking lot. Alyssa had her right arm draped around his shoulder. He thought she was leaning heavier than before.

"You OK?"

She gave his shoulders a squeeze. "Ankle's a bit sore. Must be all that movement today. Doctor said I should rest, rest, rest. I didn't do much of that."

"The doctor hasn't got an idea what's going on, huh?"

"How could he?"

He sighed. "Well, we have the piece of paper. That's a kind of evidence anyway—whether Maria's still 'real' or not."

"'Still'? You think she ever was? What if these people just exist in our heads?"

Ray shook his head. "I don't believe in solipsism. If it had been just me I would have accepted insanity and hallucination. But with the two of us… No, there's got to be more. You met Maria. She was real. This afternoon anyway."

"You sound much more sure of yourself than you did earlier today!"

"Maybe I am." He held up the slip of paper. "After this, definitely. Also…" He told her about Pete's dragon and his meeting with Marcus Hayek. "There's another bit of physical evidence," he concluded. "Not quite in the same league as this slip of paper here, but very suggestive."

"Of what?"

"Wish I knew. But it's a start."

She shook her head and touched his arm. "I'm glad I've got you to help me through this. I don't know how I would cope."

Ray patted her hand. "It's the least I can do, after dragging you into this."

"There you go again! I thought we weren't going to have this conversation!"

His hand came to rest on hers and he squeezed it gently. "But I *did*. I don't know how, but when I pulled you out of that car something happened to drag you into a mess that's none of your doing. I'm sure of it."

"I don't believe it."

"But I *know* it!"

"Ray, please…"

He took a deep breath. "Listen. You'd better at least think about the possibility—and about how'd you feel about me if it turned out that I'm right. Because it's on the cards!"

"If you hadn't interfered in my life, I would be dead." She said it with a finality and determination that shut him up. He became very conscious of her hand under his. As, it seemed, did she.

"We'd better get back," he said, somewhat hoarsely.

She didn't reply, but made no move to encourage him to take his hand away.

"Lys?"

"Yes?"

"You know what's going to happen here, don't you?"

She didn't ask what he meant. "There's no way it isn't," she agreed.

Oh, what the hell...

He took his hand off hers and put it behind her head to draw her to him. There wasn't, he noticed distantly, even a token resistance. She came willingly—and this time they didn't hold back. It was all out there in the open—at least between them: an admission of the inevitability of, and their complete mutual consent to, what had started the moment he'd stood on the brake when he should have pressed down on the accelerator.

They separated. "We'd *really* better go back now," she said, quite out of breath.

He looked at the car's digital clock. "Shit!"

She laughed throatily and leaned back in her seat. "Time flies when you're having fun."

He leaned over and kissed her again: quickly; not allowing it to linger, because that would have led to more. But they didn't drive off yet, but sat and talked for quite a while; until the clock reminded them that they would surely be missed.

11.

By the time they got back to Tantrevalles Gallery over an hour and a half had passed. The event was still in full swing; though Ray gathered that they had missed the formal opening ceremony. The governor was still here. He must have arrived shortly after they left. Now that he was here, security, which prior to the governor's arrival had been visible but unobtrusive, was more openly active. Ray thanked his lucky stars that both he and Alyssa had their invitations with them. They were stopped upon entry and their names were checked off against a clip-boarded list.

The governor and his wife were circulating between the exhibits; surrounded by an entourage of guards and gallery officials—which, Ray noted from his vantage point at the upper level, included Debbie. Ron, however, was nowhere in sight. Debbie appeared both efficient and yet ill at ease. Every now and then she looked around as if searching for someone. Ray guessed that she was looking for Ron—who had obviously absconded to somewhere unknown.

Oh well, the exposure would do Debbie no harm at all. Ray noticed that her charms weren't lost on either the governor or his wife. Each for different reasons, no doubt.

He became aware of Alyssa close beside him at the railing. They had decided that it wouldn't do any harm to be seen together here. After all, one meets a lot of people during such occasions, and they could pass each other off as casual acquaintances. As long as they kept *some* distance from each other. No touching. No intimate movements. After the episode in the car it wasn't easy.

Now, back in the context he at least partially shared with Debbie, Ray felt like a bastard. Which he probably was.

No—nothing 'probable' about it. Most definitely.

Alyssa seemed to sense his mood. It was uncanny, actually, just how much she knew already knew him.

She leaned a bit closer. "I don't think you should blame yourself too much."

He glanced at her, amazed that she knew this, too.

Alyssa gave him a knowing grin. "This is bigger than the both of us. I don't think we could fight it if we tried."

"I feel like some really pathetic, philandering, middle-age crisis twerp." He shook his head. "Don't misunderstand me, Lys. This...thing..."

"You're right. You're just so totally right. It's about the most amazing thing in my pathetic life."

"Not pathetic."

"Pathetic enough. And, there's another part of me that feels really and truly bad about it all. Terribly sorry for Debbie. Because she's done *nothing* to deserve this!" He shook his head. "What a mess."

"Ray?"

"No." He shook his head. "I wouldn't want it any other way." He grimaced. "That's wrong, of course! I *would* prefer it...tidier, I guess; with nobody to get hurt. But I wouldn't want it without *you* in it. Hell I don't think I could even *imagine* it."

He felt a tension flowing out of her. "Good," she said softly.

He glanced sideways. "You've got to believe that."

"I do."

The urge to put his arm around her and do a lot of other things besides was almost overpowering. As it was, they just allowed their gazes to cross briefly before pretending to pay attention to the scene below them.

Debbie finally happened to look up in his direction. She recognized him and froze briefly. She made as if to wave, but then obviously thought better of it and redirected her attention to the governor and started to explain something related to the exhibit before them.

"Lys?"

Alyssa turned around, Ray following her example. Alyssa's friend Susan stood there, her arms tucked possessively around that of an athletic-looking thirty-something stud. The top of the neck was as thick as the head, flaring into solidly textured trapezes that flexed and rippled under a thin layer of skin.

"Lys, this is John. John, Lys."

Her glance flicked to Ray. No sign of recognition—though, according to Alyssa, she should have known him from last night.

Susan looked back at Alyssa, who hastened to introduce Ray. Susan sized up the situation and visibly reserved her decision. The signals were probably contradictory. A definite something in the air on one hand, and yet no obvious physical connection on the other. Besides, if the hunk beside Susan was anything to go by, Ray was definitely not her type. She probably disapproved of him. He thought that the look she gave Alyssa had an element of 'where'd you pick this one up?' in it.

Ray caught himself. He was feeling smug; rather too much of it. Though he dismissed the sentiment immediately he sensed it, he couldn't help but have it linger. It was, he admitted, a male self-esteem thing. Pathetic, really. Probably a middle-age thing, too. But there was something incredibly ego-boosting when a beautiful woman, who could have her pick of just about any of the fashionable hunks or rich sleaze-balls around here, chose to spend her time with a guy who really wasn't looking his best right now!

Not that, even at his best, he was all that attractive; certainly not in the way that apparently got women turned on. Though he was in a shape most thirty-year-olds would have reason to envy, most of that was hidden to casual inspection. He wasn't in the habit of strutting through public areas in tight T-shirts emphasizing his physique. And it wasn't immediately visible that he had, in days past, broken in horses at his parents' home in Montana; or that he had won just about every shooting competition going.

A regular He-Man.

Ray caught himself.

Sad, really, what kinds of props one needed—despite knowing better. But real nonetheless.

And he was *still* feeling smug.

Sad man!

Still, when he thought back to the car...

Her kissing him. Kissing this pink-headed, hairless freak.

Is my self-esteem that low?

Maybe he did need some help.

No doubt about it. But not the sort that the medical profession could provide.

"Wanna go somewhere else?" Susan asked her friend. She flicked a quick glance at Ray—and finally picked out his wedding ring. Her eyes widened a tad, and for just the fraction of a second. He only caught it because he happened to be looking at her face at that very moment.

Alyssa shook her head. "I'm going to talk to Ray for a little while longer. Why don't you take the car? I'll get a cab home."

"You sure?" Susan seemed relieved. Ray got the impression that she had plans for John and herself, and that she was asking Alyssa more out a sense of obligation than anything else.

"I'm sure," Alyssa told her.

Susan tugged on John's arm. "Let's go then. See you later Lys. Nice to meet you, Ray."

Ray nodded agreeably. The two disappeared in the crowd.

Ray and Alyssa turned back to the balustrade. "What next?" she asked him.

"Tonight you mean?"

"Yeah."

"Well, when Debbie's done I'll have to go home, I suppose."

"Tomorrow's going to be a long day," she said pensively.

"Why?"

"Because for the first time in months I won't know what to do with myself."

"What do you normally do on Sundays?"

"Oh...stuff. Laze around. Read. Watch videos. Try to switch off from the week. That's unless the boss calls and wants something done. Which happens—but not too much. He tends to respect our weekends. Unless it's some shit like today, with that creep Samuel..."

"Well, take it easy tomorrow then. Do what the doctor ordered. Rest the ankle. Is it sore now?"

She nodded. "Quite."

"Want me to get you an aspirin or something?"

She nodded. "That would be nice. I haven't been drinking, so it should be OK."

"Yeah, I've noticed you clutching the orange-juice!"

"Just being politically correct," she smiled. "Don't drink when you've got to drive."

"Sometimes 'politically correct' actually *is* correct." He glanced around for one of the circulating waiters. He spotted one and strode across to him. "You wouldn't happen to know where I can get an aspirin? Paracetamol? Whatever."

The man nodded. "Yes, sir. You'll find a dispenser in the bathrooms." He grinned. "Aspirins and condoms."

Ray went back to Alyssa. "Wait here. I'll get you some."

"Thanks."

He went off, sauntered through the elevator lobby and, following the discreetly-placed signs found the men's toilet easily enough. It was empty, save for the man who left as he entered. The only indication of a human presence was the closed door of one of the toilet cubicles.

Ray dropped four quarters into the dispenser and got four encapsulated aspirins in return. He dropped them into his pocket and, since the urge was upon him, headed for the urinal. When he was done, he zipped himself up and turned to go.

As he did his eyes fell on the closed door. From his angle he could see well under the lower edge of the door. He took a step and then stopped.

Something wasn't right. Feeling just a tad foolish he took a step back and looked again. Something, he decided, definitely wasn't right. The visible parts of the legs, with their trousers down around the feet, looked…odd. Funny angle. Like…

Feeling even more like a pervert Ray hunkered down to get a better view. It was from this perspective that he saw the dangling hand. And the blood.

Shit!

He straightened and went to the cubicle; nudged the door with his foot. It wasn't locked, but swung open—only to jam against something; that something being the slumped-forward corpse on the seat, leaning slightly sideways and somehow jammed against the paper dispenser.

The cause of death was pretty obvious: a gaping hole in the side of the head. And another couple in the back. Bullet wounds.

It took Ray a moment to recognized the corpse.

Ron Hadlow: Debbie's boss.

Fighting his urge to retch, Ray stepped back and hastened out of the bathroom. Only when he was outside did he remember that he had the cellphone hooked to his belt.

Should he call the cops or notify whoever was in charge around here? Should he do anything at all? There was virtue in avoiding involvement.

He stood irresolutely for a few seconds. Then he took the cellphone and dialed 911.

12.

Ray took a long time. Alyssa wondered what was holding him up. Behind her was a small commotion. She looked around and saw Ray talking to a couple of waiters. They appeared to be in some state of agitation. Ray himself looked drawn and tired. Alyssa pushed herself off the balustrade and, supporting herself on the crutch, hobbled toward where he stood.

He finally took note of her.

"What's the matter?" she asked him.

He made a small gesture. The cellphone was in his right hand. "I found a dead man in the bathroom."

"What?!"

He twitched his head as if to dislodge an unpleasant image or memory and reached into his pocket. His hand came out with a foil-pack holding four aspirins.

"Sorry for taking so long."

"It's OK. Are you all right?" she asked, worried.

He shrugged. "Yeah, I'm OK. It just wasn't a pleasant sight."

"Do you know who it was?"

"Yeah. Debbie's boss." She uttered a soft sound. Ray looked at her emptily. "He was murdered."

A man in an expensive suit came running toward them.

"Better go!" Ray whispered to Alyssa. "You don't want to get dragged into this." His eyes pleaded with her and she relented. Reluctantly, but she could follow his reasoning. They were in a precarious situation in more ways than one.

"I see if I can talk to you later," he said quickly before she left. "Otherwise I'll call you as soon as I can, OK?"

"Be careful," she told him.

"I will."

The man in the expensive suit was upon them. Ray faced him and Alyssa used the opportunity to back away discreetly. She retreated to the balustrade and made a show of sipping her drink as she watched the scene unfold. She felt the aspirins in her hand and took three of them. Her ankle was hurting like hell.

The cops showed up with sirens and the whole shebang only a few minutes later. She guessed that Ray must have called them on his cellphone. The exits were sealed. The PA system announced that nobody would be allowed to leave the place until their names and statements had been taken. That excluded the governor of course. No surprises here. But then, he had the advantage of an implicit alibi.

Damn! Speaking about alibis…

What were she and Ray going to do about that?

She saw him standing between a couple of plain-clothes cops who were asking him questions. He was shaking his head. One of the men wrote something in a small notebook.

She tried to catch his eye and finally succeeded. She screwed up her face in what she hoped was a reasonable attempt to tell him that she had to talk to him. He nodded minutely. Alyssa turned away and hoped for the best.

Down in the lower level the cops had set up a makeshift interview desk. People were filing past it, identifying themselves, by various means, sitting down, making statements which were duly recorded on small hand-held dictaphones, before being allowed to leave through the wide entrance.

Behind her she felt a presence. Ray stopped beside her.

"You went for a walk," he said lowly without looking at her. "Unless there's a pressing need to come up with anything else—which I doubt—that's probably the best."

"What about you?"

"I'll make up a similar story. Except that I went for a drive."

"Do you think that's wise?" she wondered.

"I don't know *what's* wise," he admitted. "The way things are going I have no idea what to do? What do I know what's changed from the way I think it was? Anyway, I think that, under the circumstances this is the safest. If it becomes necessary we can always change our story. I'm sure the reasons for fudging it will be understandable."

"You mean like that we are having an affair?"

He glanced at her sideways.

"We are, aren't we?" she said.

I guess we are at that.

She smiled to herself.

"Anyway," he said, "I'll do my best to keep in touch. And now I'd better attend to Debbie. This is going to hit her pretty hard."

"Please be careful," she said softly.

"You, too."

"I promise."

He moved away. Alyssa saw him descend along a ramp to join his wife, who was being interviewed by a uniformed and a plain-clothes policeman. She didn't appear to notice him at first; but then, when he finally attracted her attention, she just shook her head. Alyssa thought that Ray was right. Debbie seemed to be in profound shock. She turned away from her husband and said something to the cops, before pushing her way through the crowds and out of sight. The policemen directed their attention to Ray, who stood there, looking after her in bewilderment.

13.

"Mr. Shannon?"

The detective, a wiry black man, scanned him with unsettling frankness.

"That's me," Ray confirmed.

"Miles Carter," he detective introduced himself. "This," he indicated the overweight uniformed policeman with him, "is Sergeant Thighe."

"Your wife is upset," Thighe said.

"Ron was her boss," Ray pointed out. "It must have been a terrible shock."

Detective Carter nodded, never taking his eyes of Ray's face. "Quite a coincidence," he mused.

"What?"

"That you, of all people found the body. Especially since it must have been in there for at least two hours."

Ray considered the detective. "How's that possible?"

"How did you discover him?" Carter countered.

Ray explained.

"And you're in the habit of peering underneath toilet doors?" Thighe interjected.

Ray was at loss to explain the cop's palpable antagonism. Unless these two were acting out a good-cop-bad-cop routine...

"No," he said curtly. "It was just a question of noticing something that didn't seem right."

"A lot of people must have come and gone," Carter insisted. "*They* apparently didn't notice."

"People aren't very observant," Ray pointed out.

"Don't I know it," Carter noted wryly. "You wouldn't believe it if I told you."
"I would."
Detective Carter nodded. "Yeah, I guess you would."
"What did you do next?" Thighe asked.
"I went to the door and pushed it open."
"You didn't think to knock? I mean, there might have been someone alive in there. Taking a dump. Or did you know the man was dead?"
Ray thought. "No and no," he said slowly.
"What?"
"No, I didn't think to knock. Probably because the latch showed the 'vacant' label. And no, I didn't know there was a corpse. Not consciously anyway. But maybe I *did* sense that there was something out of the ordinary."
"'Sense'?"
"Whatever. Come to think about it, seeing the skewed legs and the dangling hand... bloody dangling hand...Maybe the smell, too. I suppose maybe I *did* know he was dead."
"'He'? How did you know it was a man?"
Ray didn't believe he'd heard right.
"It is a *male* toilet, Sergeant!" he said, putting as much sarcasm into the statement as he could. "And those were trousers around *his* feet. Bit of a giveaway, don't you think?"
From Carter same soothing noises. "I'm sorry, sir, but it's our job to ask questions."
Ray looked at the black man. "Stupid questions."
Carter smiled thinly. "As I said, you wouldn't believe me if I told you just how stupid some *answers* are." He considered Ray for a moment. "Did you touch anything at the scene?"
"No."
"But you opened the door."
"With my foot."
"Your foot?" Carter echoed.
"Are you in the habit of opening doors with your foot, Mr. Shannon?" Sergeant Thighe said.
Ray shrugged.
"Why this time?"
Ray shrugged. "Don't know." He really didn't. "I guess something must've told me..."
"You 'sensed' something again?" Thighe asked, not bothering to keep the sarcasm out of his voice.
"Not 'again'," Ray corrected him. "It was the same event...remember?"
"So," Carter continued, "you claim that you felt there was something amiss and you acted accordingly."
"Something like that," Ray admitted.
Carter nodded. "That's fair enough." He gave Thighe a quick look, which Ray interpreted as an order to lower the annoyance level.
"We'll be asking everybody this same question, sir," Carter continued, "Don't feel singled out, just because you discovered the body."

"What question?"

"We need you to account for your whereabouts during the time you were here. You know, people you talked to. When you spoke to them. Anything that'll allow us to reconstruct your movements during the evening."

"You mean, I need an alibi."

"Something like that."

Of course.

"I can probably provide that—for the time I was here."

Detective Carter raised a questioning eyebrow. "You weren't here all evening?"

"No."

"Where did you go?"

"For a drive."

"Why?"

"I needed to get out of the crowd. I only came here because of Debbie—and she was very busy. I chatted to a few people, and then I told myself that I needed to get away. The whole thing was getting claustrophobic."

"Is this your usual reaction to crowds?"

"Sometimes. Today it was. Mainly because of the accident…"

"Accident?"

Ray pointed at his face. "My complexion doesn't usually rival that of a cooked lobster. And I *do* have some facial hair."

"What happened?"

"I was caught in the pileup on 285 and came too close to some igniting gas fumes."

"When was that?"

"Yesterday. Driving home after work."

Detective Carter looked at his massive companion, who shook his head. Ray, with preternatural clarity saw where this was going. Well, not quite 'where' it was going, but it was clear that it wasn't going *his* way. He knew what Thighe was going to say almost before the man opened his mouth.

"What accident on 285? What time?"

Ray, thinking furiously, wondered how he could recover as much ground in this mess as possible. He shrugged with fake carelessness. "Late yesterday afternoon. It was a stupid accident resulting from some idiot cutting across lanes. Another couple of idiots following too closely—as usual! and 'bang'…

"I stopped and got out to help. Came too close to the scene when a gas tank blew up. It's amazing how fast this stuff diffuses through hot air."

Thighe made a note on a little pad of his. Carter nodded thoughtfully. "You're still in shock, you say?"

"I'm still trying to come to terms almost with having my face fried to a crisp. I'm also kind of self-conscious right now. Skin freshly anointed with gel. No eyebrows. Bald like an egg. Stuff like that."

Carter considered him frankly; not entirely, it seemed, without sympathy. "So, you went for a drive. Where to?"

"Stone Mountain. Didn't drive into the park though. Then I went back again. The long way. Must've cruised aimlessly for quite a while. Don't really remember *where* I went."

"That took you how long?"

"Maybe an hour and a half."

"And when did you came back?"

"The opening ceremony was over. Debbie was showing the governor and his wife around. Standing in for Ron, I suppose—who didn't seem to be around."

"What did you think about that?"

"His absence? Not much, really. I'm not overly familiar with Debbie's business. But I gathered that she wasn't prepared for this."

"What do you mean?"

"Well, she kept looking around, like she was searching for someone. Ron, I suppose."

"How long had he been gone?"

"I don't know. I wasn't here, remember?"

"So you say," muttered Thighe.

Ray chose to ignore the remark. "Anyway, I decided I needed a piss. So I went to the john. The rest you know."

Carter nodded. "Quite. Well, thank you, sir. That's all for now. We'll probably have to talk to you again. You will be around town, won't you?"

"I have no plans for going anywhere."

"Good."

Ray produced his wallet and extracted a business card which he handed to Carter. "You'll probably find me here."

The detective took the card, studied it briefly, and put it into his pocket. "Thank you for your help Mr. Shannon. I'm sorry you had to be the one to find the body. It's probably been a shock—what with you being stressed anyway…You know, the accident and all."

"It was," Ray agreed.

"I commend you for your presence of mind in calling us immediately—and for making sure the area was sealed off."

"I watch a lot of movies," Ray smiled. "Part of my job."

"Your job?"

"I design A.I. modules for computer games. Strategies and tactics. Character reaction patterns. Story development. All of which is pretty much on par with writing novels or screenplays. And when something like this happens in real life, as it were, the mind kind-of treats it a bit like a game. I suppose it's the unreality of it. The kind of stuff we only *expect* to see in movies or games."

"Hmm." Carter looked at Ray for a few silent moments. "An interesting philosophy, Mr. Shannon."

"'Psychology' is more like it. I'm still amazed how detached from the whole thing I feel even now. As if it hadn't really happened."

"Well, it did," Thighe noted curtly. "This is not a game, Shannon."

Ray turned to the policeman. "*Mister* Shannon to you, officer!" he said with all the venom he could muster. The overweight pig was getting on his nerves. Which, he thought belatedly, was probably the intention.

"That will be all," Carter said in his soft but intense voice. "Thanks again for your help."

Ray frowned. "Something bothers me."

"What?"

"Can you tell me when he died?"

Carter shook his head. "I'm afraid at the moment I can't discuss this."

"Well, it's not really important," Ray wondered aloud. "But the man was *shot*, right? How come nobody seemed to have heard anything? It must have made a racket in that room. Especially since he was shot…what?…I thought I saw at least three wounds…"

"An interesting question," Carter agreed.

And there'd been no shell-casings either. At least he hadn't seen any. Which meant that it had either been a revolver, or, if someone had used a semi-auto, that he ('he'? why a 'he'?) had actually collected the spent casings.

And no noise? Meaning a silencer had been used? That made it look like a *very* pre-meditated killing.

No doubt Carter was having similar thoughts. Ray shrugged and went off to find Debbie. The sense of the two cops looking after him was like a physical prod in his spine.

14.

Ray found Debbie a little while later. She had just emerged from the ladies' bathroom and looked like shit.

"You OK?" he asked her. A stupid question, but what else could he say?

She stared at him as if she'd never seen him before.

"Let's go home, " he said.

She looked as if she was going to say 'no', but then a shadow of resignation flitted across her empty face and she nodded listlessly.

The drive home was conducted in a silence that hung like a thick fog in the air. Debbie was distant and cold: physically present only; and resenting even that. She got that way every now and then; especially when they'd had a real bad argument. Which wasn't the case this time, but Ray guessed that having your boss murdered could well have the same effect.

When they got home and the garage door had closed behind them she disappeared immediately. Ray found their ensuite locked. He shrugged and stood there, contemplating the bed for a moment. He couldn't possibly go to sleep now. Not after everything that happened to day. One might have thought that he would have been exhausted, but, if anything, the cumulative effect of the events of the day was one of heightened alertness.

He knocked on the bathroom door. "Debbie?"

"What is it?" her voice came back faintly. It sounded as if she was crying.

"Is there anything I can do?"

"No. I'll be OK."

"I don't think I can sleep right now," he said to the door. "I'll just stay up and read for a while."

There was no reply, and somehow he hadn't expected one. He turned and went back into the small room which doubled as a kind of library and office. The walls were completely covered in bookshelves, and most of the shelves were full. Near the window stood a small desk with a keyboard and a thin LCD screen. The computer was tucked away in a specially designed compartment underneath the desk.

Ray didn't turn it on, but got the laptop out of his briefcase. He extracted a phone connector, plugged one end into a wall-socket and the other into the laptop's modem connector. He plonked himself down on the sofa in the corner and, after making himself comfortable, fired up the web-browser and connected to the Journal-Constitution site.

Saturday headlines. Atlanta news. The pages looked subtly different from the way it had when he'd looked at it this morning. Which wasn't unexpected, because they updated it constantly.

After about five minutes Ray gave up. The report about the accident on 285 had disappeared. Surprise, surprise. It seemed like, over the period of about one day it had sort-of faded away.

Somewhere in the house he heard Debbie putter about. She appeared at the doorway, wearing a light nightie.

"I'm sorry about being so pissy," she said lowly. "It's just that..."

Ray looked at her. Despite the words she seemed distant and not-quite-here. The face exhibited a frightening emptiness; a bleak void.

"It's all right," he said soothingly.

"I'll have to go to work tomorrow," she said. "With Ron..." The words choked in her throat.

He made a move to put the laptop aside and get up to go to her, but she shook her head. "I'm fine. I'm going to bed."

"I'll try not to wake you," he said, sinking back onto the sofa again.

She shrugged—a gesture of utter indifference—and left. Ray stared at the space where she'd been for a few moments. Then he took a deep breath and returned his attention to the screen. He remembered something and reached for his briefcase. A few seconds of fumbling around came up with a printout from this morning at work.

He sighed with relief when *this* at least was exactly as he remembered it.

Like that piece of paper Alyssa had given him. He reached into the back pocket of his trousers, withdrew his wallet, and retrieved the blue slip of paper.

Physical evidence.

Of *what*?

That he wasn't insane!

It would be nice to know that.

And Alyssa wasn't insane either.

On impulse he got up and went to the bedroom. The light was still on. Debbie, her eyes red from crying, was sitting at her dresser, taking off her makeup.

"Debs?"

She stopped her ministrations and turned to look at him.

Ray pointed at his face. "This accident..."

"What about it?"

How was he going to phrase this without sounding weird?

"Well, I'm having memory lapses again..."

"How can you forget something like *that*?"

"Shit, I don't know. It's just...the details...They're just getting kind of...hazy."

Her face actually acquired some sort of animation. "Just as well you're seeing Dr.

Lopez on Monday."

He was?

Ray nodded. "You're not kidding. Which reminds me, have you written that appointment down somewhere? I'm liable to forget that, too, you know…"

"It's on the kitchen calendar," she said shortly.

"Good," he said, with genuine relief. "Now, about the accident. Help me Debs, will you? What did I tell you about it?"

She looked at him strangely but in the end yielded and told him. About the barbecue on Thursday night. When she had suggested eating out, but he wanted to do this stupid barbecue in the garden. How he'd been so scatterbrained that he'd forgotten that he'd turned the gas on already—and when he came back and tried to light it…

She'd always told him that gas barbecues were dangerous.

"What exactly," she concluded, "is it you can't remember?"

Ray shrugged. "Whether I used matches or that…sparky-thingie."

She frowned. "I don't know. Doesn't matter, does it?"

"No it doesn't," he agreed, "but it just bugs me that I'm can't remember."

"I'm sure Lopez will sort it all out. He really helped Marcie."

'Marcie'?

Who was 'Marcie'?

Ray bit back the words wanting to come out. "Thanks," he said. He went over to her and, despite her stiffness, placed a kiss on her cheek. "Sleep tight."

She said nothing. Ray went into the kitchen and looked at the calendar beside the back door, where they wrote down all their appointments, so that there was a central reference of sorts.

'Dr. Lopez, 2.10 pm.'

He didn't even know where to find 'Dr. Lopez'! Then he saw the card attached to the top of the calendar with a paper-clip.

A neurologist, huh?

Well, why not? It was all a charade, but maybe there was something the guy could come up with anyway. Something that poked a hole into the mystery.

Ray returned to the library and sat back down on the sofa. He made another attempt to find any trace, even the flimsiest, of the accident, but finally gave up trying. It was gone—and there was no doubt in his mind that, if he picked up the paper…

The paper! They had a 'physical' copy around here somewhere! It was delivered every day. For Debbie mainly.

Ray got up again and found the JC in the kitchen. As expected there was nothing—literally *nothing*—about any accident on 285.

Shit!

He tiptoed back to the bedroom, but the light was out now. Quietly as he could he returned to the library and closed the door behind him. He picked up the phone and sat back down on the sofa. Since they had two lines to his phone account he could leave the modem connection running and call someone at the same time.

He bethought himself and decided to use the cellphone instead.

"Hello?" Her voice was like a tonic. An oasis of certainty in a quagmire of confusion.

"It's me."

"Ray. I'm so glad you called!"
"You OK?"
"I am now!"
"What happened?"
"The cops. Very persistent people. They weren't very happy with my lack of an alibi. Wanted to know all sorts of things."
"How did you go?"
"I think they bought it. But I suppose I'm actually on the 'suspect' list."

A pause, while Ray digested the information. "How did you fare?" she wondered then. "I saw them grill you. From where I stood…you didn't look very happy."

"I wasn't. I wish I hadn't found the body! Or bothered reporting it! There was this fat asshole…"
"The lard-ass white cop?"
"Yeah—him."
"I got the impression he didn't like you."
"You could see that from up there?"
"Yeah, body language thing."

He chuckled siccantly. Alyssa had told him about Susan's passion. It looked like it had rubbed off on her just a bit.

"Lys?"
"Problems, huh?"
"Yep."
"Something else is going wrong?"
"Can I ask you to re-tell me what you remember about our first meeting?"
"Why? What's…"
"Just tell me. Please!"

She did. It still matched his own.

"Good," he said when she was done. "We're still in synch."
"What makes you think we might not be?"
"Nothing, really—if you ignore the fact that the accident never happened."
"What?"
"Is your friend back?"
"Susan? Actually she is. Seems like the guy turned out to be not quite what she had hoped for."
"In what way?"
"Rapist type."
"Shit! Is she OK?"
"Yeah. A bit shook up, but nothing happened. It might have, of course; but Susan's done some self-defense stuff. It came in handy."

Ray sighed. "Good. Hey, she wouldn't still be awake, would she?"
"She's having a very long! shower. Trying to wash the bastard off herself, I guess."
"All right. Well, I don't know how you're going to handle this, but when she gets out—do you think you could find out just how *she* thinks you got your face burned?"

There was a moment silence.
"Lys?"
"I'm here."

"You OK?"

"Yeah."

Another few moments of silence.

"I wish you were here," she said. "I really wish you were here."

"So do I," he agreed.

"I'll call you back when I know," she said tonelessly.

"All right. Hey, Lys?"

"Yeah?"

"We'll see ourselves through this. You've got to believe that."

"I don't know *what* to believe."

"Believe *this*!"

A sigh at the other end.

"Susan's done. I'll see what I can do. You gonna call me back?"

"Call me when you're ready."

"What are you doing anyway?"

"Insomniac stuff. Searching the web. Checking on how much the world is what I think it ought to be."

"Debbie?"

"Asleep—I guess."

"She seemed very distraught."

"Can you blame her?"

"Not really." But her tone indicated that this wasn't quite what she meant.

"I'll call you soon," she said suddenly.

"Bye."

The line went dead.

15.

Susan emerged from the bathroom, rubbing her hair with a towel. Quite uncharacteristically, she had another towel wrapped around herself. An indication to Alyssa just how much she had been affected by what she called her 'encounter'. Alyssa never hadn't figured out yet how the whole thing had gone sour, but she knew Susan would get around to it in due course. It must've been a strange sequence of events. Susan liked men and she wasn't exactly inhibited when it came to…responding…to their advances. And it had looked as if she actually liked that guy. What could he have done to get her into *this* state?

But she saw in Susan's face that, as yet, she wasn't ready to talk.

Still…

"You OK?" she asked.

Susan put down the towel and made a grimace. "What a jerk!"

"Wanna talk about it?"

"Later."

Alyssa nodded. "Think you can help *me* with something?"

Susan eyed her curiously. "What is it?"

"It's about my accident."

"What 'accident'?"

Oh, shit!
"What happened to my face."

Susan snorted derisively. "Is it an 'accident' now? That's not what *I* would call it. I still think you should sue the pants off the bastards."

Alyssa eyed her without comprehension.

"Hello!" Susan said. "Remember? You're a corporate litigator! That's your baby, kid! How can you sit there and let them do this to you? *You* of all people?"

Alyssa said the safest thing she could think of.

"Burden of proof." What was Susan talking about?

Her friend shrugged negligently. "I won't be pleasant, of course; but you could use that stuff under controlled conditions. Expert medical witnesses, appointed by the court. If you're worried about the lobster face, maybe you could try it on your chest."

Alyssa was beginning to figure it out. "They'll claim their trials were exhaustive. That I'm at fault—not their product. A statistical freak. Unless I can establish that they *should* have found it during their trials..."

Some cosmetic product! That's what it had to be.

"Van Salle have a record of sloppy human trials," Susan pointed out. "I gave you the file, remember?"

"Yeah, I know." Alyssa was prevaricating as she tried to construct a coherent picture of what Susan's 'reality' might be.

Funny way of looking at things, really. And maybe even stranger that she, Alyssa, was taking to it with a dizzy kind of ease.

What kind of a freak am I?

Maybe not a freak at all. Merely coping, moderately competently, with what Ray claimed might well be a 'natural' phenomenon external to themselves.

Whatever it was, she'd better get her act together here. Starting with a big rule that she had to make the centerpiece of her life:

Don't assume *anything*!

Nothing was certain. Everything could be different to the way she remembered it. She had no idea why, but there it was.

She came back to immediacies. Her accident—which, to Susan, had been...what?

What about her singed eyebrows and hair? How did that fit in with everything?

Except that right now there was little sign of any of these effects. She'd carefully combed out the singed bits and pieces and plucked her eyebrows until they were reasonably—well, remarkably, if the truth be told—symmetrical. Only her skin still exhibited a slight redness, but even that was clearing away nicely.

All in all, whatever was left behind was consistent with an allergic reaction to a cosmetic as much as it had been with what *she* remembered.

It looked like Ray had suspected something like this.

Why? What had he found out?

Possessed by a sudden sense of urgency she told Susan that she might consider suing the bastards after all. Susan was visibly pleased. Alyssa thought she detected a predatory glint in her eyes. The girl was sharpening her claws already!

"Sleep tight," she told her friend and picked up the cellphone.

"Who you're gonna call?"

Alyssa shrugged. "Someone who might help me with this."

"At one-thirty in the morning?"

"He's an insomniac."

Susan's eyebrows rose. "Lys? What are you up to? Is this someone I should know about? What have you been keeping from me?"

What was going on?

You've met the guy! Tonight!

Alyssa shook her head. "Nobody you'd be interested in."

"I thought I knew everybody there is to know in your life! You've been keeping secrets!" she said accusingly.

Alyssa laughed. "Go to bed. I'll talk about it tomorrow. Maybe."

"You'd better!" Susan gave her a last knowing look and flounced off.

Alyssa dialed Ray's cellphone.

"You were right."

"What did she say?"

"She thinks its an allergic reaction to some cosmetic I've used. Wants me to sue the company."

There was a chuckle at the other end of the line. "Lawyers."

"Hey!"

"Present company excepted."

"You're just subscribing to the popular image of the legal profession. Bloodsuckers and opportunists."

"Not me! I'm trying to assume nothing. It's a sobering experience."

"I was telling myself the same thing."

"Unfortunately I ignored my own advice." He told her about his conversation with the cops.

Suddenly she was *very* worried.

"What are you going to do about that?"

"I'd hoped you might be able to tell me!"

"I'm not a criminal lawyer."

"Well, if these guys decide to follow this up I might need one. Actually, if they compare notes—our absences from the scene—they might even decide to connect us."

"Maybe it's better that way."

"I don't think so, Lys. *Please* try to keep out of this!"

"I may not have a choice."

"But if you do…"

She sighed. The man was being perfectly unreasonable. They could provide each other's alibi!

"Trust me on this," he said in her ear.

She was unconvinced, but relented anyway.

"For the moment."

16.

Her reluctance was obvious from the tone of her voice. He hoped that she wasn't just humoring him. Hard to tell, really. He didn't really know her well enough yet to sort out such nuances.

But he knew he trusted her. Within this madness that's one thing he had to be able to hold onto. Otherwise he would go surely nuts.

"Maybe you should go to bed, too," he told her.

"I'm not tired."

"Try it anyway."

"I'd rather talk to you."

Yeah, well, if the truth be told, he felt pretty much the same.

"What shall we talk about?"

She laughed. "Anything. Everything."

"Be nicer to be face to face."

"But we can't do that."

"No."

"Tell you what. I'll call you when I'm tucked into bed. Maybe it'll help me go to sleep."

"So now I'm boring, huh?"

A chuckle on the other end.

"Gimme a few minutes," she said and hung up. Ray put the phone down and retrieved a headset attachment which he plugged into the small unit. If he was going to talk to Lys for a while this would be much more comfortable. And safer.

Ray put the computer on his lap again, paged back to the AJC site, and studied the news. Then he picked up the paper from beside him on the sofa and compared some of the items. They appeared to agree. The contexts of paper and website matched perfectly.

Ray turned a few more pages. He came across an article about newly flaring problems in the Middle East. President Madison was sending the Secretary of State on a mission to defuse the situation.

'Madison'?

Ray's hand shook as he put the paper down.

The cellphone vibrated against his leg. With a shaky hand Ray picked it up.

"You can talk me to sleep now," Alyssa told him.

He didn't answer immediately.

"Ray?"

He let out a breath. "Yeah, I'm here."

"What's the matter? Falling asleep yourself?"

"Far from it," he said. "Lys, who's the President of the United States?"

"Jack Trent."

"And who was the one before that?"

"George Bush."

"Which one?"

"There's more than one?"

"Father and son."

"Father, I guess."

"What about Bill Clinton?"

"Clinton? I've heard the name."

"Arkanas governor. Good talker."

Lys laughed. "Oh, him! He was nominated, all right—but then he couldn't keep his dick out of a pretty campaigner. The Republicans found out. That was the end of Clinton."

"Does '9/11' mean anything to you?"

"Should it?"

"Osama bin Laden?"

"Hmm. Isn't he the guy someone in Africa handed to the U.S.?"

"You tell me."

"They locked him up at Guantanamo, I think. For all I know, he's probably still there."

When Ray didn't answer immediately: "You don't agree?"

" 'Agree'? I'm not sure that means anything right now. To my memory, Clinton became president. During his eight years in office he had his dick in more than just one place it shouldn't have been. He sweet-talked everybody and sundry, but ignored the really important issues. Osama bin Laden remained at large and became an icon for world-terrorism. On September 11, 2001, planes, piloted by terrorists crashed into the World Trade Centre and the Pentagon."

"What??"

"But none of that happened wherever we are now, it seems. It's definitely more like your world than mine."

"Whatever that means."

"Tell me," he said, "who was the first president of the US?"

"William Jackson."

"That not what *I* learned in history class."

Silence on her side of the connection.

"Do you still know your Presidents?" he asked her.

"Most of them."

"I'm all ears."

She recited their names. She got most of them—and in the right sequence. With the small snag that three of the names he'd never even heard of.

"What does all that mean?" she wondered. "That even you and I can't agree on what's real? Now I'm *really* scared!"

So was he. There was no denying it. On the other hand he sensed that here was another bit of data to be added to his fact-file.

"Maybe it's not so bad," he said, trying to sound confident.

"It looks pretty bad to me!"

"We agree on the things that matter to us," he reminded her. "That 'reality' we share completely."

"But..."

"Look, don't let this get to you. Let's just keep talking about those things that matter. Forget about the big picture. Let's flesh out some more details."

He hesitated, thinking about what truly mattered here.

"About you and me," he told her. "Because we're the only reference points in this mess. And that's what we have to hold on to."

Sunday

1.

Neither of them got any sleep that night. Daylight was a pink hue when they finally agreed to hang up and try to sleep; call back as soon as either of them woke. Ray went back to the sofa, where he propped a cushion under his head and presently—his head full of images of Alyssa: child Alyssa, teenage Alyssa, college Alyssa, grown-up Alyssa—exhaustion claimed him.

When he woke up it was almost noon. The air-conditioning, for some reason or other, was off, and the place was an oven. Ray squinted into the glare of daylight seeping through the curtains. His mouth felt like it was plastered with cow-shit. His neck hurt from lying in a twisted position, and he had a headache to match. He dragged himself off the sofa and into the shower. A cold one—and even that didn't quite dispel the heaviness that seemed to weigh him down.

When he came out of the shower he checked their bedroom. As expected, Debbie was long gone. He looked around for a note but found nothing. He called the up-market art gallery/store where she worked. Debbie answered.

"I didn't want to wake you," she told him.

"Thanks."

"When did you get to sleep?"

"Late."

"Figures."

"What time will you be back?"

"We close at four, but I'll have to stay on and do some things."

"So—what time?"

"Maybe six or seven."

"What're we going to do for dinner."

"I don't feel like eating."

"All right, I'll make myself something then."

"You going out?"

"Maybe. Don't know yet."

"Well, I'll see you when I get back."

Ray was preparing a very late breakfast of scrambled eggs and toast when the phone rang.

"Mr. Shannon?"

Ray recognized the voice immediately. "Detective Carter! How nice of you to call."

"I have a few more questions about last night."

"Shoot."

"I'd rather speak to you in person. Mind if I drop around?"

"Suit yourself. Just give me an hour, huh? I'm still waking up."

"How about two o'clock?"

"That would be good. Leave the unpleasant Sergeant somewhere else, will you?"

A chuckle on the line. "I'll see what I cam do."

Ray hung up with a sick feeling in his stomach. He picked up the phone again and called Alyssa. She answered after several rings. Her voice sounded drowsy.

"Wakey, wakey," he said softly.

"Torturer," she said weakly.

"Just thought I'd let you know that I'm up. The cops are going to pay me a visit at two. Once you got yourself up and awake, can you call me? I think I may need the name of a decent attorney."

"Sure. Gimme half an hour." She sounded *much* more awake.

"Thanks."

"How are you?"

"Like I was hung over. And that without a drop of alcohol."

"I know how you feel. I'll call you soon."

Less than half an hour later the phone rang again. But it wasn't Alyssa.

"Ray Shannon?"

"Yes."

"My name's Frank Nuovo. I'm an associate with Heckler and Barlow: Alyssa's firm. She told me you needed legal advice."

Ray heaved a sigh of relief. He explained the situation. Frank Nuovo promised to be over within the hour. And, no, he wasn't to speak to the police without him present.

"Sorry about screwing up your Sunday," Ray said.

Frank Nuovo laughed. "I hate Sundays anyway."

Nuovo showed up less than an hour later. He was a small, compact kind of guy in his mid thirties, who stood with the straight back of many small people. He wore a yellow Nike T-shirt and shorts. The small briefcase in his hand was an incongruous addition to the image.

They shook hands and, over a Coke, Ray filled Nuovo in about the details of the case. Nuovo questioned him closely about the interview with the cops the previous night, insisting that Ray repeat everything with as much detail as possible. When it came to the point where Ray had brought up the accident he paused.

"I have a problem," he confessed.

"What kind of problem?"

"Don't know yet. I'm seeing a neurologist tomorrow. It's probably a stress-related thing though. Point is I have…well, memory lapses. Distortions. Blank spots. I think I told these guys that I'd received my singed face at the scene of an accident on the 285. Fact is, it happened when I lit the barbecue on Thursday night. That stuff about a vehicle accident…I must have dreamt it—but for a moment there it seemed like it was what happened."

Nuovo studied him attentively. "You've had this…condition…for long?"

"It's been getting more acute."

"And you're seeing a doctor on Monday?"

Ray nodded. "Yeah. Should have done it a while ago, but…well, you know…"

"Any other medical matters I need to know about?"

Ray shook his head. "None I can think of."

Nuovo nodded. "All right then. This is the drill. I approve every question by the police. If I don't approve, you don't answer. If I shake my head, you don't open your mouth. If I nod, you can talk—but be careful and deliberate—and *watch* me! If I shake my head, you shut up immediately. That clear?"

"Clear enough to me."

Nuovo nodded. He smiled thinly. "Alyssa told me that you two were together last night, but that you don't want to drag her into this affair. Why?"

Ray shrugged. "My wife, if nothing else. She's upset enough. The dead man is her boss—and a friend. Besides, Lys's and my little trip would only be misinterpreted—unjustly so. We didn't sneak off to a motel or anything like that. We just went for a drive."

"That's what she said, too."

"Probably because it's true. Anyway, I really want to keep Lys out of this, if that's at all possible."

"You may not have a choice. And the police aren't going to be pleased if they find out that you haven't been candid with them."

"You telling me that I *should* drag Lys into this?"

Nuovo shook his head. "It's not a question of 'dragging'. She is involved in this, whether you like it or not."

"Let's hope we won't have to," Ray said. "I'm willing to incur the displeasure of the police. After all, I've done nothing wrong."

Nuovo shrugged. "Your call. I was just advising you about what I thought is the best course."

"But you'll support me with this?"

"We'll have to skirt the subject very delicately. As I said: watch me carefully—and weigh every word you say in front of these guys."

"What if they bring up the thing about the accident?"

"Tell them what you told me. I can't see any problem with that."

2.

Detective Carter—'Lieutenant', to be precise—was not amused to find Frank Nuovo at Ray's place. Ray was faintly amused when he saw their combative stances. The detective with Carter, an underling with the curious name of Midget—he was over six foot—appeared equally bemused.

When Carter questioned the wisdom of Ray's recourse to legal assistance, Frank Nuovo smiled.

"My client feels that, in the light of your questioning last night, this follow-up merits the presence of a sympathetic witness—and some legal counsel."

Carter made the best he could of what was an inconvenience and proceeded to go over the same ground they'd covered the previous night. Frank Nuovo, who had positioned himself strategically, so that Ray could see his face without having to crane his neck, kept nodding slightly throughout the questioning. Only when Carter touched on Ray's slip about his 'accident', did the lawyer interrupt.

"My client corrects that particular statement to the effect that the accident occurred at his home while lighting a gas barbecue."

Carter, ignoring Frank Nuovo, raised his eyebrows, folding his forehead into a bunch of wrinkles.

"Would you care to explain your statement last night?"

Frank shook his head and Ray said nothing.

"We may do so tomorrow sometime."

Carter turned and looked at the lawyer. "What are you trying to do, Frank?"

"There are medical issues to be considered. As I said, we should know more tomorrow and will notify you as soon as we do."

Carter nodded thoughtfully. "See that you do," he said curtly.

He turned back to Ray. "Mr. Shannon, do you own a gun?"

Ray looked at Nuovo, who nodded. That hadn't come up in their prior discussion. But, under the circumstances, it appeared like a reasonable question.

"I do." Actually he owned two: Glocks. But only one had been bought from a gun-dealer, and was on the books somewhere. The other had been a private sale.

"Where is it?"

"In my study." The other gun was affixed out of sight underneath the dashboard of his car.

"Could you please go and get it?"

Nuovo nodded again. Ray got up. Carter motioned to his sidekick. "Let's accompany Mr. Shannon."

They followed Ray into his study. "It's in a holster affixed to the underside of my desk," Ray told the detectives. "And it's loaded. So, maybe you'd better get it yourself."

Carter nodded and gave a signal to the Midget. The latter went to the desk, bent down, and looked underneath. He took a Ziploc bag from his pocket, slipped on a latex glove, withdrew the Glock from the holster and dropped it into the bag, which he sealed.

Carter looked at Ray.

"I'm asking you, in front of these witnesses, if you agree to us removing the gun from these premises to subject it to forensic tests."

"On what grounds?" Frank Nuovo wanted to know.

"The murder weapon was a 9mm semi-automatic. Probably a Glock. Four shots fired at close range. One in the head. Three in the heart and the lungs. Since Mr. Shannon is one of those individuals at the gallery who does not have a sufficient alibi, inspecting his gun and ruling it out as the murder weapon can surely be only to his advantage."

He looked at Ray. "Unless you feel differently, of course."

Ray glanced at Frank. The lawyer's look seemed to tell him that it was his call.

"Take it," Ray said. "As you said, it can only help if you rule it out."

"Quite." Carter took the bag with the gun. "Why do you own a gun, sir?"

Ray shrugged. "Home security."

"You are proficient with the use of this weapon?"

"I grew up on a farm in Montana."

"Meaning?"

"Meaning 'yes'," Ray said dryly. He pointed at a framed target hanging on the wall. Carter stepped over and considered the tight grouping in the center.

"Nice shooting. Glock?"

"Yep."

"Fifty feet?"

Ray nodded.

"*Very* nice shooting." Carter nodded thoughtfully. "One more question, Mr. Shannon. Did you know that the victim, Ron Hadlow, was having an affair with your wife?"

Ray felt like someone had whipped him across the face. His heart missed a beat and he found that he couldn't breathe.

Debbie?

An affair?

Debbie?

With Ron, the asshole?

A little voice told him not to be so surprised. Besides, what was he going on about? As of lately he hadn't, exactly been Mr. Faithful.

But...Debbie?

He felt their stares like a physical thing, and it brought him back to the present with a jolt.

"No," he said. "I didn't."

Carter made a skeptical face. "You told us yesterday that you pride yourself on your observational prowess. Are you telling me now that this is something you missed completely? That it comes as a total surprise?"

Ray sighed. "Well, it did. Maybe it isn't anymore...now that you've told me. I mean, hindsight is the best sight, right? But, no, I *didn't* know. I never thought..." He drew himself up. "Anyway, how do *you* know?"

Carter's face looked faintly smug. "It seems to be common enough knowledge among some people. Many of them considered it ironic, to put it mildly, that it should have been you who found the body."

That would be Debbie's 'arty' crowd: a bunch of jerk-offs.

How long had this been going on for?

He forced himself back to focus on the present. "Is that all?"

Lieutenant Carter nodded. "For the moment. Pending the examination of your weapon."

"Which I can have back *when*?"

"If it turns out not to be required...Tuesday. Maybe Wednesday."

"Good," Ray noted, putting a measure of disdain into his voice. "Then, if you're done..."

The policemen left. Ray closed the door behind them and looked at Frank Nuovo. "What do you think?"

"You're their prime suspect."

"What?"

The lawyer touched a finger to his nose. "This tells me they're zooming in on you. Even if the gun's clean..."

"...which it is!" Ray interrupted.

"Yes, of course, but even that's not going to divert them. I know Carter. I know how he functions. You're right up there at top of his shit-list."

"Fuck!"

Nuovo shrugged. "Don't worry. If you're innocent they won't be able to touch you.

But you may need Alyssa for your alibi."

"Let's jump off that bridge when we come to it," Ray told him.

Nuovo made a wry face. "Your choice. I'm just advising."

"You're going to continue to act as my attorney?"

"If you want me to."

"I do."

"All right." Nuovo opened his briefcase and withdrew a thin sheaf of papers. "Here's our standard retainer contract. Read it and let me know what you think. The moment you sign it it's official and you're our client."

Ray scanned the jargon-laden text. "I think I'll get Lys to explain what all that means," he grinned.

Frank shook his hand. "You do that," he chuckled. "I'm sure in the choice between me and you she won't hesitate. I get the impression she's rather fond of you." He grimaced. "Don't know how you did it. I've been trying to get…well, 'closer'…to Lys for a long time. Without perceptible results, if I may say so. I wonder what you've got that pushes her buttons." He grinned to take the sting out of the words.

Ray saw Frank to the door and waited until the lawyer had climbed into his silver BMW. He gave him a brief wave and went back into the house.

Debbie?

An affair?

It went round and round in his head.

How long?

Months?

Years?

How long had his marriage been on the rocks? And, if what the detective had told him was true—and somehow Ray knew that it was—then why, on the other hand, did Debbie still seem to care? This whole doctor stuff. What was it to her if he, Ray, lost it?

I care what happens to her as well. he told himself. Just because there's someone else it doesn't necessarily mean that one stops caring.

The strange twilight world of marital infidelity!

Ray went back to his study and plucked the cellphone from the recharger. He dialed Lys's number. She answered immediately.

"How'd it go?"

He told her, including the bit about Debbie.

Alyssa made commiserating noises, but Ray sensed that she was relieved. It didn't surprise him. He was relieved, too. Debbie's transgressions, no matter what lay behind them, lent Alyssa's and Ray's relationship an air of ethical legitimacy. It didn't absolve him from responsibility in whatever had happened or was happening, but it eased the burden of guilt—because guilt there was aplenty; and it was only now that he was capable of acknowledging it to himself.

"The truth is," he admitted to Alyssa, "that this gets me off the hook. I still feel like a jerk and a heel, but it's becoming manageable."

"You didn't choose this," she insisted. "Neither of us did."

"Bigger than both of us? You really believe that?"

"Don't you?"

"I'd like to think so," he said, "and it's probably true, too. But we make choices; and sometime yesterday—or maybe Friday night—I made a choice to fall in love with another woman but my wife."

He stopped dead when he realized what he'd just said. On the other end of the line there was a pregnant silence.

"I'm sorry, Lys," he said softly. "I didn't mean to..."

"Will you *please* stop riding the guilt wagon?" she interrupted.

Ray chuckled. "Yes, ma'am."

"Good."

"Wanna meet somewhere?"

"Definitely."

"When?"

"As soon as possible."

"I'm going to bring that contract Frank left with me. Maybe you can translate it into English for me."

Her laughter echoed in his ear. "I'm going to bring my collection of *TIME* magazines for the last year. Maybe we can figure out what's what, eh?"

"Excellent idea! Where shall we meet?"

"Have you had lunch?"

"Not yet."

"You like Pizza?"

"Who doesn't?"

"There's a Mellow Mushroom in Roswell Road."

"Yeah, I know that one."

"See you there?"

"Half an hour."

3.

He'd used the 'L'-word. And from the way it had made her feel...

Alyssa put the cellphone down and took a deep breath. For the umpteenth time today she asked herself why she wasn't going crazy—considering everything that had happened in the last couple of days. Or maybe, whether she *was* actually already insane, and just simply didn't know it.

My worst nightmares and my wildest dreams. What a roller-coaster ride!

Six impossible things before breakfast. Alice had *nothing* on what was happening to her!

Susan was up and about. She had the ears of a cat and no doubt had heard most of Alyssa's end of the conversation with Ray. Fuel for wild speculations.

What was she going to tell Susan? She had to come up with *something*.

She found her friend in the bathroom, flossing her teeth.

"I'm going out for a while."

"To meet with *him*?"

"Yes."

"Gonna tell me who he is?"

"Someone I met at the party last night."

"Not *that* guy? The one with a head like a sculptured egg?"

"Susan!"

"I'm shocked, babe!"

"Looks aren't everything."

"Don't I know it," Susan said darkly, her light mood evaporating. Last night was coming back to her.

Alyssa hugged her from behind.

Susan said nothing.

Alyssa released her. "I've got to go."

"Just watch out for yourself."

"Ray isn't like that," Alyssa told her friend.

Susan turned around and looked at her. She saw something unexpected and her eyes widened. "Whoa! There's really something going on here!"

"Yep."

Susan shook her head. "Well, maybe you're right. I certainly shouldn't be talking…"

"You just ran into a jerk," Alyssa said gently. "It happens."

"Yeah." Susan returned to her flossing. "That'll teach me to mix with the art-crowd."

"You could have run into that prick anywhere."

"True," Susan mused, the thread between her teeth. "Take care of yourself, huh? When will you be back?"

"Don't know. I'll call you."

"Yeah—do!"

"See you!"

Alyssa went into the spare room where she kept a collection of old *TIME* magazines in a cardboard box. She picked up what she thought was about half a year's worth and put them into a small airline bag she retrieved from under her bed. Then she went off to meet Ray.

4.

They must've looked funny. Munching pretzels, then pizza, and leafing through *TIME* magazines. They sat together, squeezed onto one bench, and poked through the mags, finding aplenty that neither of them remembered. Snapshots of a world that was only partially theirs.

They also found out that their individual worlds differed in some marked respects. Not in anything that had happened since their meeting, but things before that. And the further back they went, the more differences there seemed to be.

"Where's this going?" she said when he took a napkin and drew a couple of intersecting circles onto it. And another behind it, and another in a staggered pattern. Then he connected them to form the image of two merging tubes.

"Sorry, I'm not very good at drawing."

"What is it supposed to be?"

"Individual world lines. Well, not quite. Context lines, rather."

"The overlap represents the amount of context we share. The rest is what's different.

The stuff in the foreground is the present. Behind that the past."

"And the further back we go the less we share and the more is different."

"Exactly. Now, of course, in a way that's what happens when any two people meet. As they get to know each other and spend time with each other their contexts merge more and more. So, in a way, this is a psychological diagram."

"But it's more than that."

He nodded and took a bite of pizza, washed it down with a swig of Coke.

"Much more. It's also a picture of physical reality, if you will. The problem is..."

She knew what the problem was. "Where's the rest of the world?"

Ray drew some more circles until in the end the napkin was full of squiggles and surreal-looking intersecting tubes stretching away into the distance.

"The rest of the world, if we look at it just in terms of the worlds of *people* is just this: shared contexts—or not, as the case may be."

Something was missing here. She knew that Ray was leading up to something. Sod him! He was playing games and—she saw—enjoying it.

She dug an elbow into his side. "Ouch!" he exclaimed.

"Get on with it!" she whispered.

"With what?" he asked innocently.

"Whatever," she hissed.

Then she saw that he was grinning.

"Bastard."

He looked her full in the face. "It's just a theory, you know. I could be completely wrong. And even I'm not, I have no idea what good it would do us."

She pushed against him. "All right by me, mister. Any explanation is welcome right now."

Their faces were very close. Too close. Pizza or not, she wanted that kiss *now*. So she closed the last few inches and gave him a quick, greasy kiss. She found a very satisfactory response.

"That's better," she said. "Now. Back to theorizing."

"I don't know if I can."

She grinned. "We'll take another break in a minute."

"All right."

He turned back to the napkin and stared at it for a moment, then plucked another one out of the dispenser.

"But there aren't just people," he continued. "We both have *memories* of things that we both know either have never been real in this world we're in.

"Still, we manage to interact—on the whole pretty effectively—with all those who seem to be blissfully unaware of all this."

He looked at her. "I know this sounds crazy, but this whole thing's crazy..."

"I don't care. I just want *something* to hold onto."

"I don't know *what* it means, but, unless we want to assume that the whole world's gone crazy around us, or that everything can change into just about anything else... unless we accept that—which I can't..."

He pulled a blue slip of paper from a back pocket of his jeans. He fumbled a bit more and came out with the printout of the AJC web page. "This here is the clue. There's us. Our memories."

"I have no idea what you're talking about," she admitted, feeling stupid.

"This printout," he said. "It's a physical object. The characters on it are physical objects adhering to its surface, shaped by events which happened sometime in the past when I did the printout. Yesterday morning.

"This object has persisted despite the fact that, according to the apparent 'reality' around us, what's written on it could never *have* been written because it relates to something that never happened. And not only that, but I bet you that if I tried to verify that I actually did that printout by some method—which I don't have, by the way, but I could have, theoretically—I would find that it was never done."

He put the printout down and picked up the blue slip. "Here. A note written by a woman who, according to what we've been told, doesn't work in the place where you *know* she told you she works. Another physical object that shouldn't be here. But it is. As are *we*: yet more physical objects which bear testimony to a curious physical phenomenon, whose existence, to the best of my knowledge, has never proposed by anybody."

"Would you mind speaking English for at least part of the time?" she said crisply.

He put a hand on her arm. The touch soothed her. For a moment, despite everything, she felt *safe*.

"I'm sorry," he said. "I'm trying to reproduce my own lines of thought. I'm not very good at explaining this, am I?"

She hooked her arm under his. "Go on."

"All right. There is a theory in physics—often dragged in to explain the paradoxes of the subatomic world—which postulates that, in a very real sense, every physical event splits the universe into at least two tracks. Two forever separate realities. In one of them the event went *this* way"—he pointed the thumb of his right hand to his right to the right—" and in the other it went *that* way." He pivoted his hand to point the thumb in the opposite direction.

"That's a simplification, of course, but basically heart that's what it is. Each time anything happens that could as well have not happened, or happened differently, the universe splits into different timelines—which remain separate from each other into the future. And in due course in each of these resulting universes the same thing happens again, and then they split as well, and so on and so on.

"You can see where that leads: to the creation of a near-infinite number of separate universes, each of which is slightly different from the other."

"And they're all *real*?"

"Yep."

"And we are in *all* of them?"

"Yes. Different—more or less—but real."

"Sounds crazy—but I'll accept it for the sake of the argument. What's that got to do with us?"

"Well, something about that theory has always bothered me."

"I'd say," she muttered. "It's crazy. A gazillion copies of me?"

"Not just you," he corrected her. "Of the whole of universe. And, yes, it is crazy. But 'crazy' isn't a good enough reason to dismiss it."

"It is for me."

"Much more bothersome," he continued, "is the asymmetry of it. We start off with one universe and we end up with an infinity of them."

He took another napkin and drew what looked like an inverted tree.

"See what I mean by asymmetry?" he said. "It kinds of offends one's sense of symmetry, doesn't it. But what if…"

He continued the drawing; only now he re-connected some of the branches.

"Ah."

"Ouch!"

"Sorry!" Alyssa released her fingers, which had dug into his arm.

"I get it! This here…it's the other way around. It's not worlds splitting apart—but *coming together*."

She could see that he was genuinely pleased with her. Maybe even proud.

He nodded. "And somehow we're caught in the middle of this."

She touched the blue slip of paper. "So this is a…leftover…from…what? A past—one of those universes?—in which we *were* in that restaurant? But somehow that past doesn't seem to exist any more. Why not?"

"Maybe it's just been absorbed in some strange kind of way," he said. "When two branches merge, something's got to give. Whatever is left has to be consistent."

He grimaced. "Just speculation, remember? Truth is, I don't understand any of this. Maybe when worlds that are incompatible in some way come together one of the strands has to disappear. Like water in sand. I only know that it's the best explanation I have come up with so far."

He gazed out the window at the traffic on the road outside. "Maybe this is a normal physical process: just the inverse of what happens when quantum events split the universe. Maybe it happens all the time, only normally we don't ever notice, because the mergers happen so smoothly that it doesn't make any *difference* that they happen. It's only when there are discrepancies—like in our case—that things don't go so smooth. At least not for us."

He shook his head. "I wonder how often this happens. To people, I mean. Like us. Or maybe just to people alone— who haven't got anyone to share their confusion and bewilderment. I wonder how many people go crazy because their world's turned upside down and inside out."

He looked at her and smiled. A bit sadly, it seemed to her. "Maybe it explains a whole lot of other things as well. Like what happens when people remember so totally different things about what should be the same event. Maybe it's not always question of perception and memory. Maybe sometimes it's just plain common-garden physics."

They sat quietly for a few moments, each preoccupied with their own thoughts. Her hand crept along his arm to find his. She interlaced her fingers with his.

"So, what can we do?" she whispered.

He shook his head.

"Survive it," he said bleakly.

5.

Ray derived no pleasure from the 'explanation' he had just provided. It sounded sensible—if anything could be called 'sensible' right now—but it didn't explain the 'why'; nor did it offer any suggestion as to how they should deal with their predicament. Certainly, it wasn't something he cared to broach to anybody but Lys. It was the stuff of science-fiction, not something to propose seriously. He could just imagine explaining the whole thing to Carter.

"I'm sorry, Lieutenant, but you see, we're not *quite* from the same world as you."

"That's fine, Mr. Shannon. Now, if you don't mind, here are a couple of guys in white who would like to take you away somewhere."

In contrast to Ray's gloomy disposition, Alyssa seemed to have benefited from what he'd told her. Despite his dismal pronouncement on their prospects she had lightened up considerably. All of which in turn helped to provide him with some measure of hope; despite everything.

He wanted to tell her that it wasn't going to make a shred of difference whether they knew or not. But he didn't. Right now he didn't want to spoil the optimistic mood. The moment was just too precious, in more ways than one. There was an easy closeness between them that he hadn't felt with anybody for a long, long time. He looked at their interlaced fingers and gave a gentle squeeze. She laughed. It came from deep within her.

"Crazy," she said. "Totally crazy."

That it was.

"But not *this* part."

"Definitely not."

"I know this isn't pleasant for you," she said, "But I can't say I'm disappointed at your...domestic...problems. I know it's selfish, but..." She shrugged, not looking guilty at all.

"It's all right," he told her. "It gets me off a rather awkward hook. I really had no idea how to handle this...thing."

"'Thing'?" she said archly. "Is that what you call it?"

He grinned. "Well, it doesn't quite qualify as an 'affair'. Not yet. And I don't think there's a word invented for people like us. There may never be."

She laughed. "You're right. You know, two days ago I didn't even know you. And now..."

"Now what?"

"Now...well, now you're *it*." Her face inched closer, but it stopped just short of touching his. "And all that because of some stupid maniac coming out of nowhere."

Her words triggered off a flash of memory.

"That's it," he said.

She pulled back a couple of inches. "What?"

"That car—it came out of nowhere. Literally. One moment it wasn't there, and then, *bang*! Like the guy who suddenly was just *there* when I pulled out of my car-park."

"I guess it must have started around then. Maybe even before. And it lasted at least until that car hit you."

"You mean that car just didn't exist in *this* world?"

"But it did in another—and when they came together the driver lost it. Understandably so."

"But the accident," she objected. "It's...disappeared. It's as if it had never been."

"Maybe it just took a while to be 'assimilated'," he said. "Remember that some time passed. When I did this printout, the whole affair had already been demoted to something far less significant than it had been in the first place. And less than a day later it has been effectively wiped out. Except in our minds, of course. Somehow, *we* remember."

"And we have this." She indicated the pieces of paper on the table.

"None of which constitutes 'evidence' that we can show to the police," he reminded her. "You know that as well as I do. It's good enough for *us*, because it supports our shared context; but it'll never be anything more than that."

"Well, it's our sanity I care about," she said and moved her face closer to his. He closed the gap and kissed her again. For a few moments her presence was the only real thing in his world.

"Wow!" he whispered when they separated.

She looked at him dreamily.

"Is this magic or what?" she said lowly.

"My vote goes to magic."

6.

"What about that woman at the restaurant? Maria."

They had found a surprisingly quiet spot along one of the many parks adjacent to the Chattahoochee. Away from barbecues and screaming kids. Ray was lying on his back and Alyssa, her sore ankle carefully positioned for maximum comfort, had draped herself halfway across him. Her head lay sideways on his chest, tucked just under his chin.

"Maria?" Ray echoed. "I don't know. Maybe she just doesn't work at *El Gitano* in our current stream. Maybe she doesn't even exist."

"So she's just…gone?"

Ray grimaced. "I have no idea. But it's a scary thought. One moment you exist and the next, poof…"

"Now you're scaring me!"

"I scare myself."

"What if she exists? Somewhere in this world? Just *who* is she? Does she have any inkling of what else she was? Like when I talked to her?"

He stared at the blue sky. She could see that her questions bothered him. By now she'd figured out that he wasn't the type to let such things rest. He'd dig away until he thought he'd figured something out. Just like he had come up with this goofy but weirdly coherent theory; which she had been willing to buy, hook, line and sinker, because it gave her *something* to focus on. Something to order her world around.

So, Ray's theory had a few rough edges. But did that matter? It seemed to hold together—if one accepted the assumptions behind it.

"Maybe she, whoever she is now, has a few strange memories of her own," he said.

"I like that better than the notion that she'd just stopped existing!"

"Definitely," he agreed.

"And what about your friend, Peter? Where's he? And how is he connected with you and me and the accident? And what about your funny double-lane ramp?"

She felt his chest shake as he chuckled. "You're full of questions, aren't you? Sorry, but I have no idea."

"That's all right," she said into the cloth of his shirt . "I forgive you."

His arms around her tightened. For a while they just lay there silently, savoring their moment of peace.

Above the treetops a sudden breeze was developing. A thousand leaves rustled in unison, producing the sound as if of a waterfall. Alyssa raised her head and looked up. Just visible above the trees a tower of cumulus clouds, promising a summer thunderstorm. They'd have to leave soon. Far too soon! Return to their respective lives and sort things out. She would have to find some convincing answers to Susan's questions. Ray would have to face Debbie.

"Are you going to tell her that you know?"

He grimaced. "You think I should?"

"I don't want to tell you what to do."

"I know. But I need help."

"Well, I think you should. Get it out into the open."

"I agree."

"Are you still going to see that neurologist tomorrow?"

"I have to."

"Why?"

"We have to adapt to the prevailing...well, 'reality' I suppose. That goes for you as well. We're in enough trouble as it is without fighting the system. That means we both go back to work tomorrow. And I'll go to see that neurologist."

"And then?"

"Seems to me like planning too far ahead is a bit dicey right now."

"Hourly calls!"

"Promise."

7.

The confrontation with Debbie was not edifying; especially when she told him that she was just doing what *he* had been doing for years. She even gave him names and dates. Called him a 'philandering s.o.b.' and told him that she wasn't going to spend another night in the same house with him.

At that moment Ray finally *understood* that the woman shouting at him wasn't Debbie at all. Not the Debbie he'd known anyway. Not *this* Ray's wife.

What did that mean? In another 'past', as he had come to think of it, had he really been like that? Sleeping around? Cheating on his wife, and driving her into the bed of a creep like Ron Hadlow? Ray didn't like to think that he was capable of being that kind of guy, but then he admitted to himself that, given the frightening ease with which he had turned from a monogamous husband into a love-struck mid-forties hard-on, it wasn't all *that* outlandish. A bit of the 'other' Ray definitely lurked in him as well.

The confrontation magnified Ray's sense of being in a world that wasn't his; of being somebody else than he should be.

A cold shock ran through him when he realized that the Ray whose world he now inhabited might well have been capable of...what? Murder? Killing Ron Hadlow?

For what reason? What could he possibly have gained by icing the prick? Ron and

Ray had nothing to do with each other; Debbie being the only connection. And if the other Ray had really been the kind of guy Debbie was depicting, even jealousy didn't really come into this as a motive.

When Debbie was done with him and had stormed off into the bedroom to collect some stuff and take herself to a hotel, Ray dumped himself into an armchair; totally exhausted and drained. He tried to remember the Debbie he had known. What she had been like over the last few days.

There had been genuine concern about his welfare. That's why she was so down: she, like him, could see their marriage falling apart at the seams. Nothing visible, but with rot all through it. Chemistry out the window. Talking, but not communicating.

Friday, after the accident, when she had picked him up from the hospital, it was still all right. Not good, but all right. Afterwards, at *El Gitano*: a bit distant, but nothing worse than usual. The post-mortem. That, too, was in line with expectations.

Then came the evening of the gallery opening. Before leaving the house. Still nothing unusual here. But between arriving at the party and the discovery of Ron's body things had deteriorated with devastating swiftness. And now it had become just about as bad as it could get.

Ray felt an odd void inside him. It took him a moment to figure out what it was, but then he thought he knew. It was a sense of loss; of something gone forever. Debbie and he might not have been as close anymore as they once had been; they mightn't even have loved each other anymore; but they had been an integral part of each other's lives, and they had shared a significant number of years. They had struggled and failed and triumphed together. Had had a past together. No matter how far apart they had grown: what had been had been, and nobody could take that away.

Still, it appeared that the only traces of that history existed in his own head. The Debbie that was rummaging around in the bedroom, slamming doors and sobbing, probably had no memory of many of the things he still bore within him. That Debbie had memories of somebody who wasn't him. A creep, from all appearances.

Ray experienced the same kind of sickness he'd felt yesterday morning. His wife, the one he had known—and loved!—had effectively ceased to exist.

Lys's question came back to him.

Where—if 'where' made any sense in this context at all—was 'his' Debbie? If one accepted the 'merging timeline' theory he'd propounded to Lys, then what happened when, like now, two strands came together? What happened when Debbie #1 and Debbie #2 merged into—were replaced by?—Debbie #3? Did one of them just cease to exist? Or both? Who or what was Debbie #3?

This was one of the major problems with his theory. Unlike the accepted—though purely hypothetical—notion that each event generated multiple, diverging copies of existing universes—which wasn't inherently paradoxical—the reverse idea, that there might be a subsequent merger of previously disparate continue—was; because if 'mergers' they were, then something had to give.

The rules, please!

The slamming of the front door disrupted his thoughts. Debbie was gone. He could hear her car start up and the squeal of tires as she backed it out onto the road and roared off.

What Ray thought of as the 'absorption-hypothesis' made more sense than the idea of a mere cessation of existence of one 'version'. During the last couple of days he'd witnessed several developments which made him think that this was the more likely course of events. Gradual changes from situations that seemed to belong into his former universe to others which conformed to the reality he found himself in now. Like superimposed images, blending into each other. One of them proving dominant and, in the end, displacing the other or maybe both morphing into something that was both and yet neither nor.

Except for himself and Lys, of course.

Was this what had happened? That in this instance the 'wrong' versions had retained their dominance—thus throwing them out of synch with everything else?

Did it matter?

Ray realized that he was exhausted, in more ways than one. Physically, he felt like he'd been run over by a truck. Mentally, he sensed, he was on the verge of collapse. He probably would have done so already if it hadn't been for Lys. Her presence, her very existence, was what held him together right now. That and maybe the fact that he'd found at least *some* 'explanation' for what was happening: a theory that fit into his scientific paradigms.

Actually, if the truth be told, he felt quite smug about having come up with it. Even if it didn't help him to extricate himself from his problems, it showed that he hadn't become completely dysfunctional.

His eyes fell on the book-shelved wall in his line of sight. He reminded himself that in a sense this wasn't 'his' room at all, but that belonging to quite a different 'Ray', who was him at the same time as he wasn't. Not to put too fine a point on it: he was in somebody else's house. Nothing here really belonged to him. He was an intruder into other people's lives; and the Ray whose personality was imprinted on the room around him wasn't necessarily a guy he would find particularly *simpatico*.

Let's snoop!

He got up and scanned the room. It was quite familiar. The basic decor was the same, as was the furniture. A slightly different arrangement, but nothing glaring enough to attract his attention.

Or maybe we wasn't as observant as he thought he was. Maybe...

Maybe things weren't the same now as they had been, say, last night. It was possible. Any damn thing was possible right now. Any assumption was potentially dangerous.

Ray continued to scan the room, and as he did, the differences began to crystallize. Arrangements on the shelves. The pictures on the few leftover free wall spaces. His desk...

His desk.

He went over to it and opened a drawer.

Definitely not *his* desk.

He pulled out the drawers one by one. Now he really felt like he was snooping on someone else; riffling through another life. He turned on the computer. Even here things were subtly different. Everyone working with computers for any length of time imposes a certain order, appearance, personality on the machine. The arrangement of the desktop. The placement of icons. Installed software.

The Ray whose computer this was, also had copies of certain of his programming projects on this machine; taking them home from work to fiddle with them during the wee hours of the morning. Ray went into some of his programming projects and found more subtle differences: methods of indenting code; commenting; the naming of variables; a hundred other little things, all of which added up to a definite picture of this machine belonging to someone *else*.

Ray looked up from the screen and around the room. He went over to the nearby wall that was nothing but a floor-to-ceiling book case and bent down to retrieve a couple of photo albums from a lower shelf. They were, he noted, still in pretty much the same place where they had been.

(Here he caught himself thinking of this other life as being in the past, rather than a 'parallel' present.)

Ray noted that there were fewer albums than is 'his' study, and that the styles were different as well.

He started leafing through them. Some photos were familiar; others he'd never seen before. And there were other differences. Poses. Settings. Motifs for landscapes. Groups of people he'd never met in his life.

'His' life.

Ray put the albums down. Following an impulse, he went back to his computer and clicked on an icon denoting an address-book. The program started up and asked him for a password.

A password for an address book?

Ray tried some from the collection of those he'd used in the past. To his surprise one of them worked: 'muthafucka'. That surely told him something else about his 'other'.

The entries in the address book: some he knew; some he didn't, especially the women. If this list was anything to go by, his 'other' was quite a ladies' man; possibly more than Debbie had ever suspected. No wonder the address book was password-protected.

Ray thought for a moment, then got his laptop. If his 'own' reality was anything to go by, it contained, among other things, a mirror of many of the files and programs of his desktop system, as well as some stuff from work.

He started up the laptop. The first thing he noticed was that—*as he remembered!*—the laptop did not contain the address-book program he had on the desktop machine. And there were a lot of other differences. It looked and felt much more like what he—what he thought of as the 'real' Ray!—remembered and was familiar with.

The laptop, Ray decided, should be considered another piece of physical evidence that he wasn't insane after all.

His eyes fell on the time display at the bottom right of the screen. He compared it with that of the desktop machine. The laptop was a couple of hours fast. Following a hunch Ray positioned the cursor over the clock to get a display of the date.

Actually, the laptop was a full week ahead: exactly where it *should* have been, according to Ray's reckoning. All of which meant that the laptop kept *his* time.

Ray looked at his watch: the same thing here.

It looked like there were some serious synchronization issues…

A week—minus two hours. What did it mean?

Monday

1.

"I think you're right," Alyssa told him when he called her before going to work on the next morning. "After our talk last night, I did some poking around in Susan's mind."

He laughed. "I like the way you phrase that. Makes me think of a surgeon opening up someone's skull."

"Thanks! Anyway, her expectations of me...I don't know where she could have gotten them from—unless the 'me' she's known is *very* different from who I'm now."

"What kind of differences are we talking about?"

She hesitated. "Like me and men. Seems like I'm somewhat dysfunctional in that area. According to Susan, I go for studs in their early twenties—with no emotional overhead, as it were. Tiny brains, big...you know. One night stands only. A week with a guy is a *long* time for me. Professionally, I'm a predator. That's why Susan's so perplexed that I'm letting this Van Salle thing slide. Come to think about, I've wracking my brains trying to remember a cosmetics manufacturer called 'Van Salle'!

"Anyway, it seems I'm a litigator's dream. Susan thinks I've got a lot of sublimated hostility—which comes out in the courtroom—and in the rest of my life as well. She called me a 'ball buster'. Apparently it's all my father's fault. Seems like I was molested when I was young."

"Which you never were in *your* life?"

"No. I've got *good* memories of my parents. Dad especially. To think that he's gone..." her voice died out.

"Hey easy!"

She sighed. "I'll have to go and see them. I've got to know. And I dread going to the office tomorrow!"

Ray knew how she felt. He, too, had to face his colleagues. When they looked at him, who was it they would see? What were their secret thoughts going to be when they confronted *this* version? How was he meant to act to conform with their expectations?

"I'm thinking of just quitting," he said. "I don't know if I *want* to live as my 'other'. From the sounds of it he was a real prick."

"I don't think I like 'me' much either," she admitted.

They said goodbye and promised to keep in touch: on the hour. If one hadn't called, the other would.

"I miss you dreadfully," she said.

"Ditto. Wish you were here."

2.

When she came into the office, Jeff Samuel was already waiting for her. Waiting? She wasn't even late! What was it with this guy?

Horace Dimbleby—a.k.a. 'Horrie'—her boss, was entertaining the likely, and potentially lucrative, new client. The two were immersed in an intense-looking exchange, interspersed with occasional bursts of chuckles, and having the air of a man-to-man kind of talk. Something told Alyssa that they were discussing her; a suspicion confirmed when the two broke off the moment they saw her approaching them. The put-on look of complete indifference gave it all away.

Bastards. Especially Horrie! How could he do this to her? How low could you sink to rope in a client? Tempting him with the promise of a piece of the action that had nothing to do with patents, copyrights, and litigious competitors. Alyssa felt like dragging Horrie into his office and giving a piece of her mind.

But she didn't. For a number of reasons, not the least of which was that she wasn't sure that it would work. It would have—in her 'own' world. But in this one…

Who knew what kind of a sleaze Horrie was here? Maybe his 'other' matched that of the Alyssa whose place she currently occupied. In her experience, legal offices tended to accumulate personalities which, in the issues that mattered, had similar predilections. You didn't find a 'nice' guy in an office filled with creeps, and vice versa. If such a mismatch existed it usually didn't last for long as the odd-one-out was either levered out or moved of his or her own accord.

As she hobbled toward the two men she glanced around the office, attempting to get a feel for the place. The postures of the secretaries and para-legals. The way in which people walked. The way they looked up at one. Furtive or openly; smiling or just forcing it—if that. The decor.

The place was pretty much as she remembered it: an open-plan office, arranged in the form of a rotunda, with the secretarial and supporting pool of employees occupying the center, and the offices of the associates and partners arranged around the periphery. But the people had changed. The background buzz of mutterings and low conversations, punctuated by an occasional loud remark or retort, or maybe even laughter—all that was gone. Interactions had an air of considerably more artificiality and decorum about it. 'Subdued' was the term that sprang to mind.

In contrast to this was the behavior of the 'upper' layers of the firm, who dominated the scene not only with their voices but also their demeanor. Posing. Strutting. Swaggering. Behaving in such a fashion that the dogs-bodies might be forgiven for drowning in their own perceived insignificance. Which, in the eyes of those Alyssa mentally labeled 'the emperors', they probably were.

It was not, Alyssa, decided, a place she would like to work in. Already, after only a few seconds here, she was certain that she would leave here; sooner rather than later.

"Alyssa!" Jeff Samuel greeted her by stretching out his hands as if welcoming an old friend. She could see Horrie raise an knowing eyebrow. What he thought she could only guess at. And what was going on in the mind of Mr.Samuel was even more of a riddle.

She stopped, let go of the crutch and leaned it against a nearby desk. She took Jeff Samuel's hand and gave it a quick shake. As he other hand closed around the back of hers to envelop it like a precious gem she fought an urge to tear herself away.

Jeff Samuel had a predatory glint in his eye that had nothing to do with legal matters.

Horrie, you total fucking creep!

"I'm glad to see you," Samuel told her, trying to hold her gaze. She wouldn't let him and looked at Horrie. "Sorry I'm late." Not that she was, but it would be expected.

Horrie appeared mildly surprised. Maybe, Alyssa thought, her 'other' wasn't in the habit of apologizing for things like that.

Her boss nodded at Samuel. "Well, I'll leave you to it then. You're in good hands."

He excused himself and presently departed, leaving Alyssa to deal with the last person she wanted to speak to right now. But there was nothing to help it. She led him into her office, declining his offers of assistance politely but firmly. Then she sat herself down and began the lengthy process of working out just exactly what it was Jeff Samuel wanted from Heckler and Barlow.

3.

Something had remained the same: nine o'clock staff meetings on Monday mornings. And when Ray entered the meeting room where everybody was already assembled, he saw with relief that, apart from Jack all the faces were the same. A closer observation revealed that their haircuts weren't quite as he recalled them. Neither were their clothing preferences. And Mark had a beard.

Close enough.

Now that everybody was here, John started the meeting in his usual brisk style, gave a rundown of last week's highlights, and then asked Fred at his right to start the usual round of everybody talking about what they'd done since they'd last met. The state of their work. Where they were going. Maybe problems that others could help with.

Here, too, nothing glaringly inconsistent with Ray's memory. Everybody was doing pretty much what he would have expected them to.

When his turn came, he produced something suitably vague; which he hoped was consistent with what he had gleaned from his brief exchange with Jack on Saturday.

"I've still got a few bugs but I think I know where they are," he finished.

He heaved a sigh of relief when Anita beside him took her turn. Presently the meeting finished and everybody returned to their offices. Ray stopped at the door and told John that he had a doctor's appointment in the afternoon. John nodded equably. "If you can't make it back afterwards, that's OK."

"Thanks." Ray withdrew. He went back to his office and closed the door. He tried to do some work, but found himself quite incapable of concentrating.

A short time later the phone rang.

"Mr. Shannon?"

"Lieutenant?"

"I was just verifying your whereabouts."

"I told you I wasn't going anywhere."

"I also wanted to ask you a question."

"Shoot."

"Well, about that actually."

"What?"

"Shooting."

"You tested the gun?"

"Yes."

"Well, can I have it back?"

"Not yet."

"Why? You didn't match it to the bullets. So what's the problem?"

"How do you know we didn't?"

Ray laughed, but it sounded false in his own ears.

"Come on, Lieutenant! I *know* you couldn't have found anything because it wasn't used in the murder. And you wouldn't be calling, but arresting me if you *had* found anything."

"Correct," Carter agreed. "But there's the matter of your non-existent alibi; which is the cause of some significant problems."

"I think," Ray told him, "that you should really take this up with my attorney. In fact I'm going to refuse answering *any* questions unless he's present."

"Why are you so touchy about these things?" Carter asked curiously. "Surely, you must realize that you're not acting like someone who considers himself above suspicion."

"I *am* above suspicion," Ray said. "But only in my eyes. And now let me give you Frank Nuovo's number."

"Don't bother," Carter said curtly. "I have it."

"Well then…"

"I *will* be wanting to speak to you."

"I'm rather busy," Ray said. "So, I imagine, is Frank Nuovo. Unless you're actually wanting to arrest me…"

"Not yet," the detective said.

"Well then—I have work to do."

Ray hung up and called Frank Nuovo's office.

"I signed your contract," he told Frank. "Lys says it's acceptable."

The lawyer laughed. "I must have given you the benign version! If Alyssa passed it…"

"The police called." Ray gave Frank a synopsis of his conversation with Carter.

"Let them call," Frank told him. "And say nothing without me there. Nothing."

"Understood."

He called Lys's cellphone. She answered after a few rings.

"Hey. I'm in a meeting. Can I call you back?"

"When you can…"

"Everything OK?"

"I have a bad feeling about this murder. You know, I wonder if my 'other' would have been capable…"

"No!"

"Why not?"

"Because!"

"He's not a nice man."

"Neither is the Alyssa into whose shoes I've stepped," she said. Her voice had dropped. He imagined that she had turned away from whoever she was with in order to acquire a modicum of privacy.

"You wouldn't believe how *different* they treat me around here," she said. "Especially the para-legals and secretaries. Like I was going to bite their heads off at any time. That Alyssa must've been a real stinker. You know, I feel this pressure; like they hate me.

"And there's this young para-legal… I think the other me must have screwed him or something—in more ways than one. He's like drooling at the mouth whenever he sees me, in am excited-scared-puppy kind of way. I get the feeling he wants to talk to me but wouldn't dare unless I told him to. But I can see his eyes on me. Sneaking a peek at my butt and tits. A proprietary sort of air—despite all his cowing and submissive demeanor."

"Maybe he just fantasizes about you."

"Yeah, maybe... And Ray, have you noticed that the date is *wrong*?"

He'd neglected to mention that.

"I'm sorry. I was going to tell you." He hesitated. "How far ahead are you?"

"A week. *Exactly*."

"Are you sure?"

"Well, my watch was out by a couple of hours. But I adjusted that on Sunday. It doesn't show a date so I never thought to check. Until I came into my office this morning—and saw the calendar on my desk. You know, it didn't register with me at first; but then..."

"You and I both," he told her. "Seven days and two hours, give or take a few minutes."

"You think this is important?"

"*Every* anomaly is important. I just don't know what it tells us. About my theory. Maybe just too...simple. Hell, I don't know. I'm sorry."

"Ray, I'm scared."

"We'll work it out," he told her with more confidence than he felt.

"Got to go," she said.

"Be careful."

"I will. You, too!"

When she was gone, he leaned back in his chair and swiveled it so he could look out the window.

He *did* have a bad feeling about the murder. What was it that Carter had wanted to ask him? Maybe it would have been an idea to at least listen to the question and *then* refuse to answer it. That way he would at least have known something more about the general direction of Carter's own ruminations. Questions could be almost as—and in some cases more—revealing than answers.

Ray sighed. Too late now. He just hoped that it didn't matter.

He spent the next few hours trying to do some work, but found that, whatever he did, it produced only minute steps forward in the development and debugging of his program modules. In the end, and with a sigh of relief, he called it quits and left for lunch.

He called Alyssa. She told him she'd free herself, no matter what it took. They met in a small cafe on Peachtree amidst the lunchtime crowd. He was so glad to see her he could have kissed her there and then, and damn the public. By some minor miracle they managed to claim a small table and while he was holding the fort she went off to get something to eat.

Later they sat munching salad buns and sipping Coke. She told him about her morning. Compared to the stress she'd been under, he'd had it easy. At least he could withdraw to his office. She had been exposed to clients and office-staff for four solid hours.

"I'm exhausted," she said. "My other self must've been a total workaholic nut. She wouldn't have had one free minute in the day. You should have seen the others—

including Susan—when I insisted that I go for lunch! Susan cornered me in my office and asked me right-out if I was seeing you again. To her mind, that was the only possible reason why I would act so strangely."

"What did you tell her?"

"That I was seeing you. 'Which motel,' she asked—and did I really think I could fit it all into one hour." Alyssa shook her head. "My other me must've been one randy bitch."

Ray grinned. She saw it, and the scowl left her face. She laughed, then suddenly fell silent, and—to his amazement—blushed. "Maybe that's what we *should* have done," she said softly.

Their eyes met across the table.

"Maybe," he said, just a tad hoarse.

Alyssa leaned closer. Her hands touched his.

"What time are you finished tonight?" he asked her.

"I'll *make* myself finish by five."

"Good. Where shall we meet?"

"How about outside my apartment? We can leave one of our cars there and take the other."

"Bring a toothbrush."

"Definitely."

She smiled. There was a good feeling between them. Unspoken, but nonetheless binding, promises. The closeness brought about by shared thoughts and a mutual affection that was rapidly growing out of control.

He looked at his watch. "I've got to go."

"Want me to come with you?"

"I'll be OK."

"I'd like to. Please!"

Actually, he *did* want her to come. Just so that she was there. Not that he expected anything interesting to emerge from the visit, but somehow...

"What about your afternoon appointments?" he objected.

She smiled because she knew she'd won. She picked up her cellphone from the table and called her office.

"Marcie? Alyssa here. Something's come up. A kind of emergency." Alyssa winked at Ray and shrugged. "I'm afraid you'll have to cancel all afternoon appointments."

She listened.

"No, I don't think I'll be back today. Tell Susan I might not be home tonight either." She winked at Ray and blocked the microphone slit with the tip of her index finger. "Might as well make use of a beautiful day," she whispered. "We can drop by my apartment on the way. For the toothbrush."

She returned her attention to the phone and rolled up here eyes. "No, Marcie! Tell Mr. O'Neill I'm truly sorry, but I'll definitely make time for him tomorrow. Oh yes, and tell Susan I definitely won't be home tonight."

She put the phone down again. "There. That'll rattle them. The other Alyssa wouldn't have *dreamt* of doing anything like this!"

She eyed Ray. "You're not planning to go back to work, are you?"

He grinned. "If I ever was, I'm not anymore."

Alyssa smiled demurely. "Why, what would have changed your mind?"
They laughed as they went back to their cars.

4.

Alfredo Lopez M.D. operated from a private clinic in Roswell, which he shared with eleven other medical specialists. In between them, the partners in this enterprise shared sufficient funds to equip their clinic with some very hi-tech diagnostic equipment, some of which they used to generate yet more revenue through its use by outside physicians.

Ray hated medical establishments of any kind, but in this instance he had no option but to oblige. The fact that Alyssa was here made the whole thing infinitely more bearable than it would have been otherwise.

After the obligatory waiting period they were ushered into Dr Lopez' office. The physician, a middle-aged, wiry individual, raised an eyebrow when Alyssa entered with Ray.

"Mrs. Shannon," he said, surprised.

Alyssa flicked a glance at Ray but did not bother to correct the physician's mistake. They sat down and Lopez began a lengthy round of questioning Ray about his problems.

"We would like to eliminate any possible physical causes for these…lapses," Ray told him.

Lopez nodded. "That's very sensible," he said. "Far too many people assume that the roots of their problems are psychological, when in truth there's often an underlying physical condition."

After more than half an hour of extensive questioning—which included queries about Ray's work, diet, family medical history, his daily habits, as well as other issues—Lopez made him lie down on an examination table and proceeded to give him a thorough physical examination.

When he was done he sat back and shook his head.

"Nothing superficially obvious. What we should do next is to take your blood and send it away for tests. And, while you're here, I'd also like to generate an EWP map."

He looked at Ray. "EWP: Encephalographic Wave Profile. Our staff will be able to do this. If the equipment is available, would you be free? Now?"

Ray declared that he was. Lopez made enquiries and confirmed that the scanning machinery was currently not in use. A nurse entered the office.

Lopez turned to Ray. "This will take about half an hour. Give or take a few minutes."

"What's involved?"

"It's a very sensitive and completely computerized high-resolution scan over the entire surface of your brain. The technique is still new and still requires the full benefit of an extensive patient database to establish the parameters of 'normality'—as well as the correlations to specific pathologies. Still, the protocols are now well established. Short of an MRI or PET scan it's probably one of the most useful screening techniques. It's also considerably less expensive." He made a small gesture signaling his regret that such banal matters as 'expense' should interfere in the practice of medicine.

"The procedure is simple. You will be placed under a hood. Inside it is an array of sensors, which will record the electrical activity on the surface of your skull.

"You will be shown a series of tachistoscopic images on a computer screen and subjected to a series of auditory stimuli. All of these are designed to elicit particular, standardized responses. These will be compared with our database and should give us a reasonable indication as to whether further, more extensive tests will be required."

He looked at Alyssa. "Mr. Shannon will have to be alone for the procedure. Your presence is likely to contaminate the results."

Alyssa shrugged. "As long as I can be nearby somewhere."

Lopez smiled. "That's not a problem." He eyed her curiously. "I sense that you're… concerned."

She nodded. "Very."

"At this stage," the neurologist said sympathetically, "I do not believe that there's anything to be concerned about. Unless something very unforeseen is revealed, I am almost certain that your husband's symptoms *are* the results of stress; not of a physical condition. This test should provide supporting evidence for my tentative assessment—or help me to correct it and determine just exactly what is causing your husband's present distress."

5.

Ray was shown into a room, which contained a mirror and an examination table, at the end of which was the device Dr. Lopez had referred to. Ray was made to lie down and a hood, attached to a jointed structure of linkages, was fitted over his head, so that it disappeared almost totally inside it. A transparent window allowed him to look at a flat LCD display which was moved into a position above him.

The attendants departed and closed the door. Alyssa was confined to watch Ray through a one-way mirror from the adjacent operator's room. He knew she was there, but quickly forgot all about her as the procedure continued.

It went faster than he had anticipated. The screen displayed a series of images; too fleeting for him to discern or analyze what was on them. At certain intervals sounds impinged upon his ears from nearby speakers. Simple sounds. Tones. Melodies. Screams. Whispers. Cacophonies. Clashing cymbals.

When it was over they came in again and released him from his strange headgear. Alyssa came in behind them.

"Dr. Lopez will get in touch with you when the data have been analyzed," a nurse told him.

Ray gave them his cellphone number. "You're more likely to get me at this number than anywhere else."

They left the clinic and drove back to Alyssa's apartment, where Ray waited outside while Alyssa went inside to fetch some necessities. Ray didn't want to come in; just in case Susan had returned early.

As he waited in his car—the windows wide open to admit a breeze, sultry though it was—he found himself thinking about Lieutenant Carte, who still had his gun. And then he thought of the other one and reached under the dashboard where he kept it in a holster and well out of sight.

His groping fingers found nothing; not even the holster.

Ray straightened slowly and took a deep breath. A nagging question that, since late last night, had been lurking somewhere in the back of his mind, but which, so far, had never been made explicit, now could not be ignored any longer. There were two possibilities. One, that his 'other' had never possessed a second gun and that it had never been in the car. The other, that he *had* owned the second gun, that it *had* been in the car, and that it had been removed.

Ray opened the door, got out of the car, and poked his head under the dashboard. He found what he had been looking for: a triangle of holes drilled into underside of the plastic fittings. Ray, feeling sick again, pulled himself out of his contorted position. Behind him he heard footsteps. Alyssa came toward him with a small soft bag in her right hand. She stopped when she saw his face.

"What's the matter? You look like you've seen a ghost."

Ray shook his head. "I'll tell you later. Shall we go?"

"Your car or mine?"

Ray considered the question. An uncomfortable thought emerged from the jumble in his mind. He looked around furtively, wondering just how intent Carter was on getting his hands on Ray—with, as it now seemed, some justification.

And now he had dragged Alyssa into this mess as well. Intentionally or not; it was immaterial.

Shit!

"Are you all right?" She looked concerned, vertical frown-furrows between her eyes.

He shook his head. "'m going to leave this car at my work," he said. "We'll take yours."

"You're not going back to your place?"

Ray shook his head. "No. Let's just drop off the car and go. We have to talk, Lys. Seriously."

It was, as he had already noticed, characteristic of her that she didn't press the issue. She had a fine sense of time and place. And that was only one of the things that he liked about her. She was... He groped for the right word word. Certainly she was a much better person than he deserved. And he had to do everything he could to get her into the clear if the shit really hit the fan.

They dropped off his car in the parking lot, in view of his office window. On the way there, Ray went to some pains to spot any possible pursuit—but, try as he might, he could not detect any. Which didn't mean a damn thing, of course. In the city area, with all the traffic, *he* would hardly spot a skilled tail or set of tails.

They took the I-575 north and just kept on going. Past Marietta, toward the Chattahoochee National Forest and Cherokee. As Atlanta fell behind, Ray felt himself unwind. It was a gradual process, but after an hour he was almost relaxed.

They found a sign pointing at a tiny motel in a town he'd never heard of; and there they stopped. By now it was dark, and out here the stars were actually visible. There were no restaurants about, but they didn't care. This was where they'd spend the night. It felt right. Their hosts offered them supper with the family, and they accepted. The owners of the motel were a couple in their late sixties, who had moved here from Atlanta almost ten years before, in order to spend the rest of their lives away from the city, which they called a 'cancer on the face of the Earth'. Ray was inclined to agree.

They spent a pleasant couple of hours with the people and then went for a walk in the dark to feel the vast expanse of the firmament above them.

"Ray," said Ray, "meaning the *other* 'Ray', probably killed Ron Hadlow."

There, it was out.

Alyssa, to her credit, didn't miss a step. It took Ray a moment to realize what that meant.

"You guessed?"

"When I saw your face," she agreed. "What happened?"

He told her about the gun.

"Our alter-egos in this world weren't very nice people."

Ray shook his head. "They weren't. And what about us? Have you noticed how readily we've *accepted* this? Here we are, talking about 'others' and 'alter-egos', and about being in a different world, as if it was the most natural thing in the history of the universe—when it's freakish and scary and doesn't make any sense at all."

She tightened her arm around him. Since she was the taller one, the traditional male-female roles had been inverted: her arm was around his shoulder, his around her waist.

"I haven't," she admitted. "I'm just hanging in there by a thread. Without you I'd be a nut-case by now."

"Without me you wouldn't be here," he said, convinced that it was true. "You would have congratulated yourself on sneaking into that space in front of me and gone on home to your apartment and to a normal and sensible life."

"Sneaking? What do you mean? I didn't sneak into anywhere."

"Yes you did…" He stopped. "That *wasn't* you, was it?"

"What are you talking about?"

"That was the other Alyssa! You…merged…into this world immediately after that! At, I'd guess, exactly the same time as that crazy jerk came out of literally nowhere and hit your car. Or, to be more precise, we both merged into a third 'path' that didn't belong to either of us. "

Alyssa whistled tonelessly. "And you weren't that asshole who was tailgating me either. Though I thought you were…"

"You never mentioned anything about that!"

"It didn't seem to matter anymore. Not after we'd become like…this…"

She chuckles. "I thought you'd just had a bad day. People, even nice people, sometimes do stupid things when they're angry or frustrated. I remember seeing you in the mirror and telling myself that I wished you were someone else…"

"Who?"

"Just *some*one. Not just the faceless driver of a car on a freeway."

And Ray suddenly remembered…

"Lys?"

"Yes?"

"I'm just trying to imagine… What it would have been like if everything had gone along it 'normal' way. And do you know something? I can't! And do you know something else? I know this sounds strange. Considering what I've lost—what *we* have lost. The terrible situation we're in right now…

"But if I had a way of re-setting it all back to the way it was…"
"Would you?"
"And lose you?"
"I guess that goes hand in hand."
"I'd rather have it this way."
"So would I," she said softly. "We're throwing away a whole *life*, you know? How can we do this? And how come that this is what I actually *want*? What's happened to me? To us? If it doesn't matter to anybody *but* us… If the people in those other lives aren't even real anymore…"

She stopped and wrapped her arms around his neck.

"More more real than anybody or anything."

Echoing his sentiments exactly. He was still bewildered, but that would pass. Maybe one day he would understand how he could just *surrender* everything that had been his…life…his wife, his friends, his whole context—how he could just leave it behind, and be it in what might well be a completely different *universe*! and just give himself over to this strange…

Not now. Maybe one day.

Right now it was Alyssa who filled his world; her touch, her scent, her warmth.

So he kissed her, and the light breeze carried away their soft sounds, and they completely were alone but for the stars and the dark silhouettes of the trees all around them.

"Let's go back," she whispered.
"Let's."

6.

Their room was small, furnished in a traditional kind of way, with a quaint rustic touch. An ornate shade hid the light-bulb on the ceiling, and there was a small-wattage light on the table beside the queen-size double bed.

They turned off the main light and drew the curtains. Then, in the dim light of the bedside lamp they undressed each other—slowly, and with delicious deliberation and a breathless kind of anticipation—that led into something neither of them fully understood; but neither did they want to, because this was their night: their first; when they dropped caution, reluctance, inhibition, the guardrails; to surrender…

Tuesday

1.

A ray of light shone through a crack in the curtain and into Ray's right eye. He woke into an ocean of delicious memories, and the feel and scent of her beside him on the bed. She was turned on her side, her face beside his shoulder, her breath playing rhythmically over his skin.

He lay still for an indeterminate time. Then, slowly, such as not to wake her, he turned his head and looked at her. Her face, just inches from his own, was half covered by her hair. Her nose poked through the cover; her breath stirred a few loose strands.

As he watched her one eye opened briefly, blinked, then opened again and fixed on his face. Underneath her hair he could see her mouth twitch. He noticed that when she smiled a couple of small lines appeared in her face at the sides of her mouth.

Ray turned on his side. "How are you?"

The smile broadened. "Very, very good."

He pushed aside the hair from her face. She wriggled closer.

"That, Mr. Shannon, was very lovely. We must do it more often."

"Anytime."

"Let me go to the bathroom, and we'll do it again."

"Now?"

"You said 'anytime'!"

"I did, but…"

She gave a small triumphant laugh and rolled over and out of bed. His eyes followed her as she disappeared into the bathroom. When she was gone he rolled over and reached to the bedside table to retrieve his watch. He held it close to his face.

Ten thirty?

Shit!

He dropped the arm with the watch as silent laughter shook him. What else had he expected? They'd been asleep for just over four hours.

Alyssa returned and he surreptitiously let the watch drop from his hand and onto the floor beside the bed; out of sight and out of mind. Alyssa crawled back onto the bed and draped herself over him.

" 'Anytime' is now," she said, smiling—and he forgot all about the time.

Considerably later, slick with perspiration, and pleasantly exhausted after a feat he wouldn't have considered himself capable of, she asked if he knew what time it was.

"Well on the way to noon, I guess," he said.

"What?!"

His arms held her back. "Hey, what did you *think*?"

She relaxed. "I didn't."

"Just as well."

She giggled like a little girl. "My, we *are* bad."

"I guess you turned your cellphone off as well."

"You guess right."

He kissed her again—on the mouth; the curve of her neck; lower.

Lys made contented noises.

"You purr like a cat." He ran his tongue along the cleft between her breasts.

"A very happy cat," she agreed. A hand slid around the back of his head and held him close. Her scent filled his world.

Eventually, reluctantly, he desisted from his caresses.

"We'd better rejoin the world. Our hosts are going to wonder what's up."

"They'll probably guess," Alyssa said. She kissed him again and rolled off the bed. Ray retrieved his watch and looked at the time. Close enough. By the time they were out of here it would be afternoon.

They showered together and enjoyed that, too. They offered the owners the fee for an extra night. The woman waved the suggestion aside. "We haven't turned anyone away because of you." Her eyes twinkled knowingly.

By mutual agreement they didn't turn on their cellphones until they were in the car. Then, with Ray driving, Alyssa called her office and contrived a story to explain her absence. Ray listened with rapt admiration. Lawyers…

He checked with his answering service and found several messages waiting for him: one from Frank Nuovo, another from Lieutenant Carter. Plus one from a certain Ralph Johnston; a name Ray had never heard before. A fourth call had come in just a short time ago. A message from Dr. Lopez, and could Ray contact him as soon as possible.

Ray called Frank first.

"Where are you?" the attorney asked him. "Carter isn't happy. Says he's going to arrest you as soon as you surface."

"Why?"

"Because you skipped town."

"I went away for the evening. With a friend. I needed a break."

"Carter doesn't see it like that."

"What do you think he's going to do? He's left me a message to call him. What should *I* do?"

"Let me talk to him. Unless they have something substantive to pin on you, he hasn't got a case. Where are you now anyway?"

"Just passing through Marietta."

"Are you alone?"

"No. I told you I went away with a friend."

Frank Nuovo chuckled. "Do I know that 'friend'?"

"Is it any of your business?"

"In this instance, yes."

Ray looked sideways at Alyssa who had finished her call and was listening. She guessed the contents of the conversation and nodded.

"It's Lys."

"I see."

"Any problems with that?" Ray asked.

"Actually, yes. Given that she's effectively your alibi…"

"I told you, I didn't want her dragged into this!"

Alyssa touched Ray's arm. "There is no other way," she said. "We're in this together;

whether you like it or not."

"I don't think either of you have any choice in this matter," Frank pointed out. "Carter's already indicated that he's aware of your relationship—and that you were away together for the time in question."

"The time in question?"

"The time when Ron Hadlow was murdered—about one hour before you found him. And he *wasn't* killed where you found him. Someone dragged him there—and by the time whoever it was did it, the body was well exsanguinated. That's why there weren't any bloodstains. Someone carried—rather than dragged—him into that toilet and dumped him there."

"Why? That's stupid!"

"I think so, too. So, for that matter, does Carter. But the evidence allows no other conclusion."

Ray finally saw where this was leading.

"So, with Lys and me actually being away from the opening…that makes it worse, right? We could have…"

"Something like that. Carter wants the stuff you wore that night at the gallery for forensics. And Alyssa's as well."

"She's a *suspect*?"

Alyssa's eyes widened, but she recovered quickly. She shrugged and made a gesture, which told Ray that, as far as she was concerned, the fact was inconsequential.

"You could say that," Frank's voice said in his ear.

"You'll better talk to her then." Ray unplugged his headset and handed the cellphone to Alyssa. "Here. I think maybe you should hire Frank to represent you as well."

She took the phone.

"Don't worry," she said to Ray, before she put it to her ear.

A few minutes later she put it down.

"Well, that's it," she said.

"I'm really sorry," he said, and meant it.

"It was inevitable. They would've made that connection anyway. Besides, we're in this together in more ways than one, remember?"

"What now?"

"Now we give that Lieutenant Carter everything he wants—before he contrives a reason to have search warrants issued for both our places."

He wanted to apologize again but didn't. She was right. This thing had always been bigger than either of them, and his attempts to control it had probably been futile from the first moment.

"I'd better call Lopez," he said. Alyssa, about to catch up with the next call on her list, looked up. Ray shrugged. "Here goes nothing."

Lopez sounded strangely reluctant to speak freely over the phone. "You wouldn't happen to have some time free today? I can *make* some time…"

Ray felt Lys's regard on him like a physical touch.

"What time?" he asked the neurologist.

"Four sound OK?"

"I'll be there."

"I'll see you then."

Ray pressed 'clear'.

"What is it?" Alyssa asked.

"I don't know. He wants to see me this afternoon."

"I'm coming with you," she declared.

He really wanted her to. But...

"What about your appointments? They'll be pissed off at you."

Alyssa shrugged. "They already are. Or maybe 'perplexed' is more like it. I spoke to Susan a moment ago. She told me that Horrie is in a bit of a state—especially since I've missed an appointment with Jeff, the asshole. Horrie's seeing a big, fat client slowly slipping from his grip."

"Why doesn't he just assign him to someone else?"

Alyssa shook her head. "It's not a simple as that. There are procedures. He can't do it just on a whim. Besides, I think he's banking on Mr. Samuel's hard-on for me to clinch the deal. So, he's been tap-dancing and telling stories about me being sick. None of which, I suspect, our Mr. Samuel's going to buy. And Horrie'll know that, and he's going to be even more furious."

"You're not going to help matters by not showing up at all," he argued.

Alyssa gave him a funny look. "Don't you *want* me to come with you?"

"I do," he affirmed. "Honestly, I do! But..."

"Then I'm coming," she said—and he knew her well enough by now to recognize the steely determination behind that tone.

He grinned.

Alyssa leaned closer.

"What?"

"What what?"

"Why are you grinning?"

A sudden gust of wind disrupted the steady slipstream from the moving vehicle and blew her hair across the side of his face and head. She gathered up the loose ends and tucked them under the ribbon that was holding it in place in a thick ponytail.

"Well?" she asked.

He laughed. He reached over and rested his hand on her left leg.

"Thanks."

She put her hand on his briefly, before he relocated it to the steering wheel.

One more call to make. "I wonder who Ralph Johnston is," he muttered.

Alyssa had heard him. "Johnston?" she asked.

Ray nodded.

"There's a lawyer of that name. Family cases."

"Debbie!" He realized with a shock that he hadn't thought of her *once* since she'd walked out of his life.

"A divorce lawyer?" He asked Alyssa.

"That kind of stuff," she agreed.

"Can't say I blame her," Ray said, subdued. "The man she knows is a bastard. Maybe even a murderer."

"But you're not."

Ray dialed Johnston's number. It turned out that Alyssa had been right. The man advised Ray that his wife had initiated divorce proceedings. Ray promised to get back to him as soon as he had found representation himself.

He disconnected and shook his head wryly. "I've never used an attorney in my life; except for buying a house, of course. Now it looks like I need *two*!"

Alyssa laughed. "We have a way of making ourselves indispensable," she agreed.

Ray glanced at her sideways and reflected that, while generalizations probably still held true, even the legal profession boasted members who didn't conform to its overall sleazy opportunist image.

"You're grinning again!" Alyssa gave him a playful jab in the arm.

He just laughed. Despite everything he felt just too good for words. Though his life had been turned inside out and upside down, right now it was better than it had ever been. He wondered whether that had anything to do with having been laid in the most satisfying manner he could possibly have imagined. But he knew it was more than that. Though the massive glandular relief of last night definitely came into it, it was only a part of something much bigger—of the strange discovery that a hollow part of him he hadn't even known was there was finally being made less empty with something warm and gentle. Something so unexpected and overwhelming that he still found it hard to believe that it was really happening.

"I love you," he said. He hadn't intended to say it, but it just happened. And now it was out there, and no way was it going to be shoved back into the bottle in which it had been hiding.

She said nothing for a moment, but he could feel her eyes on him.

"And that's something to grin about?" she finally retorted.

"It is for me," he told her.

She slid as close as she could get and tucked her arm under his. "You could have told me last night, you know! For most guys that would probably have been the time."

"I only figured it out just now," he said.

"Better now than never," she agreed. She leaned her face against his arm. "I love you, too," she said. Almost too softly for him to hear it over the wind.

"I know."

"You do, huh?"

"I figured it out."

"All by yourself?"

"I had help."

"I'd say! Quite a lot."

"Yep."

"You know, if we weren't driving along an interstate at almost sixty miles per hour…"

"I know…"

2.

"Thank you for coming," Dr. Lopez told them as they sat down opposite him. Along the wall, clipped to a light box which was now turned off, they saw a series of charts and printouts.

"You sounded kind of urgent," Ray said.

Lopez wagged his head. "I do not wish to alarm you, of course—and quite possibly there's nothing to be alarmed about, but your scans were...well, unusual. That's probably the correct term, since they don't match against anything in our database."

Lopez held up a hand to preempt the question on Ray's lips. "I should be more accurate," he said apologetically. "They *do* match against certain patterns, but not in a way that we've seen before, and only after I and one of my colleagues did some very imaginative data-processing."

He got up and asked them to step closer to the charts on the lightbox.

"With your background you'll probably appreciate some of these printouts better than the average lay person." An apologetic gesture in Alyssa's direction. "Sorry, but it's the truth."

Alyssa nodded. "Go ahead. I'm not insulted. Just keep the jargon at minimal level."

"I'll try." Lopez turned back to the charts. "These are altazimuthal projections of an idealized hemisphere which corresponds to the upper portion of your skull. Displayed on these projections, in color-codings which represent a number of different parameters, we have the results from the scan we did yesterday.

"These here," he said, pointing at a large, laminated poster on one side, "are similar displays, averaged over a database of patients and volunteers who were deemed to be 'normal'."

Lopez stood back to allow Ray and Alyssa a closer look at the comparison chart and Ray's results. It didn't take Ray long to identify at least four of his scans that seemed to exhibit similar colors and distribution patterns as the comparison charts.

"We use computational methods to match the patterns, but in the end the only one who can make a final assessment is myself. So I *always* check up on the results."

"These appear normal." Ray indicated two of the graphs.

The neurologist nodded. "Quite. The conclusion appears inescapable that for these parameters your brain is 'normal'—within the expected margins of error."

"But not these." Ray pointed at those printouts which didn't match the standards at all.

"They don't match anything we've ever seen," Lopez agreed. "For a very good reason, as we finally figured out—just before midnight..."

They sat down again. "Let me explain what exactly we're doing here. We have an array of eight hundred sensors, distributed evenly over that area of your skull below which there is cerebral matter. The sensors measure the electrical activity on the surface of your scalp. Spectra of the fluctuations at each point are computed once every half second, and averaged over anything between two to five seconds, depending on what is being calculated. A computational cycle is synchronized with the presentation of one or more tachistoscopic images in between the random dot patterns you see on the screen for most of the time. That or one of the sounds you heard.

"When we performed the scan on you, the result at first sight were...puzzling. That is, until one of my assistants came up with the idea of using individual measurements and subtracting a set of 'normal' patterns from our database of patients. From the difference we generated a cross-correlogram over the length of an averaging cycle."

He gave Ray a look of enquiry.

Ray nodded. "Go ahead."

Lopez made an apologetic gesture in Alyssa's direction. "I'm sorry, but this is as simple as I can make it."

"I'd be happy with the bottom-line to all this," she said dryly.

"Of course." Lopez pointed at the charts on the wall. "What we found was that your husband's activity record consists of not just one, but *two*, basically similar patterns of activity, displaced from each other by somewhat less than a second."

The neurologist looked at Ray questioningly. "I have to ask this, Mr. Shannon; but is there a record of...mental disorder...in your family. Or in your past, for that matter? Schizophrenia? Extended periods of a persistent sensations of *deja vu* perhaps? Anything like that?"

Ray did all he could to keep his facial expression under control.

"Not that I know of." This was true—up to a point.

The neurologist shook his head.

"You mean there's...like *two* of me?" Ray asked. "Temporally displaced by how much? Just under a second?"

"That's an interesting way of putting it."

Lopez picked up a piece of paper from his desk. "I think that under the circumstances it would be advisable to take some further tests." He looked at the paper. "I have taken the liberty of tentatively booking you in for an MRI and a PET scan at Emory University Hospital tomorrow afternoon. You're under no obligation to do this, of course, but under the circumstances I would strongly advise to get to the bottom of this as soon as possible."

He cleared his throat. "I should also like to point out that these scans will be free of charge. I have booked them under a research agreement this clinic has with the hospital."

"Research?" Alyssa asked.

Ray grinned to himself. The legal eagle sniffed something on the wind.

Dr. Lopez nodded. "Your case is unique, at least in my experience. An invaluable addition to our database."

"With the appropriate consents for each step and each procedure," Alyssa interjected.

The neurologist smiled. "Of course. Your husband's contribution will be invaluable to our research."

"I'd like to speak to my wife for a moment, please," Ray said. "In private, if that's possible."

"Of course," Lopez replied. He stood up and walked to the door. "Call me when you're done."

When he was gone Ray looked at Alyssa. "What is it?" she asked.

"I want Lopez to do a scan on you."

"What for?"

"Call it a hunch."

She stared at him. "You think..."

"I'd bet on it."

"What does it mean, Ray?"

"I don't know, but we have to find out if you're the same."

"What are we going to tell Lopez?"

"We're just going to ask him to do it. It'll be the price of my cooperation."

"If I am the same he'll start wondering."

"He'll do that anyway."

"You really think that's a good idea?"

"We have to know, Lys."

"I hope you know what you're doing!"

"So do I."

When Lopez heard their request he frowned. "There's something you aren't telling me."

Ray nodded. "You wouldn't believe me if I did—so I'd rather not. But I promise you that if you do this—and if Alyssa exhibits the same patterns as I, that I *will* tell you. Mind you, you're still not going to believe me, but at least you won't be able to accuse me of withholding information."

Lopez considered them for a few moments. His face was faintly troubled. "This isn't some kind of a joke, right? I'm really…"

"Doctor," Ray interrupted him, "these results are real—yes? They exist. They are a scientific fact—determined by yourself after a significant amount of work and thought. The only question is, are you willing to follow them where they may lead, no matter how disturbing you might find the outcome?"

The neurologist leaned back in his chair and bit his lower lip. His dark, Latin eyes fixed on Ray with the stare of a basilik.

"Why do I have the feeling," he said thoughtfully, "that I should drop this matter right here and now? Maybe refer you to one of my colleagues specializing in abnormal psychology."

Ray grinned. "Because you're curious."

"Exactly." Lopez leaned forward. "But I don't want to hear anything about voices from outer space, telepathy, or UFOs! If that's where you're leading me, forget it."

"I'm not," Ray assured him.

It's going to be worse.

But he didn't tell Lopez that.

"Could we do Alyssa's scan today?"

Lopez nodded. "Do you have the time right now?"

Alyssa glanced at Ray and nodded. "Why not?"

Lopez stood up. "Why not, indeed? To be honest, I'm curious myself now. Not that I have any reason to suspect that there's even the shred of a reason to go ahead with this. But I must confess that I'm intrigued. Why, I ask myself, would your husband make such a request?"

"Call it an informed hunch," Ray supplied.

3.

Ray watched the procedure from the control room, where a technician was operating the computer controlling the experiment. The man had been only too happy to explain details of the experimental procedure to someone with a scientific background who understood the intricacies of data acquisition. Ray sat and looked over the man's shoulder as the progress of Alyssa's test was displayed on the screen.

When it was done, and even before Alyssa emerged again, the tech had initiated the post-acquisition analysis program. By the time she came out, it had been completed.

Results appeared on the screen. The tech was plainly fascinated by what he saw. He picked up the phone and told Lopez that the experiment was done. When he had hung up he turned to Ray and Alyssa.

"Amazing."

"Same thing, right?" Ray asked him.

"It looks that way. Even the phase is the same—within the resolution of the experiment anyway."

He proceeded to explain the displays on the screen. Ray felt Alyssa's hand sneak into his. Their fingers interlaced and tightened around each other. He looked from the screen and into her face.

"What does it mean?"

What indeed?

Ray thought he had an inkling, but as yet the details remained unformed and unclear. But one thing was for certain: here was a form of physical evidence that could not possibly be denied by anybody.

Lopez came into the room. He bent over the tech and studied the screen. Then he straightened and looked at Alyssa and Ray.

"I'm all ears," he said.

Ray shook his head. "Let's wait for the results of the scans tomorrow." He raised his hand to forestall Lopez' incipient objection. "Dr. Lopez, the truth is even I am not certain that what I'm going to tell you is going to make any sense. I really would prefer if we could wait until tomorrow—or whenever we get the results from those scans."

Lopez made as if to object, but held himself back. He nodded with evident reluctance. "Just for interest sake: would you like to tell me what you're *expecting* to see on those scans?"

"I have no idea. But if I my hypothesis is correct then it's going to be like nothing you've seen before. And, as for the MRI scans, I'm not too sure they'll even manage to get acceptable images."

Lopez raised an eyebrow. "That's a *very* interesting prediction."

He looked at Alyssa. "Just tell me one thing. Why both of you? You are not related by blood…" He paused. "There is no genetic link, is there? Second cousins maybe? *Some form of connection?*"

Ray shook his head. "Not that we know of."

"Then how…"

"Let's say that we both have, in the very recent past, been subjected to a similar… physical…process."

"What kind of process? And do you claim that this is in some way connected to your recent lapses of memory?"

"I do. That is the part you'll find extremely difficult, if not impossible, to believe—which is why I want to see tomorrow's scan results, before we sit down with you and tell you a story that is probably the most outrageous you'll ever hear.

"Believe me: compared to this, the *X-Files* are going to seems like a weather report."

"'X-Files'?" Lopez said, plainly puzzled.

Ray opened his mouth but shut it again. He looked at Alyssa.

"Do *you* know what I'm talking about?"

She nodded.

"Oh, shit."

He only realized that he'd said it aloud when he saw Lopez' face.

"Sorry; didn't mean to... Anyway, this really isn't the time. Trust me."

"We're not crazy, Dr. Lopez," Lys said. "Though you'll probably think so when you hear what we have to say."

The tech, Ray noticed, was eyeing them curiously—as was the nurse who had attended to Alyssa.

Lopez' expression was that of a poker player.

"Do you still want to go ahead with this?" Ray asked him.

Lopez nodded. "If it turns out that you are delusional, I get the feeling that, at the very least, it's going to be highly entertaining." He smiled thinly. "Every now and then something happens to disrupt everyday routine and the predictability that goes with it. In your case I even sense something beyond the ordinary. A certain mystery." He sighed. "Let's have our discussion tomorrow. Or maybe first thing on Thursday morning. How does that sound?"

"Very good."

Lopez shook their hands and saw them out the door.

4.

"You know what this is going to look like to our friends and co-workers," Alyssa commented as they went back to her car.

"What do you mean?"

"Well, us not showing up for work, for one thing. Turning off our cellphones. Going off on unannounced jaunts to strange motels in the woods. Stuff like that."

She was right, of course. Ray reached into his pocket and turned on his cellphone. There were three messages: one from Nuovo.

"I've got one of those, too," Alyssa commented, looking her own phone.

"You call him," Ray told her. "There's a message here from John. He hasn't heard from me all day."

John wasn't amused. "What's the matter with you, Ray? You disappear from sight without a word and a contact. Is something the matter? Something I should know about?"

"Possibly," Ray admitted. "Look, John, I'm sorry about this, but it's been a... difficult...day. I've spent several hours with the neurologist."

"Are you OK?"

"Maybe. I have to go for some scans at Emory tomorrow."

There was a pause at the other end of the line. "Look," Ray said, "I know this a bad time, but..."

"No—don't worry," John told him. "It's OK. Just keep me informed, huh? Will you be back on Thursday?"

"I have to see the neurologist first thing in the morning—but after that I hope everything'll go back to normal. Until we know more about my...problem."

"I never knew... Why didn't you say something?"

"Because I didn't either. It all happened rather suddenly."

"Well, just look after yourself," John advised him. "And keep in touch. If you can't, tell Debbie to."

Now was definitely not the time to tell John about Debbie.

"Will do," he said. "Talk to you later."

He turned to Alyssa, who was leaning against the side of her car, talking to Frank Nuovo, from the sounds of it. Presently she finished her conversation and broke the connection.

"Looks like we're both in the shit."

"Carter?"

"Yes, he wants to talk to us. Tomorrow, nine a.m. Frank will be present at both interviews."

"Does he know what happened?"

"Frank mentioned that we were 'indiscreet'. Carter also feels that we ought to be at his disposal at all times, and that us turning off our phones is unacceptable practice." She shrugged. "All of which is just plain chicanery. But there you have it."

"I really didn't want you in this," he told her. "I'm sorry."

"I *am* in this," she pointed out. "I have been from the moment we met on 285. There's no way to disconnect what happens to us."

Something in the way she said that invoked a poignant memory, which was all the more painful because of the guilt that now came with it. When Debbie and he had gotten married, in a civil ceremony, she had insisted on writing her own celebrant's benediction. Ray had forgotten the lines—though Debbie had kept the text somewhere—but there had been something similar…

"What's the matter?"

He shook his head. "Nothing." He grimaced. "I lie. Guilt, actually."

"Debbie?"

"Yes."

"Want to tell me what went wrong?" She hesitated. "I mean, if there had been nothing wrong…you and I…we wouldn't be, would we?"

"No, I guess not." He made a fatalistic gesture. "It wasn't completely right from the beginning. Don't mistake me. We had a good relationship—for most of our marriage. But we didn't want the same things. Never did."

"Children?"

"That was one thing. By the time she'd made up her mind that she wanted some, she was at the stage where it would have been too risky. She never said as much, but I think she resented the fact that I never pushed harder for a family. And maybe I should have. Maybe she just needed a bit of pushy persuasion."

"Which she might well have resented in due course as well," Alyssa pointed out. "Did you ever discourage it?"

Ray shook his head. "No. I just wanted her to make her own choice."

"Maybe that's what she couldn't handle," Alyssa said. "Maybe she mistook your tolerance for indifference. It can appear that way, you know?"

She eyed him sideways. "Did you want kids?"

"I don't know," he admitted. "I still don't." He regarded her thoughtfully for a few moments. "And, Lys, I don't want to screw up another relationship…"

She pushed herself off the car and stepped closer to him. "Don't you worry. I would never resent being given a choice. It think it's one of the most precious gifts anybody can give." She put her arms around his neck. "You'd make a good dad."

"Are we heading that way?"

"When things have quieted down, and we have ridden this out... I think I would like to have children with you."

The way she said it made it into something more than a declaration of the willingness—or even desire—to reproduce the species. Instead, it became a very personal thing between just the two of them. Not just a biological event. And that, he suddenly understood, made all the difference.

Debbie would never have looked at it as personal as that; much less put it into words.

That was *his* Debbie, of course! The one that didn't exist anymore. Replaced by another who didn't just hide a part of herself from him, but who'd gone out and had an affair.

Which isn't surprising, given the jerk-off I am in this version.

He really had nothing to brag about. Even in 'his' world, he had failed just as much as Debbie had. Maybe if he'd been more forthcoming about what he wanted...

Screw 'if'!

All of this was gone. Finished. Sunk into an oblivion more profound than anything one could possibly imagine.

But how?

His mind still refused to wrap itself around the very concept of 'realities' just disappearing into nothing.

How do I decide what's 'real'?

Ultimately—and maybe only—by experiencing it. Again and again he came back to that.

But who, or what, was the 'I' that was doing the experiencing? And what did those phase-delayed EEGs mean? Were there two of him, inhabiting the same brain? Phase-duplexed in some strange way—like multiplexing signals over a transmission line? Was the 'other' Ray still around somewhere? And if he was, then why wasn't he—*which 'me' are we talking about anyway?*—aware of being around in this brain...twice?

"Ray?"

"I'm OK." He pulled her to him. "I'm sorry. I'm just...lost. I don't *who* I am. Am I the first, or the second of those patterns? Or both of them? If I'm both, then how come I'm not aware of being the other? Same goes for you? How come you're *you*, and not somebody else?" He buried his face in her hair. "This is so fucking confusing!"

And then he remembered what she'd just said. "But I tell you what. There maybe a lot I don't know...but, if we get through this...I really would like to be the father of our children."

"I know."

5.

Alyssa went back to her apartment to face Susan. She felt she had to. She still felt a strong bond to her friend—even though she wasn't quite 'Susan', of course.

But who?

Susan was home when Alyssa came in. She stopped doing what she was doing, took Alyssa by the arm and guided her to a chair.

"Sit down."

Alyssa opened her mouth to say someting but Susan made a quick gesture.

"No! Just wait."

She went into the kitchen and returned with a bottle of red wine and two glasses. She carefully placed them on the coffee-table, filled them up and handed on to Alyssa, taking the other herself.

"Drink!" she ordered.

There was still a goodly measure of 'her' Susan left in this one!

Alyssa did as she was told. Susan supported her glass on the armrest of her chair.

"Talk!"

Alyssa feigned puzzlement, though she knew it wouldn't help her any. Not with Susan.

"What about?"

Susan's eyes narrowed dangerously. "Lys!"

She started at her friend for another few heartbeats and took another sip of her wine. "How about we start with the visit we had today from a certain Atlanta cop, who started asking some very peculiar questions?"

"Carter?"

"Ahh, you know him. Well, I'm all ears?"

"What did he want?"

"He asked questions. A lot of them. Mainly stupid questions. And he sounded as if he expected answers! Asshole."

"What kind of questions?"

"Hey, don't play that game with me. Remember, you're in answering mode!"

"You know what happened at the gallery on Saturday,"

"You're involved in that?"

"Indirectly."

"I bet it's because of that…person… That hairless marvel you were talking to—and doing other things with…"

"Yes."

Susan looked at Alyssa expectantly. "Yes? Come on; don't let me drag it out of you!"

"The police suspect that he's got something to do with it."

"Why?"

"I don't know. Maybe because he discovered the body. Maybe because the victim was screwing his wife. Maybe because he had left the opening during the period that the murder was committed."

Susan raised her eyebrows. "Now we're getting somewhere! Well, did he do it?"

Alyssa shook her head. "Of course not."

"And you know this how?"

"Because I was with him for all that time."

Susan regarded her quizzically. "I really didn't think he was your type."

"It's not like that."

"Oh-oh."

"What?"

"Lys, what's the matter with you? You haven't done something really stupid, have you?"

"Like what?"

"Oh, I don't know. Fall in love maybe?" She pointed at the glass. "Drink—and confess!"

Alyssa took a sip, for purposes of procrastination more than anything. What should she tell her friend? What *could* she tell her friend?

"All right—I confess."

"You're in love? Shit! I don't believe it." She stared at Alyssa. "Is this why you've been acting so strangely?"

"What do you mean?"

"You don't know? Tell me you're kidding!"

"Well, it's been kind of difficult…"

"Difficult? I'd say! Do you know that within a mere two days you've turned from our number one rainmaker into someone Horrie has been overheard to label a 'woman'? You know what it means when Horrie refers to anyone as 'that woman'?"

"Horrie's been a total asshole," Alyssa said. "He was having a male salivating session with Samuel. Over *me*! I'm not going to take that particular crap from anybody. Especially not Horrie."

"Horrie owns the firm," Susan reminded her.

"He can shove it for all I care," Alyssa said darkly.

"You don't mean that!"

"Wanna bet?"

Susan shook her head in exasperation. "What's gotten into you? Horrie's done this before. It's all part of the game, remember? That's the way we rope 'em in; and that's the way we screw them. It's not like it's such a novelty, and you've…"

She stopped when she saw Alyssa's face. "Look, Lys," she said softly, "we're friends, right? We don't have to lie to each other. But you know and I know and just about everybody in that office knows that you…"

"Don't say it!" Alyssa hissed. "Just don't. It may be true, but I don't give a shit. It's not going to happen again."

"Wow!" Susan shook her head and leaned it all the way back so she stared at the ceiling.

"Wow!" she said again and looked back at Alyssa. "Kid, you *have* changed! Is that what love does to people?"

Alyssa shrugged. "Maybe."

"Maybe?" Susan echoed. "Is that all you got to say?" She grimaced. "That guy must be something else! What is it? Soulmates? Or just a big dick?"

"Don't be coarse," Alyssa reprimanded her.

"Coarse? Me? No way! I mentioned the 'soulmate' bit before I got to the basics!"

"Well, that's what it is. I know you'll find this hard to understand—but he's the man. The one and only."

"Are you out of your mind? You've known this guy for how long? Like a couple of days? And he's married? Where's your brains?"

Alyssa gave her friend a wry smile. "You wouldn't believe me if I told you," she said cryptically.

"I probably wouldn't," Susan said caustically. "Anyway, seems to me like this guy's got you into major trouble. I mean, that detective was asking about *you*, not your friend. Wanted to know all sorts of things. Business dealings, friends and acquaintances, recent travels.

"It looks like your association with…what's his name anyway?"

"Ray."

"It seems like your association with Ray isn't too good for you from a business point of view. If you're his alibi—and he's yours—I can see that really being problematic. Our clients won't be too happy to see one of us involved in a murder investigation in this way. Especially if all the sordid extramarital affair details come out." She eyed Alyssa. "You've slept with him, haven't you? Looks like his wife isn't the only one who gets around. Not exactly Mr. Faithful himself, is he?"

"It's not like that," Alyssa retorted before she could help herself.

"It isn't? Well maybe you're right, but it's going to look that way! And who gives a shit about the truth when appearances are so much more exciting?"

"It's the truth anyway," Alyssa said.

Susan sighed. "What are you going to do?"

Alyssa shook her head. "I have no idea. But I won't be in tomorrow either."

"Why not?"

"Ray's got some…problems. He's booked in for some tests at Emory. I'd like to be there with him."

"Why?"

"Just because."

"What's the matter with him? Is it something serious?"

"That's what they're trying to find out."

Susan's expression softened. A trace of compassion seeped into her overall critical demeanor. "I'm sorry, Lys. Whatever I think about this guy…"

"That's OK." Alyssa emptied her glass in two hefty swigs. Susan watched her curiously.

"Gonna tell me what you see in him?"

Alyssa sighed and held out her glass. Susan refilled it, and her own as well.

"It's like… Oh, I don't know. It's just *there*. No real 'reason' behind it. And it doesn't need it."

Susan exhaled sharply. "Like that, huh? You're in deep shit, girl!"

"Tell me about it."

Alyssa's cellphone rang.

"That him?" Susan enquired.

Alyssa nodded and got up. "Stay there," she told her friend, "I'll be back."

6.

Ray came home to an empty house. 'Empty' in a sense that he couldn't quite define. But the sensation was real. It wasn't as if Debbie had taken the moving van to it while he had been away.

No, it wasn't that. And it wasn't her absence either. He knew what that felt like—on the night she had worked late and he'd been home.

Worked late, my foot! Screwed Ron Hadlow was more like it.

Anyway, it didn't matter. The emptiness was not caused by her non-presence, but by the knowledge that she had actually left. That, no matter what else happened, his wife of more than a decade was not a part of his life anymore. And it didn't matter that they'd grown subtly—and not so subtly in *this* world—apart during the last few years. The other was still around. A part of one's life. And that was gone now.

Like my whole fucking life is gone 'poof'!

Yeah, well, not all of that was bad. There were compensations. A loss need not be a negative thing—and in this instance... Well, it wasn't.

A part of him found that simple truth hard to take. That same part just wanted his old life back. With all the warts. There was a certain comfort in continuity; the kind of comfort people derive from traditions and rituals; the security that's lost when change invades one's life and twists and churns it around. The reason why 'May you live in interesting times.' was a curse, and not a blessing.

Ray found, however, that another part of him welcomed what was happening with open arms and reveled in it. There was a heady feel to this mad rollercoaster ride he was on; where nothing was quite what it seemed and where, despite all the dangers, he had found a dizzy kind of fulfillment that he'd never felt before.

Predictability be damned! Predictability was vastly overrated.

Ray padded through the empty rooms. The scent of Debbie, her perfumes and cosmetics, her being, was still strong; a pervading presence. Ray poked his head into the bedroom, wondering if Debbie might have been back to get some more of her things. But there appeared to be no change. The bed was still unmade. Her dressing table had the usual paraphernalia scattered across it in Debbie's untidy and yet organized sort of way. The wardrobe door was half-open as she'd left it on Saturday night.

Ray wondered where she'd gone. To her parents? Not likely. Probably to Martie's place. He wondered whether he should check; but then realized that there was no point. She wasn't a part of his life anymore. Correction: this Debbie had never been a part of his life. Period.

He wondered what this Debbie had been like. Was she, like the other, a control freak, who just couldn't bear uncertainty and the threat of unknown changes looming? Or had she been more adventurous and risk-taking—as might be indicated by the fact that she was actually having an affair?

Ray caught himself there. How did he know that 'his' Debbie had not been having an affair with Ron? Certainly, with the wisdom of hindsight—or was it 'parallel-sight'?—there had been signs which might well have pointed in that direction. Her long hours at work, catching up with 'paperwork', certainly gave pause for thought. So did Debbie's devotion to her job, which, in Ray's estimation, exceeded that required even for an assistant manager.

Of course he had been working similarly long hours, but in his case at least he could be sure that he hadn't been fooling around. Not like the 'other'.

What do we really know about those closest to us?

Following a curious impulse Ray went to Debbie's dressing table and pulled out the drawers. Cosmetics; lipstick; perfume; scraps of paper; a ball-point pen; a women's magazine; a prospectus of *Things*, Ron Hadlow's gallery/shop; a hair-dryer. Ray rummaged through it all, wondering what he was doing. Trying to figure out this woman, he supposed.

Finally he gave up. There was nothing here.

He closed the drawer. A slight crunching sound. Ray pulled the drawer out again. A small white square of crinkled paper, caught somewhere in the drawer, fell on the floor. Ray picked it up and smoothed it out. It contained a name: 'Jack'. Underneath a phone-number.

Who was 'Jack'? Ray didn't know anybody of that name. The number didn't ring any bells either.

Ray folded the paper and stuffed it into his back pocket. He hesitated and took it out again, then went into his study and plonked himself into a chair. After staring at the telephone number for a few minutes and contemplating his options, he picked up the phone and dialed.

A man's voice answered. None Ray recognized. No name. Just 'hello'.

Ray, following a hunch, asked to speak to Debbie. He made a token attempt to disguise his voice by placing his free hand like a tube around his mouth.

There was a brief pause at the other end of the line. Then the man's voice came back. "You must have the wrong number. There's no one here by that name."

Ray verified the number.

"That's correct," the man confirmed.

"There is no Debbie Shannon at this number?"

"No. Who *is* this?"

Ray grinned. He had gone this far. Why not take it a step further?

"Lieutenant Carter. Atlanta Police."

There was a sharp intake of breath at the other end, which was immediately suppressed.

"I don't know who Debbie Shannon is, and there's no one here by that name,"

The prick was lying through his teeth. Ray didn't have to be a cop to figure *that* one out.

"Thank you, sir," he said in his best imitation of police officer politeness. "Sorry to have troubled you."

"That's all right, officer."

"However, there's one more thing..."

"Yes, officer?"

"Who am I speaking to?"

The silence at the other end was deafening. As if the man had stopped breathing.

"Sir, it won't take me two minutes to find out," Ray reminded him.

"Jack McTierney."

"And this number, Mr.McTierney? It is your home? Your office?"

"My home."

"Thank you," Ray concluded. "I appreciate your cooperation. If you happen to run into Mrs.Shannon, please tell her that I have a few more questions regarding last Saturday night."

He hung up and stared at the wall.

'Jack' hadn't meant anything to him, but 'McTierney' was another matter. A silent partner in *Things*. Ron Hadlow ran the show, but McTierney owned almost forty percent of it.

What was going on here? Debbie having an affair with not one, but *two* guys? At one time?

Man!

What else was going on here?

Ray grinned mirthlessly when he tried to imagine the scene at Jack McTierney's end. If Debbie was there—and the more he thought about it, the more certain he became that she was—this call must've given her kittens. How would Carter, who surely had spoken to her, obtained that particular number? What did he want? Whom had he *really* called?

Ray jumped up, a new purpose energizing him. Something had been going on. Stuff involving Debbie, Ron Hadlow and Jack McTierney.

A romantic triangle? Involving *his* wife? That made it into a romantic square, if he was also counted in. Three men and a woman. An interesting configuration—and not one you often saw in the movies!

Ray went back into the bedroom and started turning it upside down. Wardrobe, clothes, drawers, bedside table, under the big rug, the dressing table again. Everything.

When he was done he wasn't one step closer to figuring out anything. That piece of paper with Jack's phone had been the only useful trace of anything untoward.

He went back into the living room and looked around. If she was going to hide anything that she didn't want him to come across—by accident, that is; there being no apparent reason for him to actually *look* for it—where would she leave it?

His gaze fell on the bookshelf and traveled down until it stopped on a row of coffee-table books about fashion, general art collection, identifying artworks, house decorating. Things he didn't exactly exhibit lively interests in.

Ray went over to the shelf and took out the books; placed them on the table and tipped them on end, with the covers folded out; shook them to see if anything emerged.

Something did. A stapled printout of a database or spreadsheet. Ray put it aside and continued to riffle through the books. But there was nothing else. He took the printout and got himself an orange juice from the refrigerator. Then he sat down and tried to decipher what it was he was seeing.

Since he wasn't an accountant the whole damn thing made little sense to him. Rows with names and figures. Names of artworks—or so it appeared. Prices. Maybe sales figures or profits. The whole damn thing made no sense. But it was dated only a couple of months ago, and Debbie had hidden it. So it had to mean something.

Ray pondered the printouts and dialed Alyssa. He told her what he'd found.

"Hold on," she said.

"Feel like coming over for a glass of wine?" she asked when she came back after a while. "It's a very nice red."

"Your friend there?"

"Yes." Very guarded. Question-answer time.

"She knows I'm coming?"

"Yes."

"No objections?"

"No."

"Huh? I thought she didn't like me."

"It's OK."
"You really want me to do this?"
"Yes."
"Give me half an hour."
"See you then."

7.

Ray accepted the glass of wine from Alyssa and sat down. Susan hadn't taken her eyes off him since he'd stepped into the place. Probably trying to make him feel uncomfortable. Successfully so.

He sat down on the love seat beside Alyssa.

"Let me have a look at what you've found," Susan told him.

Ray glanced at Alyssa. "You told her?" She nodded. He handed the papers to Susan who opened them up with a bored mien. With Ray and Alyssa watching she scanned them. Then she sat up straight and placed her glass on the coffee table. She leafed back through the printouts and frowned.

"Well, what is it?" Alyssa asked her friend.

"A record of some very creative accounting, I'd say."

"Creative?" Ray echoed.

Susan looked at the printouts. "Looks like someone's been skimming off profits. Mainly by misrepresenting them. Involving mostly artwork. Paintings, sculptures. That's if the abbreviations are anything to go by."

"What are we talking about here?" Alyssa asked. "Tax evasion?"

Susan shrugged. "*Some* kind of evasion: that's for sure."

"Why would anybody keep such records around?" Ray wondered. "They seem like pretty dangerous material to me!"

Susan chuckled dryly. "I agree. But people do. I don't know if it's for gloating over, or out of some misguided desire to keep a record of one's peccadillos. But they do." She shook her head. "You found this where?"

"Somewhere I wouldn't ordinarily look."

"Well, whoever left this stuff there is obviously aware of its significance. That doesn't prove that…your wife—that's who; right?"

Ray nodded.

"It doesn't mean that your wife is aware of what it all *means*—but since she is in the art business it very much suggests she does. Creative accounting is an essential element of successful art dealership."

Ray raised an eyebrow. "Can I ask how you know that?"

"Susan's our firm's 'interface' to the art world. She has this client…"

Susan, tut-tutted her friend. Alyssa laughed, ignoring her. "Well, he's quite a character."

Ray looked at Susan and wondered. "The name Jack McTierney mean anything to you?"

Susan gave a twitch of denial. "No. Should it?"

"I don't know," Ray said thoughtfully.

Alyssa wriggled herself into a comfortable position against him. Susan watched the proceedings with a jaundiced eye.

"What's the connection?" Alyssa asked.

"That was the name of the guy I spoke to."

Alyssa looked at her friend. "If it's an arty guy, maybe Mitch Cage knows."

Susan nodded. "Maybe."

"Feel like calling him?"

"Now?"

"It's early," Alyssa told Susan.

"I'm not too sure he would appreciate it."

"But you do have his number," Ray guessed.

"Of course."

"It could be very important," he said quietly.

Susan looked from Ray to Alyssa and back again. She sighed and got up.

"Gimme a few minutes." She walked out of the room.

Alyssa pushed even closer to Ray and, after peeking over his shoulder to make sure that Susan was really gone, put an arm around his neck and kissed him at great length and with passion.

"Nice of you to come," she breathed when she was done.

"I'm glad I did," he agreed. "If only for this."

"Want me to come with you after this?"

"Do I want to? What a question. Of course I do! But it's not..." He sighed. "Too many ghosts around my place. Debbie's everywhere. I don't want to jinx us."

"Besides, who knows who's watching the comings and goings at my place? I'd rather not have you dragged into this mess even further."

"We could find ourselves a motel," she whispered.

"What will your friend say?"

"Susan will disapprove. Susan will also have to learn to live with it."

"If you're sure about this..."

"Do you want to?"

"Is the pope catholic?"

"Let me think about that," she murmured.

Susan materialized before them. Alyssa let go of Ray and configured herself into a more decorous pose.

"Well?"

"Mitch knows McTierney all right. Everybody does. McTierney's a silent partner."

"Yes?"

Susan sighed impatiently. "A guy who invests his money in businesses in return for a share of the profits. 'Silent' because he doesn't actually involve himself in the day-to-day running. He fronts up the money and wants his cut."

"An investor," Ray supplied.

"A partner," Susan repeated. "In this instance, a partner of dubious antecedents. And we're not just talking mere shady business practices, but connections to very unsavory activities. Racketeering; extortion; drugs. Stuff like that. McTierney's 'art' connections are definitely the upmarket part of his business."

"Debbie?"

"If your wife's boss was involved with McTierney, she was bedding some very dangerous people."

"Debbie must've known!"

Susan nodded. "Looks like it. The question is who was doing the creative accounting? Hiding what from whom?"

"Debbie? I don't believe it."

Susan shrugged. "Believe what you want to. The facts are as they are."

Ray's head was reeling. It didn't help that he reminded himself that this Debbie wasn't the woman he'd known. And, in a way, it didn't really matter. It seemed that in this version of whatever was 'real' all the main players—himself, Alyssa, Debbie, Ron—had almost fully realized their potential for being total creeps. It was latent in everybody, he guessed, but where he'd come from most of those features had not developed to any great degree. But they were there. He, Ray, had exhibited a shocking willingness to cheat on his wife. Debbie had a goodly portion of the kind of dedication to her work— and her boss—that would easily have led to the outcome he was witnessing right now. Alyssa's motives for choosing the legal profession hadn't been all that different from those of the Alyssa whose place she had 'taken'. And, from what she'd told him, her attitude toward men hadn't always been the healthiest either.

All in all, although things were different here, they weren't entirely unfamiliar. A question of past choices and developed potentials—or not, as the case might be. Quite disturbing, really.

Ray retrieved the printout. He considered the two bottles on the coffee table. One was empty; the other still had some mileage left. He'd had only one glass, and would still able to drive. Better to stop here and now—no matter how much he felt like helping the women to finish off whatever there was.

Regretfully, he declined Alyssa's offer for a refill. Maybe he should leave.

Alyssa divined his thoughts. The slightest twitch of her head indicated to him that she didn't want him to. The quick glance she flicked in his direction reminded him of their plans; which she obviously intended to stick to. Ray settled back into the cushions and steeled himself to being grilled by Susan. The woman looked primed for a major offensive.

8.

"That wasn't so bad—was it?" Alyssa asked him when they were finally in his car and driving out of the apartment block's parking lot.

"Bad enough," he muttered.

Alyssa laughed. "She's just concerned about my welfare."

"I know. That's why I remained unflaggingly polite."

"That you did. I was rapt in admiration."

"Good."

Alyssa laughed. He knew she was just on the other side of tipsy, but not very far. Still in control, though significantly relaxed by the alcohol. And, he told himself when her left hand slipped up along his leg, with just a few less inhibitions.

"Naughty girl," he told her.

"This is nothing," she chuckled. "You wait until I get you behind a closed door."

"Hmm. Where are we going anyway?"

Alyssa's hand finally stopped, but it didn't help his concentration any, considering where it rested.

"I don't care," she said huskily. "Just make it quick."

Wednesday

1.

Lieutenant Carter produced a gun, wrapped in a ziploc bag, and placed it on the table before Ray.
"Do you recognize this gun, Mr. Shannon?"
"Can I pick it up?" Ray asked him.
"Please do."
Ray picked up the weapon. "It's a Glock."
"Very good," Carter's colleague, who had been introduced just as Rory Schneider, muttered dryly. Schneider was white, blue-eyed, young, well-dressed, probably ambitious, but definitely Carter's underling—and it showed.
"Anything else you would like to tell us?" Carter supplied.
Ray inspected the serial number. "It's not the gun I gave you."
"Too true."
"So—why are you showing it to me?"
"Because it's the gun you should *also* have given me."
"I beg your pardon?"
Carter shook his head. "Mr. Shannon, your wife told us about your second weapon."
Ray nodded. He knew damn well it was his gun. The right side of the grip had a scrape where he'd once dropped it.
"And?"
"And—I would like to know why you chose to be less than candid with me!"
"Lieutenant, you asked me for my gun. I gave you my gun. Had you asked me if I owned another one I would have told you so. But you didn't—so I didn't. Period."
He put the gun back on the table. "Anyway, where did you get this from?"
Carter's mouth twitched. "Where did you keep it?"
"Under the dashboard of my car."
"That's not where we found it. But you know that…"
"Of course. I noticed the gun was missing."
"When?"
"Monday evening."
"Monday?"
"Yes."
"How did you notice?"
"I checked."
"Why?"
"Because it occurred to me that I should."
"Why?"
Ray shrugged. "Why, why why? How do I know? A stray train of thought. An idle rumination. I reached down to check for my gun and found it gone. It and the holster it's in."

"This one?" Carter reached down and produced another item in a ziploc bag.

Ray nodded.

Carter, who appeared to have a stash of items behind that desk, and produced them with the glee of a stage-magician conjuring rabbits, reached down again and came out with a short, but heavy tubular object, also wrapped in a bag.

"This yours, too?"

Ray shook his head. "What is it?"

"It's a silencer, Mr. Shannon. One which happens to fit this gun of yours and which, as evidenced by certain markings on your gun, had indeed been affixed to it at some stage."

Ray picked up the Glock and peered at the muzzle. Carter was right. There were marks here—but none *he* had caused. However, the emerging picture was getting pretty obvious.

"You're going to tell me where you found my gun?" he asked Carter, who had been eyeing him with the keep eyes of a predator about to pounce.

"Why not?" the detective replied. "Though, to my mind, you don't need an answer—since you already know."

"Oblige my client anyway," Frank Nuovo said. He was standing by the window so that Ray could keep him in sight and react to any warning signals.

"We found it in a dumpster in the parking lot at the rear of Tantrevalles Gallery. In the same place we found the holster and the silencer. Plus a number of bloodstains, and other evidence that Ron Hadlow was killed near that dumpster, and subsequently carried by a person or persons unknown to the toilet where you subsequently 'found' him." The way he said it made the lawyer cast a thoughtful look at his back. But Nuovo didn't say anything, and Ray chose to ignore the taunt.

Carter studied Ray for a moment and, when no response appeared to be forthcoming, shrugged and continued. "Since the murder took place outside the gallery, and since it took place during the period you claim you were absent..." He let the implications hang in the air.

"Except that I do have a witness," Ray told him. Alyssa had insisted that it was totally pointless *not* admitting to what Carter knew anyway.

"That would be Ms. Weaver, yes?"

"Yes."

"Would you mind explaining why you chose to conceal this important detail from us until now?" Schneider, who had kept pretty much out of the discussion, asked.

"Discretion," Ray told him. "I didn't think it would be necessary to involve her."

"The whole truth usually helps," Carter told Ray. "It avoids creating the impression that one's concealing important information and cannot be trusted."

Ray shook his head. "The whole truth is usually unpalatable," he said.

Carter frowned. "Mr. Shannon; that's not a good attitude. If you're wanting to clear yourself of any suspicions..."

"My client has no need to clear himself of anything," Nuovo interjected curtly. "And unless you have anything more substantive than you have now..."

Carter shook his head. "Not yet."

Frank Nuovo stepped closer to the table and placed his hands on it. He leaned forward and looked Carter in the face. "This it is? That's what you called us here for?"

"I still have to interview Ms. Weaver. I'll let you know then if this is, as you say, 'it'!

"Still," and here Carter turned to Ray, "I would appreciate it if you would be available at all times for further questions. Indeed, I must insist on it. Your conduct in this matter raises serious questions, and it probably wouldn't surprise you to hear that you're very high up on the list of suspects. High enough so that, should you choose *not* to inform us if you're leaving this city for any reason, it would be sufficient reason to issue a warrant for your arrest.

"Do I make myself clear?"

Ray glanced at Frank Nuovo, who smiled thinly. Ray took that to be a good sign.

"Quite," he said.

"Good," Carter agreed.

"Can I go now?" Ray asked him.

"Just one more thing," Carter's sidekick interjected. "For the record: just what exactly did you do during the hour and a half you were absent from the gallery?"

"We drove around," Ray told him. "Then we stopped and talked."

"About what?"

"This and that."

"Would you like to be more specific?"

"No."

Ray felt Carter's unsettling gaze upon him.

"Just 'talked'?"

Ray nodded. "At this stage…yes."

"And you didn't think of going somewhere more comfortable? A bar maybe? Somewhere people might remember you?"

"We briefly went to a restaurant called *El Gitano*, to have dinner maybe. But they were booked out. So, we just sat and talked."

"Where?"

"I told you: in the car!"

"And where," Carter said testily, "was the car at the time?"

"In a parking lot, just beside *El Gitano*."

Schneider asked for the address of the restaurant and Ray told him.

"That will be all," Carter said. "For the moment."

"Well," Ray said, "I'm not done. In your eagerness to pin the murder on me it looks like you may have overlooked a couple of factors."

"Like?"

"Like firstly, once the governor was in the gallery, it is my guess that his security would made have made it quite impractical for anybody to lug Ron's body from where you think he was killed to the toilets. Which, I suspect, narrows the temporal window of possibilities and will probably also support my story."

Carter looked at him and nodded slowly. "And your second point? There is something else, right?"

"You might want to look around other places for motives." Ray nodded at Frank Nuovo who produced a photocopy of the printouts Ray had found in his house. Ray supplied the details of how he had found them.

Lieutenant Carter studied the sheets of paper. "The originals?"

"Are in the safe at my office," Frank Nuovo supplied. "They are available to you at a moment's notice. We just didn't want to carry them around. However, if you call at my office, my secretary will hand them to over to you."

Carter blew out his cheeks. "We will certainly investigate this matter." He glanced at Ray. "How did you know about McTierney's involvement with Ron Hadlow?"

"I don't 'know' anything," Ray advised him. "I'm guessing. It's your job to find out for sure, isn't it?"

Carter studied Ray for a few seconds in that unsettling way of his. Then he relaxed. "It still begs the question about your gun."

"Not if someone wants to make it look as if I was involved."

The detective rose. "We'll talk again. Stay in touch."

2.

"Just exactly what's your relationship with Ray Shannon?"

"You mean what is it *now*, or what was it on Saturday evening?"

"Let's start with Saturday evening."

"I met Ray at the gallery opening. We talked. We decided that neither of us really liked the ambience and that a bit of fresh air would be nice. So we went out for a drive."

The wiry black detective nodded. "Why were you at the gallery?"

"My friend and colleague, Susan, had two invitations. She thought it might be interesting."

"What's her connection with the gallery?"

"None. They were given to her by a client, who does have connection."

Alyssa decided that Rory Schneider was a creep. The way he looked at her made her feel dirty. And it was more than just intimidate-the-suspect stuff. The sexual element, the suggestive leer, shone through the veneer of his apparent indifference. She tried to ignore him.

Carter, she like much better. A professional through and through. A sharp one; and a pain in the ass right now. But a professional nonetheless.

"So, you went for a drive with Mr. Shannon. After having known him for how long? A few minutes maybe?"

"We met before."

"Where?"

"At the hospital. I had a rash in my face from a…cosmetic problem. Ray had his face and scalp singed from some accident. We met—and talked briefly. Then I saw him again at the gallery."

"So you knew him for more than just a few minutes."

"Detective—please. Just don't, OK? The fact is that Ray and I…well, we just kind-of connected. Like sometimes you just *know* that a person is OK. It was that way with Ray. And, no, I don't normally…"

'…do that kind of thing,' she was going to say. And, of course, it was true. But it wasn't true for the Alyssa that Carter would know about.

"Don't normally what?" Schneider asked her.

She could have kicked herself for letting her mouth run away with her. She was a lawyer, damn it! She should really know better.

"Trust men," she said curtly and briefly stared at him. "Like I don't trust you, for example. You strike me as exactly the kind of guy that I definitely *wouldn't* get into a car with."

She could see him flinch. He tried to respond to her stare, but she wasn't going to allow him to connect, and looked back at Lieutenant Carter. "How can you work with that creep?" she said scornfully. She shook her head before Carter could answer. "Don't incriminate yourself," she said dismissively. "I figure you haven't got any choice, do you?"

Something in Carter's expression told her that they were on the same wavelength here. But he couldn't admit it, of course. And he didn't.

"Where did you and Mr. Shannon go?" he asked.

"We drove around for a while. Then we went to *El Gitano* to see if we could get some dinner. When they didn't have any free tables we decided to just leave it and talked for a while in Ray's car—before driving back to the gallery."

"That's what Mr. Shannon told us," the black detective told her.

"Of course," she said. "If for no other reason but that it's the truth."

"What did you talk about?"

"Life."

"Which part of it?"

"Relationships." She raised a hand. "And that's as far as I'll go—so don't bother to ask further."

Carter nodded, apparently unsurprised. Schneider had fallen so silent that she couldn't even hear him breathe. One of those guys who freaked out when the truth about him is bared. Probably also resented his mother for her dominance over him—even though he was the one who allowed himself to be dominated.

"What is your relationship with Mr. Shannon now?" Carter asked her.

"We spent the last two nights together," she said briefly.

"You realize of course that this decreases the value of your testimony as far as his alibi is concerned."

"Of course. But that's the way it is. I also realize that it elevates me in the hierarchy of your suspects."

"Has Mr. Shannon discussed with you some papers he found in his house yesterday?"

"He came to me for help and showed them to me and my colleague and friend, Susan. We told him what we thought they represented."

Carter placed a few sheets of paper in front of her. "Do these look like accurate copies of the papers you saw last night?"

Alyssa studied the sheets. "I think so. I don't recall all the details, of course."

Carter nodded and rose.

"Well, thank you. And for you, too, a good piece of advice…"

"I won't leave town," she promised.

"Good. See that you don't."

3.

They parted from Frank Nuovo in the parking lot.

"Keep those cellphones on," he advised them. "Don't give him a reason to come down on you."

They promised to be good and left in Alyssa's car.

"What now?" she asked.

Ray looked at his watch. "I've got almost four hours to my scans."

"Look," he said, "I'll be OK, you know. You can get back to work."

She shook her head. "I couldn't function. Better not."

By now he knew when she was serious. "I have to go back home," he said. "Change clothes. Maybe poke around a bit more."

"Mind if I come with you?" she asked.

"Debbie could be there," he said cautiously. "I don't think she will, but it's possible."

"If her car's there I won't come in," Alyssa said.

Ray nodded. "All right. If you're sure."

"I am."

4.

The inside of his house looked like a maniac from a slasher movie had worked out here. Especially the study, the bedroom, and the lounge.

Ray froze and stared at the chaos.

"What the fuck…"

Alyssa, standing behind him, looked over his shoulder into the devastated study. She touched his shoulder. "Doesn't look like vandalism," she said.

Ray agreed. It looked more like someone had been looking for something. Maybe a few sheets of printout.

"Call the cops," Alyssa advised him.

They came about twenty minutes later. Ray had also phoned Frank, who had apparently informed Lieutenant Carter of the event. The detective—and Rory Schneider, who, Ray thought, was eyeing Lys in a way that made him want to punch the bastard out—arrived about the same time as the Fulton County Police squad car. He took one look at the scene and turned to Ray and Alyssa.

"I guess you'd be hard pressed to tell me if anything is missing."

"Definitely," Ray agreed.

Carter called in a forensic team which started going over the place with meticulous methodicity. Ray looked at Alyssa. "Sure you don't want to go to work? I'll have to stay here, you know."

"You mustn't miss your scan!"

"I won't."

"That's right, you won't," she said determinedly and took his arm. "Mainly because I'm going to be here to make sure of it."

"You're quite bossy, you know!"

"Yeah, well—you're all I've got…"

The way she said it made him feel quite odd—in a nice kind of way.

The team left about two hours later.

"Strange thing," Carter told them. He and Schneider had left and come back again.

Now he was about to leave for good. "No visible signs of a break-in. Probably came in by the front-door. Of course, anybody with the skills and tools can pick a lock without leaving much of a sign. But it's also possible that the perps entered using an ordinary key."

"According to your neighbors, nobody saw or heard a thing."

"Which suggests that it probably happened during the night." He considered them. "I gather you were somewhere else."

"Yes," Ray admitted.

"With you?" he said to Alyssa.

"Yes."

Carter nodded. "Of course," he added, "people also don't see a lot of things that happen in broad daylight."

"Still…" He excused himself and departed. With him went the rest of the police team. Ray and Alyssa were left looking after them. Then they went back inside. Ray looked around the devastation and decided that he was in no disposition to clean up the mess. Not now and maybe never. He went to the wardrobe and extracted a few necessities, which he placed into a small travel case. He cast one last look around and took Alyssa's hand.

"Let's go."

5.

The MRI scanner's RF coils were hammering away as Ray lay still inside the magnet, waiting for the scan to terminate. Presently the sound ceased. A voice over the PA system told him that it would be only a few minutes longer. He knew why: they were reconstructing the data from the scan; in order to decide whether the procedure had been a success.

Ray was not surprised when it took longer than just a 'few minutes'. The voice informed him that they needed to repeat the scan. Ray, who knew that it wouldn't do any good, said nothing. A technician and a nurse came in. He was slid out of the magnet's orifice. The tech poked in a small hand-held device and muttered something.

"Sorry abut that, Mr. Shannon," the nurse told Ray.

"Just one more scan," he said. "If they can't get it right then; bad luck." She nodded sympathetically. Presently he was inserted into the magnet again and the procedure repeated.

They took him out after that, but he could see that they weren't happy. Alyssa, waiting from him in a nearby room, looked up when he came in. One look at his face and she knew. "You were right?"

"Yep."

She looked at her watch. "You're late for your other scan."

They hurried to Nuclear Medicine, where they ran into Dr. Lopez.

"What are you doing here?" Ray asked him.

"This is my weekly half-day at Emory," Lopez said. "I've got a few moments to spare—so I thought I'd check up on you. How did the MRI go?"

"Like I predicted."

Lopez eyebrows went way up his forehead, which creased into a hundred tiny and large folds. "I see," he said thoughtfully.

A nurse came up and interrupted them. "Mr. Shannon?"

The PET scan took another hour and ended with the same results as the MRI. The techs pronounced themselves frustrated at their failure. Lopez joined them again. Ray finally was allowed to dress in his street clothes.

"All right," Lopez told Ray. "You have my full and undivided attention."

"I'm still not too sure you're wanting to hear this," Ray warned him.

"But I *do*," the neurologist insisted. "Indeed, I have canceled all my appointments for the rest of the day. Your story'd better be good!"

He glanced at Alyssa who was laughing. "I hope I'm going to find this as funny as you do."

"Oh, it's not humorous in the slightest," she assured him. "I'm just laughing in anticipation at your face…"

"How about we find ourselves a nice place to talk," Ray suggested. "Shall we go and have some dinner?"

Alyssa smiled at Lopez. "How about it?" she asked.

Lopez shrugged himself out of his white overcoat. "By all means. I have no other plans for the night."

6.

They picked *El Gitano*—for good reasons.

"You'll understand in due course," Alyssa assured the neurologist.

They ordered *tapas* to nibble on while they waited for their main course.

"Think of this as a story," Ray advised Lopez. "Pretend it's fiction."

He began his story the moment he'd left his place of work on Friday to go home. By the time the main course came he had reached the point where he and Alyssa left the gallery opening.

Lopez took it all remarkably well. He raised his eyebrows a few times and asked for the occasional clarification, but that was about it. Every now and then he glanced at Alyssa, but, finding no trace of mirth on her face either, seemed to feel no need to speak his mind—which must surely by now, Ray thought, be making some fairly harsh judgments about their intention and/or their sanity.

With the arrival of the main course Alyssa started to tell her part of the story; to the point where Ray had stopped. Then they continued on together—leaving out a few salacious details, but otherwise sticking closely to what they remembered.

By the time desert had been consumed and coffee was being served they had come to an end.

"And that," Alyssa told Lopez, "is the story."

The neurologist picked up his cup and sipped carefully and deliberately, before putting it down with exaggerated care.

"Now," he said, pursing his lips, "all you need to tell me is what you *think* is the explanation for all this." He looked at Ray. "I suppose you have one."

Ray let him have it.

When he was done, the neurologist sat back and shook his head.

"You know," he said pensively, "if this is a story…even then…it's a damn good one."

"And if it's not?" Alyssa said.

Lopez sighed. "Then you're either nuts—both of you; or else this world is a much stranger place than anybody's ever dared to imagine."

"Well, what do you think?" Ray asked him. "Do we look crazy to you?"

Lopez smiled mirthlessly. "As my psychiatrist colleagues assure me, insanity takes a dazzling range of expressions, some of which are so subtle that they remain undetected by even the most skilled of observers."

Ray grimaced. "Making up for those 'mental illnesses' which really aren't."

"There's that," the neurologist agreed. He leaned back. "Anyway, it's clear that you told me this story with a fair expectation of my probable reaction. All of which leaves me in a quandary. Because either you're playing a game with me—in which case I must confess to a mixture between amusement and irritation. Or you actually *believe* what you've just told me—which either proves that you both have serious cognitive difficulties.

"The last possibility—and this bothers me most of all—is that what you've told me is essentially true."

"It's not a joke," Alyssa said.

"I didn't think so. Which leaves me with the insanity option—which most of my colleagues would opt to go for at this point.

"And so would I. If only it weren't not for those scans." He grimaced again. "Care to tell me what you think is happening here?"

"I think there are two 'minds' here for each of us," Ray said. "Displaced from each other by a few hundred milliseconds in time. One of them is identical with the one I would identify as 'me'. That's the one I'm aware of. The who has a reasonably continuous memory of all those things we just told you about.

"The other… Well I don't know. The one whose place I've taken maybe? I haven't got any answers either. And I certainly haven't even got the conceptual framework for explaining why, whatever constitutes 'me', seems to be aware only of that one 'me'; and why I—why *we*—don't exhibit openly bipolar symptoms. Schizophrenic episodes."

Lopez smiled thinly. "One might argue that your story, if it represents something you actually *believe* has happened, constitutes sufficient evidence for the presence of a fairly serious bipolar disorder."

He made a small gesture. "But I don't believe that. Schizophrenics do not exhibit temporally phased patterns. Their patterns just have different sequences and spatial distributions. The temporal phasing, which implies that the true pattern of neural activity actually consists of two superimposed, phase-shifted patterns, doesn't make any sense at all. If for no other reason but that the patterns are actually separable—which simply couldn't happen if they took place upon the same neural matrix. If this was the case you should not be able to formulate a single coherent thought; let alone function coherently at a purely physical level."

He frowned. "In fact, I seem to remember that the second pattern is actually somewhat weaker than the first. Sam, my technician, called it an 'echo' when he first separated it. But, of course, we thought of it was having some relationship with the preceding pattern. It is, after all, almost indistinguishable. If there are differences our apparatus and protocol is not refined enough to resolve these. But if we assume—purely for the sake of the discussion—that this pattern is actually just a purely *physical* echo of... whatever..."

He shook his head. "To be honest, I don't even know why I'm talking to you about this. You've got to realize just how crazy it sounds."

"You said the second pattern was weaker than the first? How much weaker?"

Lopez shrugged. "Something like twenty percent: sufficient to be definite."

"How would you like to scan both Lys and me again tomorrow morning? And what if I made you another prediction?"

"Like what?"

"Like that this time the second pattern will be more attenuated than at the last recording. Maybe even more out of phase. For both of us."

Lopez pursed his lips and scowled at his coffee cup. "That *would* be interesting."

"Would that lend more credence to what we told you, you think?"

"Possibly. Though I wouldn't stop trying to find other explanations."

Ray chuckled. "I wouldn't respect you if you didn't."

The neurologist eyed them curiously. "So—what are you two intending on doing with your...situation? I mean, it's obvious to me that for you it is real, and that you are compelled to act as if it were real. Meaning you're living in a very confusing world. How do you deal with that?"

"There are certain things we *know*," Alyssa said. "Well, things *I* know."

"Like?"

Alyssa glanced at Ray. "About us, for one thing."

Lopez nodded thoughtfully. "An island of certainty in an ocean of confusion and doubt."

"Something like that," Alyssa agreed. "For me it's a lifeline. Without it..."

Lopez gave her a sympathetic inspection. "I can imagine." To Ray: "I suppose you feel pretty much the same?"

"Very much so."

"You see," Alyssa said, "I'm not so sure—as Ray is—that this whole thing is just 'physical'. I can't help but think that there's something else to it. Not a necessarily intent...but something more than just some freakish event involving parallel universes, or whatever it is... That we have some control over this. That whatever happens isn't just chance and physics."

"A very human way of looking at things," Lopez agreed. "Not that it proves anything, of course. But we need to believe that we're not completely helpless."

"I'm not saying that we don't have any control at all," Ray objected. "I just think that right now we haven't got any," he told Alyssa. "We may have had some: when it 'happened'; when I thought that I wanted you to look at me as something else but just another faceless man behind a wheel."

"So why not now?" she enquired. "What was different about that time?"

"I don't know," Ray admitted.

"That seems to be the bottom line," Lopez said siccantly. "Look, Mr. Shannon: you're a scientist. Surely, a rational part of you must be telling you that this whole thing make very little sense indeed. That maybe you and Ms. Weaver are living a very elaborate fantasy."

"Briefly," Ray told him.

"Briefly?"

"Yes, it occurred to me briefly. Very briefly. The problem is that this explanation makes even less sense than what we've come up with. But you know that, don't you?"

Lopez sighed. "I know nothing. And I'll reserve my judgment until tomorrow morning when I fully intend on taking you two up on your offers."

"Another scan?"

"Definitely. And if your predictions turn out to be true, I promise to reconsider my current—decidedly skeptical—position."

He emptied his cup. "And now, if you'll excuse me, I really have to go." He pulled out his wallet, but Alyssa stopped him. "No need for that. It was a pleasure to have someone hear us out. Thank you for you patience."

The neurologist smiled at her. "It was an interesting evening. I thank *you*." He shook their hands and departed. They looked after him until he had disappeared through the door.

"What do you think?" Alyssa asked Ray.

"I think he's an unusual man. Someone I'd like to get to know better—if only there were an opportunity."

"There may yet be."

"I hope so."

They paid at the till and stepped outside, into a sultry Atlanta night.

Alyssa laid a hand on his arm. "What are you going to do tonight?"

"That motel we stayed at last night wasn't bad. I'll check if they have any rooms left."

"Need company?"

"Desperately."

"I'll meet you there," she said. "I'm just going to fetch some things."

She brushed a kiss on his mouth.

"See you soon," she said and got into her car.

Ray looked after her as she pulled out of the parking lot and onto the road. When she was gone he stood unmoving for a minute or so, attempting to get some *feel* of this world that was his and yet wasn't.

How could anybody know for sure that the world around one was one's own? That the people were the ones one had known the day before?

Nobody, but *nobody*, ever remembered the same things in exactly the same way. Nobody had even *experienced* them the same way to begin with! So, what was the meaning of what he'd just asked himself?

How do I know that anybody is who he or she was yesterday?

When even billions of their elementary constituents weren't the same anymore...

Futility!

Ray shook himself and let himself into his car.

7.

The *Peach Blossom Inn* was only a few minutes' drive from *El Gitano*. They still had several vacant rooms. Ray, anticipating that this probably wouldn't be his last night, booked it for the rest of the week and paid with his VISA card. The receptionist on duty smiled as she recognized him from the night before.

"Twin occupancy," Ray advised her.

She gave him a look that was a mix of I-know-what's-going-on and I-don't-care-what's-going-on. But she didn't say anything and Ray appreciated the discretion. He really didn't feel like confronting a nosy and garrulous inquisitor. He just wanted Lys to come, so they could wrap themselves around each other, and in their mutual immersion forget that the world was a strange and very uncertain place.

He went to the room and decided to have a shower. When he came out he dressed himself in jeans and a T-shirt and turned on the TV for something to do while he waited for Lys to turn up. The program, an episode in a series called *Overman*—a series he'd never heard of! had just started. It was interesting enough to hold his attention, but finally, during an ad break near the end, he finally found himself getting restive.

Where was Lys? Half an hour max for the round trip to her apartment; maybe another half hour if Susan cornered her. Maybe longer.

He forced himself to relax. When *Overman* was finished he switched to CNN for the news. Despite his impatience for Lys to turn up he found himself fascinated by the oddly skewed world that opened up to him. A window into a strange universe. Strange—yet disconcertingly familiar. He'd always been bored with news, which only in rare cases managed to rivet his attention; too much of it being repetitious, irrelevant, or sickening. Journalists fabricating news where there weren't any, or dishonoring their profession by distorting the 'truth' they were meant to report to suit their own biases.

But now it was different. Eeverything was 'news'—to him at least.

Quite exciting actually. If he forgot his problems with the cops, his estranged 'wife', and his phased double personality, it was quite a pleasant adventure, this continuity slip; endowed with a quality very similar to watching a movie. Or maybe playing *Wild Worlds*. Only that he couldn't just walk out of this one; or select the 'Suspend Game' option from a menu.

Even the novelty of the news, however, could not cover up his growing unease when Alyssa did not materialize after about two hours. Ray eyed the cellphone. There was really no cause for alarm. Susan probably had cornered her and Lys just couldn't get away.

But then she would have called him: that much he was certain of.

Ray hesitated. He picked up the cellphone. There was a brief delay as the call worked its way through the system. Then Lys's phone ringing. And ringing. And ringing.

Then: relief!

"Hello?"

A woman's voice, but not Lys!

"Who's this?" he asked.

"Is that you, Ray?"

"Yes."

"This is Susan. I guess Lys figured out that she forgot her phone..." There was a pause. "Ray? Where's Lys?"

"That's what I was going to ask *you*!"

8.

"Behave yourself," Susan called after her.
Alyssa laughed. "No way!"
"Remember what I told you about strange men!" Susan shouted.
"I'm trying to forget!"
 The door of the apartment closed after her and she limped down the few stairs to the ground floor and out of the entrance. She launched the bag into the back of her open convertible and carefully inserted herself into the drivers' seat. The ankle still hurt. It really could do with more rest than she was giving it.
 At the window she saw the silhouette of Susan's head move past the kitchen window. She put the key into the ignition and started the engine. As she did her eyes alighted on one of the cars parked outside the apartments at the end of this particular block of buildings.
 The engine started. Her attention was distracted by the mechanics of handling a car: turning on lights, putting the automatic into reverse, backing out of her slot. When she had reversed far enough she placed the automatic into 'drive' and looked forward through the windscreen again. The beams of her lights shone across a group of cars ahead of her. Alyssa, her mind nudged by something she was unable to pinpoint, moved off. She drove around the loop at the end of the drive and back on the other side of the center row of bushes until she reached the exit. Traffic on the road was sparse. She turned left. When she was about a hundred yards down the road she happened to look into her mirror—and saw another pair of lights emerge from the apartment lot.
 In that moment something clicked in her mind. The car...
 What was it?
 Then she knew. When she first looked she'd glimpsed the silhouette of an occupant. Maybe two. A few moments later, when her lights had picked out the very same vehicle, the car appeared empty.
 There was a perfectly reasonable explanation for that, of course. Like that the occupants had anticipated being half-blinded by her beam and had decided to duck in time.
 Possible. But not what she would have done herself. More likely she would have just shielded her eyes—with her hands, or maybe an arm. Besides, what were people doing, sitting in parked cars in an apartment parking lot? There were better places to talk—or to do anything else for that matter.
 She glanced in the mirror again. The lights were behind her. There were only two cars in sight traveling in the same direction as herself. One of them had just become visible in the distance around the bend of the road. The second one, much closer, had to be the same she'd just seem emerge from the driveway.
 The signals turned red. Alyssa stopped. The other car pulled in behind her. Alyssa, keeping her head straight, tried to use her mirror to peer into the other car.
 Two occupants. Both men.
 Now she was sure.
 Police?
 Possibly.

Were they tailing her and Ray? The main suspects in the murder of Ron Hadlow?

The lights turned green. She had intended to turn right, into Clairmont and heading south. Following a sudden impulse she ignored the road markings and pulled to the left instead, crossing Clairmont and continuing on straight. In her mirror she saw that the car behind her didn't follow but turned right.

Alyssa let out a sigh of relief.

Paranoia.

She pulled to the curbside and did a U-turn, doubling back to the intersection. She turned left and continued south on Clairmont.

Unless they had expected her to so this, of course...

The thought came unbidden and caused her to inspect the lights now behind her more closely. Since they were all some distance off, it was impossible to tell.

Another set of signals. Alyssa dawdled enough to arrive when they were just changing to red. She peered at the cars coming up behind her—and noticed that one of them pulled onto the verge about fifty yards behind her. When the lights turned green it pulled out again and fell in about two cars behind her.

Bastards.

Why would they be following her? What could they hope to gain? What was she to do?

Maybe they didn't know where Ray was! Maybe that's what this was all about. They must be following her to find him. Unless she was a major suspect. Which was quite feasible...

Alyssa turned left at the next intersection and headed through northern Decatur toward the I-285. She'd have to warn Ray. She reached over to the passenger seat for her cellphone. Her groping hands found nothing.

Shit! Shitshitshit!

Where was it?

Had to be in her handbag on the backseat.

Then she remembered.

Damn! More like on her bed in the apartment!

Shit!

She glanced in her mirror. Unless she was very much mistaken, they were about three cars behind her in the next lane.

There was some way she had to get to Ray. She couldn't lead them to him—if that's what they wanted! but if she didn't show up at the motel he'd be worried sick pretty soon. She was late as it was. Susan had held her up for quite some time. Work stuff mainly. Trying to convince her that she really had to get back to the office. Work was piling up. Clients were getting restive. Horrie was not pleased.

The 285 junction came up. Alyssa decided to go south. She looped down the on-ramp and threaded herself into a steady stream of traffic. Nothing too heavy, but maybe she could lose them here. She put her foot down. The sooner she got rid of them, the sooner she could get back to Ray.

Every now and then Alyssa was overcome by a reckless desire to do something to risk her life and limb. Just to make her feel alive. When life got too predictable and boring an adrenaline rush was exactly what was needed to perk one up and out of the slump. There was something heady about telling yourself that you didn't give a shit, and just going for it. At such times the interstate, if not too heavily trafficked, was an ideal theater for her activities. Her convertible was a zippy little machine that could weave in and out of lanes and between other vehicles. Perky enough to provide the acceleration needed. Small enough to fit where larger cars wouldn't dare to go. The added thrill of having to make sure that it wasn't some unmarked cop car she was overtaking was an extra bonus.

Now it wasn't a game though. Still, she had to admit that, in a sneaky little corner of her soul, she enjoyed what she had to do. If a certain urgency hadn't been pressing on her, she would have found the experience thoroughly exhilarating. As it was, she found that the lower part of her face was getting sore from the grin she wore.

There was no way they were going to keep up with her. Not in that stupid, staid machine of theirs. And indeed, there was no indication that anybody behind her was performing the same maneuvers.

Good. When she came to the Glenwood Avenue junction she decided to get off. She headed west on Glenwood, trying to relax from her little adventure.

On her right a gas station came up.

A phone!

She pulled up beside the attached convenience store and limped inside. The lone attendant, a lanky guy in his mid twenties, his face still ornamented with a few leftover puberty zits, pointed her at a coin-phone in the far corner of the store. She got change of quarters for a dollar and dialed Ray's cellphone.

Engaged.

Damn! Who was he talking to?

She hung up and tried again. And again. And again.

She happened to look up and out through the wide windows opening onto the station's forecourt. Her heart missed a beat. She couldn't be sure, of course, but on the other side of the road...

Not possible. How could they have followed her here?

She dialed again.

Still engaged.

Urgency tugged at her. She cast a furtive glance through the windows again. It was possible, of course, that she was just talking herself into something here, but...

No 'but'. That was them. No doubt about it.

She stared at the phone and then tried again.

Don't do this to me!

She hung up and pondered her options. She could stay here until she got through to him. Or she could...

She looked again and saw that the car was gone.

A sigh of relief.

Wrong again.

God, I'm such a mess.

But was it any surprise? Who wouldn't be?

She really needed to get back to Ray. It might not be politically correct for a competent woman like herself to admit that she actually needed the comfort of a man, but who gave a shit anyway? She needed him for her sanity now—as much as she knew that he needed her. And it was high time that she got her butt into that motel and into the same bed with him.

She smiled at the attendant, who eyed her curiously, retrieved a can of soda from the cooler, paid and slowly, favoring her good ankle, limped outside. She opened the door, lowered herself into the driver's seat, poked the key into the ignition, and...

A man materialized beside her, vaulted into the passenger seat without opening the door, and pointed a gun at her; holding it low so that the attendant could not see it when they drove through his field of vision.

"Drive!"

Her heart suddenly beat right up in her throat. Her mouth was tinder-dry, and when she tried to swallow she found that it was almost impossible.

"What do you want?" she barely managed to whisper.

The man, an athletic type, dressed in jeans and a black, tight T-shirt that emphasized the muscles and tendons rippling across his chest and arms, pushed the gun a bit closer in her direction.

"Drive," he repeated. There was no doubt that he would be willing to enforce his orders. In any number of ways. His face, illuminated by the fluorescent bars lining the underside of the forecourt roof, was as expressionless as that of a fish. She had the nauseating feeling that he would actually *like* it if she gave him a reason to put additional authority behind his orders.

She turned on the engine and drove out onto the road.

"Left," the man said. She did as she was told. They went back along Glenwood, turned onto the interstate and headed north.

9.

Ray finished the conversation with Susan. Try as they might, they had not been able to figure out what Lys might possibly be doing right now. The uncertainty grated on him. Susan had suggested calling the police. Eventually that might be what they'd have to do. But not yet. Maybe another hour. There were any number of good and innocuous reasons why she was late. No point in being alarmist.

He forced himself to sit down and relax.

How can I?

What if something *had* happened?

Like what?

Ray looked around the room. Something was wrong. He knew it! It was like a dark thundercloud hanging over the horizon. What he'd said to Susan to calm her down— what he'd told *himself* to calm down! had been bullshit.

He took his cellphone and his car keys and went outside. He stood for a moment, considering his actions. Stupid, probably—but he was going to do it anyway.

He got into his car and drove it out of the motel's parking lot and to the other side of the road. He found a free space in between other cars in the dark shadow cast by a tree. If and when Lys came to the motel he would see her. As he would see anybody else who came.

Then he forced himself into inactivity.

His cellphone beeped shortly thereafter.

"Ray?"

"Lys! Where are you?"

There were sounds, as if of a brief, minor struggle. A man's voice came on.

"Mr. Shannon."

"Who are you?"

But even as he asked he knew. He remembered the voice.

"I think you remember me," Jack McTierney said curtly.

Ray saw no point in denying the obvious.

"What do you want?"

What did they do to you, Lys?

"You have something of mine," McTierney's voice came back. "Something you found in a book."

Damn! By now Carter would have it. No way was Ray ever going to get his hands on that again.

"I don't have it right now," Ray told him, a pit in his stomach.

"Where is it?"

"In a safe." Ray thought hard. He needed to *think*. "One I cannot possibly get to until tomorrow morning."

There was a pause at the other end. "All right. Tomorrow morning. Don't do anything stupid."

Ray had a sudden feeling that this wasn't happening. The whole atmosphere of being in some Hollywood movie, of what he'd felt earlier, assumed a surrealist intensity. Hell, this guy even *talked* like he was reading from a bad script!

"I want to talk to Lys," Ray said.

There was a momentary hesitation. "Briefly," McTierney told him.

Again, noises. then a dead silence, like someone had placed his hand over the microphone. Then Alyssa came on.

"Ray, I'm sorry."

What for? It's me who fucked this up. Me and my stupid games. I should have left the damn thing where I found it. Made a copy and put it back. Damn—where was my head? Lys...

He swallowed. "Don't be," he said. "I'll give them the stupid papers." He knew they were listening. "But if they touch you...if they even *think* of touching you...I'll go straight to the cops!"

"Ray," she said urgently, "they know where you are..." There was a brief exclamation of pain; the word 'bitch' somewhere in the background; the sound of a slap. Ray, in impotent fury, shouted into the phone. "Leave her alone, you bastards! You'll get your fucking papers. Just leave her alone!"

From the periphery of his vision he saw a movement at the motel. A car pulled into the drive. Two men emerged. One of them stayed by the car in a position of alertness. The other went into the office.

"Your girlfriend is brave but stupid," McTierney's voice said at his ear. Ray wanted to say something but found that his voice refused to cooperate. The image of Lys being slapped around—and maybe worse—by those creeps incited him into such a state of helpless rage that he found it difficult even to breathe.

"For her sake, I hope you don't even *think* of police."

There it went again! Through the red haze of his anger a little part of Ray saw it all in a curiously detached way. Couldn't this dickhead see that this script was totally stupid? Fucking stereotypes all over the place!

It's not a game!

I know, but it feels like it.

Well, stop feeling like that, because they'll hurt her.

"I'll call you at ten tomorrow morning. Sharp."

There was a pause.

"Shannon?"

"What?"

"It's impolite not to answer people."

"Fuck you!" Ray spat. "I mean it! If you touch her again, I'll go straight to the cops."

McTierney laughed. Ray felt like smashing the phone against the dashboard. By a superhuman effort he broke the connection. McTierney's chuckle died in mid-flight.

Ray looked at the motel. The men had driven to his apartment and were getting out. They positioned themselves on opposite sides of the door. Both had guns in their hands. Then, on some signal, they kicked it in.

Ray couldn't help but feel a grim satisfaction at this small, but significant, victory. Presently the men emerged again. One of them was holding a cellphone to his ear. Reporting back to McTierney, no doubt. They got into their car and drove off.

Ray, following a reckless impulse, turned on the engine, did a U-turn and went after them. He followed them for several blocks, until they drove onto the 285. Ray ran a red light to keep up with them, but by the time he had merged into the evening traffic on the interstate he'd lost them. Furious, hitting the steering wheel until his hands hurt, and with tears in his eyes, he gave up the pursuit and got off the interstate at the next junction.

His cellphone beeped again.

Susan.

"Is she there?"

"No," he said tonelessly.

She must have caught something because there was a momentary silence. "What's the matter?" she said sharply.

Ray saw no reason to lie to her.

Susan insisted on calling the police immediately. Ray, equally vehemently, opposed the idea. "Do you want to kill her?" he shouted.

"That's what'll happen if we *don't* call the police," she retorted. "Remember, you haven't got the papers anymore. What do you think they'll do once they find out, huh?"

"I don't understand any of this," Ray said dejectedly. "What's the big deal with these papers anyway? How do these people know I haven't made copies? They can't be so stupid as to think that I wouldn't have…"

There was a brief silence on the other end on the connection. "Good question," she admitted.

"Well? Any ideas?"

"No," she answered thoughtfully. "But I tell you what: give me half an hour or so. I'm going to call someone. Maybe we'll figure it out yet."

"Let me know." Ray disconnected himself and dropped the cellphone on the passenger seat. He stopped the car by the roadside and just sat there, staring into nothingness. Never in his life had he felt so helpless, so useless—so guilty.

And the thought of Lys...

Because of him. Because of his stupidity and thoughtlessness.

The lights of the passing cars blurred before his eyes and, for the first since many years—maybe never—Ray found that he had no answers, no suggestions, no theories, no way out. A black ooze of despair was creeping through his skull and consuming every bit of brightness there was; extinguishing every shred of hope in its relentless advance.

The cellphone beeped. Ray wiped his eyes and stared at it. Finally he picked it up.

"I talked to my client," Susan told him. "The art guy."

"Yes?"

"He thinks he knows why McTierney wants those papers. In fact he thinks McTierney would even be happy with a copy."

"What? Why?"

"My client suggests that this may be the only record of the transactions in question. He left with your wife for safe-keeping. Apparently, McTierney has recently been subjected to some police scrutiny, involving search warrants and seizures—of, among other things, records and computers.

"The records you found may have been his only remaining records of this aspect of his operations—after the cops raiding him, and with him possibly hastily destroying stuff that he needs to actually get at all this money Ron Hadlow probably cheated him out of. I seem to recall a list of codes that I couldn't make head or tail of. I think those may be account numbers. Or passwords. Maybe both."

"Why would he give them to Debbie?"

"Maybe he didn't. Maybe what you found was just one copy of something your wife gave to *him*. If she was spying on her boss on McTierney's behalf, and if McTierney destroyed the copies she gave him, so that the cops didn't find them—and if the one in your home is the only one left...

"McTierney's may not be worried about those papers incriminating him at all. But I seem to remember that there were hundreds of thousands of dollars involved here."

"But if the police had those documents..."

"I doubt he cares. Remember, they aren't Jack McTierney's, but Ron Hadlow's. They prove nothing—nothing but that Hadlow was conducting dubious business. They do not establish a connection between Hadlow and McTierney—which I doubt could be established anyway. McTierney's contribution to Hadlow's business would have been undocumented. Cash contributions. Convenient ways for McTierney to launder his dirty money. Maybe some other help, too. Lending his men to do some of the shady work. Smuggling artworks. Intimidating competitors. Stuff like that."

"So, I've got nothing."

"That's right," she said, and, for the first time, there was something like sympathy in her tone when she talked to him. "If it was McTierney who had Hadlow killed—or maybe he killed him himself; maybe because Hadlow thought he could skim off some profits and hide the fact from McTierney—there's nothing to prove it. Those papers aren't worth a shit to the cops. Not unless there's something more. A corroborating witness..."

"Like Debbie."

"That's right."

It made sense. At least it sounded as if it did.

"I've got nothing."

"That's why I'm going to call in the cops. Lys is another potential witness. They're going to do what they can to get her back alive. Believe me, Ray, it's Lys's only chance."

"If what you say is true then McTierney won't wait around that long. By the time the cops have gotten their act together she'll be dead."

"What can *you* do?"

"I don't know." But the black ooze of despair was retreating. It left behind a bleak, grim determination. They would regret this. They had no idea of how much they would regret this.

"I've got *some*thing."

"What?"

"Me."

"What would McTierney want with you?"

"I'm a corroborating witness. Not as good a one as Debbie, but I'm a 'loose end', wouldn't you agree? "

"You only talked to him. He could claim that you merely spoke to someone *claiming* to be him."

"Please!" he said desperately.

"Even if he considered you a loose end—how could you possibly use that?"

"I don't know," he admitted. "But I'm sure he's not going to do anything until he has those papers. That's tomorrow morning. More than nine hours! Give me that time!"

"What can you do?" she repeated. "You're a...what? A programmer? Not even an amateur! You have no idea of *anything* that's even remotely connected to these people. Ray, this isn't a game or a movie! I hope you realize that! There are real lives at stake—and one of them's my best friend."

She was right, of course. And yet...

The line was silent, though he thought he could hear her breathing.

"Lys really trusts you," Susan finally said. "In fact, she's crazy about you."

"I know."

"But there is nothing you can do. And I'm going to call the police."

"Please!"

He heard her sigh.

"I'm sorry," she said. "I know you want the best. But this is out of your hands."

She hung up on him, leaving him staring at the passing cars.

10.

Alyssa had never felt so deserted, lonely, and afraid in her whole life. She lay on the double bed, her left wrist cuffed to a chain which had been looped around one leg and through the frame of the creaky old bed and joined with a padlock. Staring at the ceiling she wondered if Ray had gotten away from the motel before McTierney's men had arrived there.

The room smelt musty. Moldy timber. A rotting, moth and rat-eaten carpet on the dirty wooden floor. The paint on the wall panels was flaking off, as was the ceiling. There was a window. Broken glass. On the outside, someone had nailed solid-looking boards over it. Now, that it was night, she saw nothing through the cracks. Besides, she couldn't reach there. The chain allowed her free movement on the bed itself, but, unless she was willing to pull it along with her, that was her active circle of operation. She contemplated exploring the room, but decided against it. A dim bulb hung from a dilapidated wire which terminated in a rusted fitting above. They'd left the light on. So that they could see what she was doing, no doubt. No point in provoking them. The thought of what they might do if she gave them even the slightest excuse made her flesh crawl.

The guilt of her cowardice weighed heavily on her. But when they'd threatened to carve up her face unless she told them…

That's why she had told him—on the phone; though she knew that they would hurt her. And hurt her they did. One of McTierney's goons had smacked her across the face so hard it had thrown her off the chair.

Please, let it not have been too late.

But, even if it hadn't been, the situation still looked bleak and dismal. There would be no way Ray could get at those papers. Not if the police had them. And Ray's shouts—which she'd heard though she had been lying on the floor holding her aching face—were so much bluster. His promises and his threats. There was nothing he could do. Nothing anybody could do. Whatever was done would be too late. For her anyway.

And everything was going so well…

Alyssa felt tears well up in her eyes. Tears for what might have been and now never would. For the life they might have had. Some of the promise of the last few days realized.

Was that too much to ask for? she enquired of nobody in particular. *Or was it just a sick joke?*

Answers failed to be forthcoming, and, as she considered the flaking paint on the ceiling, she told herself that she would be stupid to expect any.

Outside her room she could her the voices of her captors.

Would they kill her tonight—or only when they found out that Ray could not deliver the goods?

Ray, I'm sorry. She imagined him lying beside her. Telling him that this was not how she'd wanted it that Friday on the interstate. She just wanted someone to look at her and be smitten beyond redemption. None of the drama that followed. No car crashes; no rescues from fiery deaths; no relationship triangles.

Be careful what you ask for. Life serves up its blessings in mixed company.

Indeed.

But like *this*?

She closed here eyes and wished that he could hear her. Sense her thoughts maybe. But even as she tried to send them to him she had the feeling that they were caught up in a black vortex and swallowed up forever.

There was a noise outside the door. It opened. One of Jack McTierney's muscle-boys shoved a woman into the room.

"Company," he said, grinning.

Another face appeared in the doorway, watching the scene. The guy who'd kidnapped her.

Alyssa considered the newcomer. Smaller than herself. About her own age. Maybe a few years older. Well-preserved. Pretty, with blue eyes, now red and disfigured by smeared mascara. Well-dressed, though the garments were disheveled by a struggle. In a state of shock, evidently. Like someone had pushed her into a nightmare from which she was desperately trying to awaken.

Lys knew how she felt.

The young thug shoved the woman toward the bed. He put one loop of a pair of handcuffs around her right wrist and the other around the same chain that held Alyssa. He considered his handiwork and turned back to the door, which presently closed behind him with sickening definiteness.

Alyssa levered herself into a sitting position and touched the woman's arm. She was rewarded with a wild and panicky look.

"Come on," Alyssa said softly. "Sit down."

The woman hesitated. Alyssa gently grabbed her arm and pulled her closer; made her sit down on the edge of the bed.

"Who are you?" she asked the newcomer. But then, even before the woman answered, she knew. The smeared makeup and the whole context had confused her.

"My name," the woman said emptily. "is Debbie."

11.

Ray drove to the airport and left his vehicle in one of the short-term parking lots. Then he went into the domestic terminal and rented a car from AVIS: the only ones who had a vehicle that wasn't booked. Feeling a little more secure driving around in a vehicle the cops wouldn't immediately ID as his, he drove back into Atlanta and to his office. He let himself in, disarmed the alarm, and informed the security company patrolling the offices of *Jitterbug Software* that he would be here for much of the night. They didn't ask questions. They knew by now that programmers kept strange hours. He had the password, the right swipe card, and he knew the alarm code. That was all they were interested in.

Ray turned on his computer and, as the machine was booting up, went to the coffeemaker and started it up. A few minutes later the office filled with the heavy, slightly-burned scent of percolating coffee. Ray returned to his office with a large mug and slumped into his chair, sipping it carefully.

Susan was right, of course. He was less than an amateur. He knew *nothing* of these people. Hadn't even the first inkling of what to do. And yes, she was right about that other thing, too.

This wasn't a game...

But, while that was indisputable, it was also true that games and life had a lot of things in common. Like there were always rules. Things that could be done and others that couldn't. Constraints of action, behavior, and thought always applied. In any given situation people had a limited range of alternatives they were able to consider. Computer games, and especially the newer generation with extensive AI support and storylines of novel-like complexity, were based on that premise. The art of the designer of successful game-programs was to create situations, contexts, and opponents that were simple enough for the player to cope, complex enough to challenge him, imaginative enough to hold his attention and to keep him playing, and yet were set up to carefully manipulate him into situations where he was so distracted by apparently important peripheral issues that he missed the *real* traps the programmer had laid for him.

The design of a computer game was a battle of wits between the skill and imagination of the designer and that of the player. Shoot-them-up kinds of games—still popular with a large segment of the market—operated only on a fairly superficial level. Other role-playing paradigms concentrated on strategy. Neither was 'life-like' enough to successfully suck in the vast potential market of those who regarded either variety with disdain. These were the people who continued to prefer reading novels or watching movies to playing computer games. People who wanted a satisfying *story* to go with the interaction. And a believable interaction with their characters—one of which usually represented the player—that went with the story.

As close to 'life' as you could get.

Think of it as a game.

Ray went over to the big whiteboard affixed to one wall of his room. He wiped out the squiggles and shapes; leftovers from stray thoughts for *Wild Worlds*—not quite his own, but close. In many ways the 'other' hadn't been that different from himself.

He picked up and uncapped a pen, and began to draw a diagram between the relationships in this whole sordid business.

That's the way he always started his designs.

The players.

Their goals.

Their assets and strengths.

Their liabilities and weaknesses.

The constraints imposed by the context.

Ray forced Alyssa from his mind as a real person. She became just another figure in the game.

Another figure, maybe. But she was the queen. To be preserved at all costs.

Absentmindedly, Ray reached for his cup and took another sip.

Thursday

1.

When *Rory's Range* opened at nine Ray was the first customer.
"Hey, Ray. What're you up to? It ain't Saturday, right?"
"Taking a day off," Ray said lightly.
"Mental health?"
"Something like that."
Rory—a slightly overweight individual with a bushy mountain-man's beard, who wore a T-shirt, sporting a peace symbol encircled by the words '*Peace Through Superior Firepower*', and a big stainless Smith and Wesson in a holster clipped to his belt—grinned broadly.
"What can I do you for?" he asked in his, only slowly disappearing, New England twang. Rory had come down from up north a few years ago; leaving behind a wife, two daughters, and an accountant's job he hated, in favor of Georgia and the gun-shop his murdered brother had left him in his will.
"A life-saver," Rory had told Ray months ago. "That shit up there was killing me." Grinning. "Mind you, it ain't much safer down here—but, to tell you the truth, I'd rather have this anytime."
Ray looked around the displays. "Just having a look around."
"Anything particular?"
"Couple of handguns."
Rory chuckled. "You've come to the right place."
"Something big and something small—but with a punch."
Rory weighed him up. "Glock-man, right?"
"Either that or wheel-guns. Wouldn't trust anything else."
Rory nodded, pulled a bunch of keys on a chain from his pocket and came around the counter. Ray followed him to a cabinet in the far corner of the store. Rory unlocked a display case and, after jacking back the slide, handed Ray a Glock 17, a duplicate of the gun Carter had confiscated from him.
While Rory re-locked the case and went over to another Ray inspected the gun in his hand. If things went as they should he wouldn't have this one for long. A very expensive decoy.
Rory came back with the other gun.
"The 'pocket Glock'. Model 30. Ten round of .45 ACP and you won't even know it's there."
Ray nodded. There was something understatedly ominous about the little gun with the big bore.
They went back to the counter.
Ray asked to test-fire the guns.
Rory nodded. "Sure."
His eyebrows went up when Ray asked him for a two thousand rounds of ammo to

practice with, but he said nothing.

Ray retreated to the range and spent the next hour practicing point-and-shoot, with the guns becoming bodily extensions, rather than separate instruments that required aiming. The only way to achieve this was to do it over and over, until the brain *knew* where the gun was pointed without requiring the eyes to line up sights on a target.

When Ray was done his hands and arms were aching, but the gun had almost become an appendage.

He handed the safety specs and earmuffs back to Rory.

"I need a spare mag for each. A hundred rounds of ammo. Starfires, preferably. And a couple of belt-clip holsters. You got duct-tape?"

Rory grinned crookedly. "Going to war or something?"

"Hunting."

"Where?"

"Don't know yet. Friend's organizing it."

"Georgia?"

"Yep."

"Lemme know how it went. When're you going?"

"Later today."

Rory eyed him curiously but said nothing more. He had learned the delicate art of not taking a conversation too far into prying territory. Small talk was OK; but no more than that.

Ray paid with plastic. Rory dismantled, cleaned and reassembled the Glocks.

"Part of the service. A gun's only as good as it's clean."

Rory excused himself to attend to a couple of shooters who'd just come in the door. Ray dropped the guns and accessories into a plastic bag and left the shop.

"Happy hunting," Rory called after him.

Ray grinned and waved; then made his way to his car. He was about to open the door when the cellphone beeped.

"Well?"

McTierney.

"I have it."

"Eleven o'clock. Stone Mountain Park. Corner of Lee Boulevard and Jackson Drive."

"I'll be there. Make sure Lys is as well."

"No."

"No? There is no deal without her!"

"Fuck you say."

He hadn't expected anything else. So far events followed the predicted course.

Ray gave what he hoped was a convincingly frustrated and yet impotent sigh.

"Eleven," he confirmed.

One hour.

He got into his car and drove to a nearby mall, where he went into a menswear store and bought a sandy-colored light linen jacket. Loose enough to conceal what it was meant to conceal. Light enough so that him wearing it wouldn't arouse attention. He found a quiet spot in the far end of the mall's parking lot, tore the tags from the jacket, crumpled it to make it look worn, and put it on. He shoved full magazines into the guns, jacked rounds into the chambers, withdrew the mags, replaced the missing rounds, and reinserted them. Safeties in the 'off' position. Not a problem with Glocks, which were double-action.

He filled up the spare mags, tore off some duct tape and used that to tape the Model 30 and a spare mag to his lower back.

The Model 17 he stuck into a holster, which he affixed to he belt around the left front, where the jacket just hid it, and where it was readily accessible—and instantly noticeable for anybody who looked for that kind of thing.

Ray looked at the dashboard clock.

Time to go.

2.

The night in the company of Ray's wife, resting uneasily on the bed beside her, had an unreal quality about it. Alyssa was grateful that Debbie seemed to be too much in shock to be talkative; or inquisitive—which would have been worse.

"Who are you?"

"Your husband's girlfriend. And you must be that stupid bitch who caused all this trouble..."

Yeah, nice conversation.

Alyssa lay back and closed her eyes. *I'm about to be killed and I worry about some pathetic social cringe situation?*

She really needed to pee—but her requests hadn't been received with much sympathy.

"Piss yourself, cunt!" the young creep with the lightning tattoo on his over-muscled arm had told her.

"Stupid fucker," she'd muttered. He'd just laughed. "I like the smell of piss on a woman."

Freak of nature!

Still, she should have been happy that, so far at least, they hadn't raped her. It was clear that this wasn't far from their minds and, quite possibly, before they killed them, it might happen yet. Unless these jerk-offs were necrophiliacs—which she wouldn't have put past them.

Debbie had watched the exchange without a word. She was in a state of shock, which had persisted through the night.

Now it was morning, and Alyssa *really* needed to pee. Her bladder was a focus of agony within her, slowly displacing all other thoughts. Finally it became too much. She'd actually started *fantasizing* about it!

Alyssa glanced at Debbie who was lying there, her eyes closed; probably asleep, though one couldn't tell. She slipped to the opposite end of the bed. But the chain was too short. She couldn't get off the other side. She hesitated, and then pulled down her jeans and panties down around her ankles, so they wouldn't get soiled. She winced at the occasional stabbing pain in her left ankle, which accentuated the ever-present dull ache. Then—feeling utterly degraded and humiliated—she tried to pretend that she wasn't sitting on a mattress, but on a toilet.

After a few minutes of trying she was crying from frustration and pain. All cramped and tensed up inside. She just couldn't do it—despite the agony in her lower abdomen and back.

Come on, girl...

Finally, after another eternity of waiting, and trying and feeling humiliated and stupid, there was a release of sorts—and warm, wet stain that spread under her buttocks and over the mattress, together with the heavy reek of concentrated urine.

Alyssa forced herself to sit still—to wait until it was done. Which was another eternity later. Then she maneuvered herself off the wet patch and, by some contortionist feat, managed to pull up her panties and jeans again without getting them wet. With some effort, laced by the pain in her ankle, she managed to crawl over Debbie's still form and crouch herself on the floor beside the bed.

Her watch showed 11:23 a.m.

3.

Ray arrived at the rendezvous point about five minutes late—as he had intended. He pulled up at one side of Lee Boulevard and turned off the engine. There weren't too many people in the park at this time of the day. Not around here anyway. They'd be here soon though. By lunchtime it would be like the streets of the city.

Ray looked around. From Jackson Drive emerged a car with a single occupant. Ray withdrew the Glock from the holster.

A sound behind him. His head whipped around. The barrel of a cold gun pressed into his neck. The man holding it considered him coldly. He pushed a bit harder. Wordlessly, and making sure that he looked frustrated and defeated, Ray placed the Glock on the passenger seat.

"Asshole," the man said contemptuously. He made a tiny motion with his gun. "Out."

He stepped back to let Ray open the door.

Ray obeyed. The other car had stopped on the opposite side of the road. The man at the wheel was looking at him.

"The papers," the man behind him said.

Ray glanced at him. The right hand was hidden somewhere inside the trendy dark blazer—whichhe probably wore for the same reason that Ray wore his jacket. The only conceivable reason why one should burden oneself with that kind of garment in the current climate.

He shook his head. "No papers," he said.

"What?"

"No Lys, no papers," Ray interrupted, trying to put just the right amount of tremor into his voice. Tremor but determination. Fear mixed with stubbornness.

The man glared at him. He motioned with his head toward the other car. "In there," he ordered.

A car came around the corner, going slowly. Visitors cruising the park. Ray waited until the car had passed, then crossed the road. The man at the wheel pointed his thumb at the passenger seat. Ray went around the car and got in. Looking back he saw that the other man had a cellphone at his ear.

"No papers," he said. "Just a gun."

He listened and frowned. Then he stuck the phone into the car.

"Here," he said to Ray.

Ray took the phone.

"Yes?"

"Listen, fucker," McTierney told him. "Are you just stupid, or what?"

"No Lys, no papers," Ray repeated stubbornly.

"Fuck you!" McTierney said. "The papers—or the bitch is fucking dead! *After* my boys have had their fun of her. And they have some *very* interesting ideas what else to do with a cunt."

"Is that really worth a few hundred grand to you?"

There was a moment's silence as McTierney absorbed the fact that Ray knew more than he had assumed.

"Lemme talk to Rick," he ordered. Ray handed the phone to the driver, who took it, listened, muttered something, and then put it down.

"Stupid motherfucker," he hissed and motioned to his buddy. "We're taking him back."

Yes!

Refocusing the attention of small minds. Add a few layers of the unexpected and they were all over the place.

The other man plonked himself inside the car behind Ray and pushed his gun into the back of Ray's seat. "Belt," he hissed.

Ray obeyed.

The rental car was left behind. The Ford left Stone Mountain Park, headed back west along the A-410 and north on I-285 until they came to the A-400. The two men were silent, though Ray fancied that he sensed a certain subdued anger in both of them.

His fault. Definitely. He had inconvenienced them. Given the opportunity and license from their employer, they would take great delight in paying him back every bit of their aggravation when the opportunity arose. But that would be later. Right now the man in the back had to content himself with occasionally shoving his gun into Ray's seat—just to remind their passenger of the dismal hopelessness of his situation. On a couple of occasions when he did that the barrel hit the Glock's grip. On another it struck of the mags taped to his back. Ray heaved a silent sigh of relief when the guy didn't appear to notice.

What did not sooth him though—but what he hadn't expected either—was that they were making absolutely no secret of where they were going. Which meant either that it didn't matter—or that *he* didn't matter. It appeared that Jack McTierney was not indisposed toward leaving behind him a trail of corpses a mile long—and that Ray Shannon might well join it soon.

For a moment there he allowed his detachment to falter, The realization that this wasn't the game he was making it out to be pushed its way to the fore. He firmly dismissed it, before it could turn his bowels to jelly and caused him to shit himself right here and now. The gamesmaster who had planned the strategies for this particular game, and laid out the contingency plans for most of the likely permutations on the range of possibilities, shouldered his reality-consciousness aside.

Besides, it doesn't matter now. When he had showed up at the rendezvous—without papers, a gun in his hand, and another taped to his back—that's when he had taken the irrevocable step which made it utterly futile to fret over what might have been. Game or not, now he had nothing but the Plan. He couldn't put the novel down, walk out of the theater, or select 'Suspend Game'.

Committed.

That was the word.

Something he'd never understood. Not until now.

Oh, he'd committed himself all right. To his marriage, his work, paying his bills. Stuff like that.

But you could pull out a marriage, you could quit your job, and you could declare bankruptcy.

That wasn't commitment. It was half-hearted shit. And just how half-hearted it was had been demonstrated last Friday when he'd taken the sneakiest of all possible ways out of just about all his commitments. Hell, he'd left his *world*! If that wasn't opting out what was?

And now?

Look at me now.

Had there ever been anything or anybody for whom he would have committed himself to the extent of putting his life on the line?

Because there's no way out this time, he told himself. *No 'Undo Last Step' option. This is real-time, right-in-your-face stuff. Which will probably end with your death within the near future.*

Oddly enough, the immediacy of this thought helped him to distance himself from the situation.

When the parachute doesn't open you might as well try to fly.

They headed north on the A-400. Another ten minutes' drive later they took a minor rural exit and then lost themselves in a maze of country roads. Ray had never been out this way, and so he was soon lost.

The Glock taped to his back dug into him, causing acute discomfort. Ray tried to arch his back so that it didn't press against the seat so hard, but he had to be careful. He had anticipated their reaction so far. They thought of themselves as 'pros' and of him an an idiot amateur. The notion that the first gun was just for show had never even crossed their minds—nor had the idea that what they were doing right now was exactly what he wanted them to do.

Ray carefully wriggled himself into a less uncomfortable position, and tried to tell himself that it was a game, and that he'd planned it all out, and that these motherfuckers had no idea what they were in for.

Presently, the car left the sealed road and bounced along a moderately rutted track, until finally they arrived at a run-down farmhouse. Inside a wide, open, but decaying, barn were parked a number of expensive-looking cars that really didn't belong here.

Including Lys's red convertible.

4.

She could see daylight through the cracks now. Bright slits beyond which lay a bright sky and the wide open spaces of the outside world.

She was still sitting on the floor, leaning against the side of the bed. Her back was aching from being in this position for too long. She wanted to lie down on the floor, flat on her back. Indeed, this would have been the sensible thing to do. But something told her that she had to be prepared, and that lying down wouldn't be appropriate.

Ready for what?

What did it matter?

Lys wriggled to ease the discomfort in her lower back. She sniffed and realized just how much she stank. That and the smell of her urine in the mattress; becoming stronger as the day wore on and the merciless Georgia sun heated the house and this closed room to nauseating temperatures.

Debbie made a sound and stirred fretfully. Her free arm flopped across the bed. Her hand landed right on the damp patch Alyssa had left behind. Alyssa pulled herself off the floor and sat down on the side of the bed to look at the woman that was Ray's wife and yet wasn't. Despite feeling that, in some way, Debbie had probably reaped nothing more than her just desserts, she realized that she felt sorry for her. If nothing else they were companions in the same predicament. It created a bond despite everything.

Alyssa's mouth felt dry and parched. She tried to conjure up a flow of saliva, but when a trickle finally materialized it just made the inside of her mouth taste like dogshit—and the whiff she caught of her own breath almost made her gag.

Debbie's eyes snapped open. She saw Alyssa near her and jerked back. Alyssa reached out and laid a hand on her shoulder. "It's OK," she said lowly, her voice hoarse with the dryness in her throat. "I won't hurt you." She held up a hand to show Debbie the cuff.

"Who are you?"

Ahh, the dreaded question.

"My name's Alyssa."

"You?" Debbie's eyes widened.

"Ironic, isn't it?"

Debbie's eyes closed again. "He used me," she said bitterly.

For a moment Alyssa thought that Debbie was talking about Ray. A snappy retort came to her lips—but she suppressed it when she understood who Debbie was talking about. "McTierney?" she said siccantly. "What a surprise."

She immediately regretted her words, but they were out before she could help it. Still…

"I'm sorry," he said. "Don't take it too personally. I'm just not too well disposed toward you. Ray wouldn't be in this shit—hell, *I* wouldn't be in this mess! if your… lover? is it?—how can you *love* this creep? If he hadn't seen fit to implicate Ray in a murder he had nothing to do with… With your collusion, I suspect."

"Ray deserved it," Debbie said venomously. Alyssa was amazed at the anger and hatred behind her words.

"Do you really think you're the first?" Debbie's eyes had opened again and were fixed on Alyssa's face. Despite the smeared mascara, she detected a sardonic gleam somewhere; a harsh pleasure at the notion of being able to hurt her.

She was going to turn away from this embittered woman. But then she reminded herself that Debbie was probably right. *This* Debbie anyway. The Ray of this world probably deserved every bit of scorn Debbie could heap upon him. And it was quite possible that Debbie had been driven into this, rather than initiating it.

Except that we all make choices.

Outside there was a sound. Alyssa's head snapped up as she listened. A crunching on gravel. As if of a vehicle arriving.

Who? she wondered. It would be about now that the men sent to meet Ray should be returning.

Without the papers.

With her death warrant.

5.

"Get out."

Ray obeyed, keeping his hands down at his side, praying that the loose jacket concealed the outline of the Glock. As the man came up behind him he stepped forward smartly to avoid being prodded. If they did, they mightn't miss it this time!

On the dilapidated front porch with the sagging rusty corrugated iron roof stood a man with a machine pistol. He stepped forward and leveled the gun at Ray, keeping it trained on him as he stepped up on the porch.

In the door appeared another man. His appearance and demeanor, as well as myriad other small signals, told Ray that it was McTierney. About his own age but taller. Blond hair, with possible traces of gray. It was hard to tell. A pale face, accentuated by a sharp nose with twin protrusions of cartilage. Blue eyes, reminding Ray uncannily of those of a pig. A wide mouth, whose thin lips gave the face the characteristics of a fish.

Pig-fish.

Despite the complete absence of humor in his current situation, Ray found it difficult to suppress a smile.

Pig-fish considered him expressionlessly.

"So, you're the asshole who thinks he can threaten my men with a gun."

McTierney took a quick step forward. Before Ray could retreat McTierney's hand snapped out. It's back struck him across the face. Ray's head snapped aside from the blow. Through the sharp pain he felt a trickle of blood run down from somewhere near his right eye.

"But I'm intrigued, Mr. Asshole," McTierney said softly. "I mean what the fuck is going on in that head of yours?"

He shook his head and stepped aside. "Inside."

Ray obeyed with alacrity. He stepped into a narrow hallway, to confront another man pointing a gun at him. The man motioned toward the end of the hallway. Ray stepped past him, fastidiously avoiding personal contact. He entered a room that once must have been the lounge. A fireplace in the center of one wall. A closed door on one side, leading to he-knew not-where. Another, open, doorway beyond which he could see an old stove. The kitchen; or so he presumed.

The room itself was sparsely furnished. A table and several chairs. On two of them sat more of McTierney's men. These two were playing cards. Their guns lay on the table before them. They looked up on his arrival. Their hands, instinctively almost, jerked toward their weapons. Then they relaxed. One of them shrugged, as if Ray's presence here was of no consequence.

Behind him Pig-fish had entered the room. Ray turned to look at him.

"I'm listening," McTierney said. "Make it quick. I don't usually waste my time on motherfuckers like you."

Ray shrugged. "It's simple. No Lys, no papers."

"You've got them?" Despite the indifference Ray sensed an eagerness there. The glint of cupidity in the pig-eyes.

What did Debbie ever see in that creep? It can't have been his charm and good looks.

"In a safe place," he asserted—which was the truth. "I can tell you where and you can send someone to get them."

In your dreams...

"But first I want to see Alyssa."

McTierney considered Ray for a moment, a quizzical expression on his face. "You know," he said thoughtfully, "you're a stupid fuck with shit for brains. But you got balls." He looked around the room at his men. "Shall we give the man a reward?"

"Why not?" said the rasping voice of one of the players. "Should be a touching scene."

McTierney nodded. "Yeah." He grinned. "And ironic." He laughed out aloud. "Ironic all right! "

He motioned to one of the players. The man got up and went over to the closed door. He turned a key and pushed it open. "Here you go, Mr. Brassballs."

Ray turned to look at McTierney's twisted sneer.

"Go ahead," McTierney motioned. "Happy reunion."

Ray shrugged and stepped through the door. As he did someone gave him a shove on the shoulder and propelled him into the room. Ray tumbled forward and barely caught himself. The door behind him slammed shut. The roar of laughter echoed through the walls and washed around him.

But Ray didn't care. Because there was a gasp on his right, and there, crouching on the floor beside the bed, was Lys.

6.

The door opened, somebody said something about 'Mr.Brassballs', and a body was shoved into the room. The door slammed shut.

Then Alyssa saw who it was. They stared at each other for an interminable moment. He stepped across to her and got down on his knees.

"Ray?" she whispered, still not believing it. Then, understanding the dreadful enormity of what it meant for him to be here, she almost cried out, but bit it back. Instead she felt her eyes grow hot with tears. Everything had been in vain. Now they were all dead.

He took her head in his hands and kissed her softly. Despite the dreadful prospects of the future the touch invoked memories of magic and, for a moment, dispelled her fear.

"It's OK," he whispered.

Only then did he seem to notice Debbie. Alyssa saw his eyes widen briefly. Then they clouded over, his face setting into an expressionless mask. "Hello Debbie," he grated.

He looked back at her again, and she thought that his eyes softened somewhat.

"Ray," she whispered, "why did you let them..."

"Sshhh," he said and put a finger on his mouth. He straightened and looked around the room, then bent down again and ran his hand over the chain and to the padlock that held it together. He made a grimace and stood up again. Alyssa looked at him without comprehension. How could he be so unconcerned? It was as if he *wanted* to be here! Didn't he understand that...

There was a sound at the door. Ray took a hasty step back toward her. His hand slipped under the back of his jacket. He twisted his back. There was a tearing sound. Ray's hand came out with a gun. Alyssa bit down on an exclamation. Ray turned to her and hunkered down, holding the gun between himself and her.

The door opened. The young freak with the steroid muscles and the tattoo poked a gun into the room, waved it around, and, when he noted nothing untoward, grunted something and stepped out of sight again. McTierney sauntered into the room. Alyssa felt Ray tense up. He looked around from his crouch. McTierney stepped closer, a leer on his face.

"What do you say, Mr. Brassballs? Is this ironic or what?"

He came even closer. Ray sighed and turned back to her. He winked slowly and deliberately. McTierney stopped less than a step behind him. Ray, his face set, pushed himself off the floor in one quick fluid motion and whipped around. His gun came up with it and, before McTierney had time to do anything but look surprised Ray jammed the muzzle against his forehead, right between his eyebrows.

Everything froze.

7.

The exhilaration was like nothing he'd ever felt before. Except maybe making love. Only that this here was different.

It was more like a cosmic '*yes!*'. A defiant fist shaken at an implacable and inevitable fate—and *getting away with it*!

And he knew that McTierney knew it. The piggish eyes blinked rapidly in an uncontrollable nervous reaction.

"Shut the door!" Ray shouted. The young thug poked his head into the room—and froze when he saw his boss standing there like that. Then he shouted something and whipped out his gun.

Ray pushed a bit harder against McTierney's forehead. "Tell them!" he grated.

"Close the fucking door," McTierney shouted.

The young thug was pushed aside as two more men shouldered into the room. Their guns were trained on Ray. They froze in that position and didn't come any closer.

"Count of three," Ray grated. "And remember...we're dead anyway. One—two—"

"Get out!" McTierney shouted. "Get the fuck outa here!"

Ray grinned at the men on the far wall. It may have been the grin that did it. Whatever it was, one of them made a placating gesture and pointed his gun at the ceiling. The other followed suit.

"Out!" Ray hissed.

"OK!" The men backed out the door, which closed behind them.

Ray pushed harder against McTierney's head and forced the man to back against the wall. There, with McTierney's head wedged firmly between wall and the Glock, Ray, without taking his eyes off McTierney's face felt around the man's waist area. His hand came to rest on the familiar shape of another Glock.

"Mine, huh?" He took it in his left hand, cocked it, and jammed it into McTierney's midriff. "The keys…for the cuffs."

McTierney barked an order. The door opened a slit. A key landed on the floor in the middle of the room. The door closed again.

"Can you reach them?" Ray asked without looking back.

"I think so."

Scraping sounds across the floor. From the side of his eyes, Ray saw Alyssa struggle to reach the keys with her good foot.

"Got them!" A minute or so later she stood behind him. She dangled the handcuffs into his field of view.

"For our host?"

"Definitely." He took the Glock away from McTierney's midriff and gave it to Alyssa. "Gimme the cuffs. Know how to work this?"

"Enough to shoot him," she said and took it.

Jack McTierney's hands were cuffed together at his back. Ray pushed him toward the bed. Alyssa limped across and freed Debbie, who stood up shakily, supporting herself against the wall. She stared at McTierney as Jack shoved him onto the bed and used Debbie's cuffs to affix him to the chain.

Alyssa came up behind him.

"What now?"

From the bed came a snort of derision. McTierney was recovering some of his temporarily lost composure.

"Yeah, Mr. Brassballs. What now?"

Ray inclined his head. "Now I'm going to be a good citizen and call the police." He changed the gun to his left hand and, keeping it aimed at McTierney, reached into his jacket.

"The marvels of modern technology," he said. He dialed 911 and asked to be connected to Lieutenant Carter, Atlanta Police. After some argument and a brief but heated discussion about the legitimacy of the procedure the connection was made.

When Carter came on Ray explained the situation. No, he didn't know exactly where he was; but surely, there were devices to track down the whereabouts of cellphones!

Outside the door Ray thought to discern a noise. He took the phone away from his ears. "Hey, guys!" he shouted. "Just wanting to let you know… Atlanta's finest should be here shortly. You might consider splitting at your earliest convenience!"

He put the phone to his ear again. "If you hurry you'll probably catch them," he told Carter. "If you don't, I'm afraid you'll have to contend yourself with Jack McTierney."

He put the phone down and grinned at his captive. The pig-eyes glared back at him. Outside, Ray could hear the sounds of cars revving up and departing.

"Seems like the rats are leaving," he said.

McTierney spat at him. "You really think this is over? Do you know who I *am*?"

Ray shrugged. "An asshole?" he suggested.

"You dumb fuck!" McTierney retorted. He looked at Debbie. "The cunt's never going to testify. Besides, she won't live for long enough." He laughed. "I'll be out in a day." McTierney heaved himself into an upright position. He laughed, completely sure of himself again.

"Go find a motel and fuck each other's brains out." He laughed. "Coupla days max, I'd say."

A deep pit opened up in Ray's gut.

This is not the game anymore.

Something inside him heaved.

Here was the deviation from the master plan. Life doing its thing.

Outwitted yourself!

McTierney had stopped laughing.

Ray inclined his head as if listening. "Hear that? The rats have departed."

"They'll be back." McTierney grinned. "I think I'll make you watch when we do her over."

Ray shook his head. "No."

He studied Jack McTierney for another moment. He turned his head to look at Lys and Debbie. He saw a woman he loved more than he had ever loved anybody. And another woman he had once loved—even though that might have been in another reality altogether.

He also felt…

A presence, like of…

"No," said Ray.

I can't do this by myself. I could never do this, no matter what the stakes.

"No what?"

Damn the game.

Ray aimed the Glock.

This is a human being!

So's Lys.

So am I.

The grin left McTierney's face. He saw death.

"Just…'no'," said Ray, and pulled the trigger.

8.

In the small room the noise of the shot was deafening. Alyssa jerked violently. She had seen it coming, of course. McTierney's taunts and threats. The strange calm that had settled like a visible aura around Ray. She wanted to cry out. Tell him that it would be all right; that he didn't have to do this.

Too late.

McTierney jerked, as if punched by a fist. A big ugly hole appeared in the center of his chest. He flopped backward onto the bed, his eyes dead before his head hit the mattress, coming to rest on the wet patch on the far side.

Her ears rang from the blast. Ray stood still as a statue, the gun pointed at the corpse. Then, slowly, his hand dropped. He turned to look at her. In his blank face his eyes pleaded with her. For forgiveness maybe.

She limped over to him. What could she say? How could she convince him that there was nothing to forgive? Nothing whatsoever.

At a loss for words she wrapped out her arms around him from the back and hugged him, averting her eyes from the corpse on the bed and pushing her face into the crook of his neck.

She felt him exhale and relax minutely. He reached out and took the gun from her hand.

Then Alyssa remembered Debbie. She released Ray and looked around. Debbie stood near the door, her hands pressed to her mouth, her gaze flicking between the corpse and Ray and Lys.

Ray tucked the guns into his waistband and went over to his wife.

"Debbie?"

She stared at him emptily. He took her shoulders in his hands. She tried to shrug him off, but he held her in a firm grip.

"Debbie," he said urgently, "snap out of it!"

Alyssa saw her glance past him to the bed again—only to avert her eyes almost immediately.

"What do you want?" she said tonelessly.

"Did McTierney kill Ron? Or have him killed? With my gun? Is that what happened?"

Debbie stared at him without comprehension.

"Did you hear me, Debbie?"

"He did."

"Are you going to tell that to the police?"

Debbie continued to stare at him. The hatred in her eyes was a palpable presence.

Ray felt it, too. He pulled the still-active cellphone out of the breast pocket of his coat and broke the connection to whoever was listening. He turned away from his wife and looked at Alyssa. "Let's get out here. Maybe there's time. She's not going to help us. We have nothing." He glanced at the corpse. "In fact, now it's worse."

Alyssa considered Debbie; wondering if there was anything there to appeal to, but knowing that there wasn't. The rift between this Debbie and Ray was too great. Even though her once-upon-a-time lover had been ready to kill her. Even though Ray had just saved her life. Still she detested him so much that none of that mattered.

Maybe I shouldn't be so quick to judge. Maybe the other Ray had deserved no better. But that other Ray also would never have put his life on the line like *this* one had.

For me.

Finally it hit home.

For me?

Was she really worth *that*? To *anybody*?

She looked at Ray. He stepped back from Debbie. Defeated, even in his victory.

She thought about what he had done.

A suicidal gamble. God only knew what had gone through his mind. He'd probably made himself believe that he'd leveled the odds somewhat by planning it all out—but deep down he must have known better. Must have known that he was not going to get out of this alive.

For me.

Did it really happen? That you'd rather die with someone, than continue to live without them?

Ignoring Debbie—for whom, she realized, she could, after all, feel nothing but contempt—she touched his arm.

He turned to look at her.

Somehow he must have seen it in her eyes: that which she simply couldn't tell him, because it was too big for words, and she didn't want to demean it—but still, she needed him to *know*...

The corners his eyes crinkled into a smile. And she felt another touch of something wondrous—and still couldn't believe that it was really *her*. Of all the mysteries this was probably the greatest and most unfathomable.

For a few brief instants Debbie ceased to exist; as did the corpse on the bed, and the room which stank of blood and death and urine and sweat and fear.

For though we must first find worth within ourselves, it will be incomplete until we see it reflected in our lover's eyes.

His right hand reached out and touched the side of her face.

"Let's go."

9.

Alyssa drove. They'd found the key for her car in the ignition. The slipstream blew away the smells of piss, death and decay still clinging to her and slowly cleaned out the residues inside her nostrils. Ray, slumped in the seat beside her, stared up at the blue sky, his eyes hidden behind a pair of wraparound shades he'd found in the farmhouse.

"Where are we going?" she asked; loudly, so she could be heard over the noise of the car and the wind.

He shook his head. "I don't know. There's nowhere we *can* go." He levered himself into a more upright position.

"Lys?"

"What?"

"Will you please hear me out now?"

"If you're going to ask me to let you go off by yourself—forget it!"

"I'll be wanted for murder. This time they have an eyewitness."

"It was self-defense!"

He shook his head. "You know that. I know that. But Debbie isn't going to tell it like that."

"Then *we* have to tell them the truth."

"And they're going to believe whom? Lys, you're a lawyer, damnit! You know which way this thing is going to go." He touched her arm. "Lys, I *know* what you're thinking. But think again! Don't fuck up your life."

She braked violently. The car came to a skidding halt in a cloud of choking dust. The wind caught it and mercifully blew it away before they had to breathe too much of it.

Alyssa jammed the automatic into 'P' and turned to Ray. "Listen. Mr. Shannon—and listen good! There's nothing that could possibly fuck up with my life! Nothing. Get it?

"You wanna know why? Because it *was* already fucked up. I just didn't know it. *I* was fucked up. In fact, in a lot of ways I was so close to my 'other' that it's really scary. A few minor differences here and there, but underneath it was pretty much the same thing. A shallow, opportunist bitch, with the mental scope of a litigation lawyer and the sense of perspective of a lettuce. A few more ethical constraints than the alternative 'me', but that's about all.

"And then…this…happened. Whatever 'this' is! But it happened. Bang! Not the way I planned, of course! Hell, how could *anybody* plan something like this?

"But there it is. And then I almost got killed—again! And the only good thing in this whole shit—the only thing that's not gone wrong—is *us*. And now you're asking me to just throw this away? To return to my old fucked-up existence? For what? So I can litigate again? Go back to Horrie and suck up to priapic clients? Literally?"

He was visibly taken aback by her outburst. "But…"

"But what? But the cops are after you? Hey, who gives a shit? I certainly don't. After what I've just been through…

"Look, if we're smart about this we probably *can* get away. We'll get ourselves a couple of forged passports and leave the country. The world's big. We'll find somewhere. We're smart cookies. We can start somewhere else."

She could see that she was winning this. Good! Because she wasn't going to let *anything* screw this one up.

She leaned over and wrapped her arms around his neck. Her lips found his and she put everything she couldn't tell him in words into that kiss.

"Don't—you—ever—leave—me," she said, half laughing, half sobbing, in between kissing and tonguing him and their teeth crunching together and the whole thing getting totally out of hand.

He pulled back to get some air. She saw that he was grinning.

"I wouldn't dare," he whispered.

It was about then that she heard the sirens.

10.

'Tell them the truth.'

Alyssa found it hard to. There *had* to be a way to make this look less like an execution. But that's what Ray wanted, and he deserved it that she respected his wish.

"Shannon said 'no'?" Schneider, the creep, enquired. "What did he mean?"

"*Mr*. Shannon to you," she said testily.

"Please," Carter said reasonably, "answer the question."

"What do you think he meant?" she retorted. "What's so difficult about understanding 'no'? Are you one of those guys who thinks 'no' means 'maybe' or something?"

Carter's voice crispened just a trifle. "Ms. Weaver, I'm just trying to establish the truth."

"Then ask Ray. He'll tell you what he meant."

Carter sighed. "Let me rephrase this: what did *you* think he might have meant?"

"What he said! McTierney had just told us that he was going to send his men after us to have us killed. Ray said 'no'. Sounds pretty clear to me."

"And he said it again?"

"Yes. And again."

"Like he was thinking about it?"

They were going to try and make this into murder! Not just manslaughter.

'Tell them the truth.'

How can I? They're going to lock you up for life!

"Like he was making the most difficult decision of his life," she said, her voice so brittle that it felt like it was going to crack.

She bit down on her lower lip to stop her eyes from watering up, and shook her head.

"You stupid fuckers," she told them, putting all the venom she could into those three words. "You know *nothing*. Nothing. All you want is a second shot at an innocent man."

"Ms. Weaver..." Carter began.

Alyssa shook her head and looked at Frank. "I've nothing more to say to you."

In the corridor Frank shook his head. "Wanna tell me what happened to Alyssa Weaver?"

Her head snapped around. "What do you mean?"

"Just what I said. What happened to you? There's a definite mismatch between the Alyssa I know and whoever's in your skin right now."

She stopped and stared at him for a moment. How could he know?

Then she realized that he was speaking figuratively. Of course he was. How could it be otherwise?

"That Alyssa Weaver has ceased to exist."

Literally. At least I think so.

"What happened?" Frank wondered. "Early midlife crisis—or just confrontation with extinction?"

"All of that. And more."

Nuovo stopped at the intersection of two corridors. "I've got to go that way. They're going to do Ray in a few minutes."

"Tell him I'm..."

She hesitated, reluctant to allow another into the intimacy between Ray and herself.

"Tell him I love him."

Frank Nuovo nodded and looked at her closely. " 'And more', huh?"

"Yeah."

Frank would never know how much more.

11.

Lieutenant Carter pressed the 'record' button, stated the time of day and the names of those attending. He leaned back against the metal of his chair.

"Mr. Shannon: what exactly happened after the members of Jack McTierney's gang departed the farmhouse."

Ray cast a quick glance and Frank Nuovo, whose face was a thundercloud of disapproval.

"Don't say *anything*," had been his advice. "Anything you say *will* be used against you, believe you me. Never *for* you. And silence is definitely golden. Hell, you tell your story right on your day in the witness box and they won't even *think* of believing Debbie's contorted version."

"What do you mean by 'right'?" Ray asked.

"The truth by itself is hardly ever sufficient," Frank said dryly. "But told the right way; with the appropriate turns of phrase; the right inflections at the right places; a pause where it should be; a tremor of indecision as if of a pain too great to bear...

"Tell it right and the truth will suddenly assume the nature of an irresistible force."

Ray, after considering the matter at some length, had decided to ignore Frank's advice. The reasons for this were clear and simple.

The first was, that the only way in which his and Lys's testimony would hold up compared against the other's, the only way in which it could never be assaulted or shredded or confused or contradicted or taken to pieces and reassembled, was if they both told exactly what they remembered. And if there was one thing Lys and he shared—apart from their mutual affection—it was the synchronism of their memories.

The second reason was that, to Ray's mind, the truth in this instance had the virtue of simplicity. Any lies, divagations or obfuscations, would only complicate what was a limpid state of affairs.

He had killed McTierney in self-defense and that was that. It didn't matter that he *felt* like a murderer—that he felt like it even now, or maybe especially now that he had gained a few hours distance between himself and the event. The chain of causality was no less valid because he'd killed McTierney in response to a believable threat that would only have been realized in the future. *Any* act of self-defense was directed toward the future; whether it was immediately following the act or whether it was days, weeks, or even years in the future.

And that's how he told it into the tape-recorder. Simply and succinctly.

"Did it not occur to you," Carter asked, after Ray had finished his statement, "that Jack McTierney may have been making threats he could never have realized?"

"No," Ray answered. "McTierney believed it. There was no doubt he did. And, unless the man was suffering from severe delusions, one would have to suppose that he probably had good reason to believe it to be true."

Schneider, Carter's sleazy sidekick, shook his head. "Mr. Shannon, can you explain to us why Jack McTierney saw fit to threaten you in such a way? He was cuffed to the bed. He could not hurt you in any way. He must have considered that making such threats would cause you to react in exactly the way you claim you did."

"Maybe he did. I doubt it. He was not a happy man at the time. He'd just been made a fool of in front of his men. A man who he thought of as a total idiot and wimp, had stuck a gun in his face and forced him into this humiliating position. This was probably meant to give him some kind of satisfaction.

"And if he considered it... Well, I suppose he had made up his mind that, despite my surprising behavior, I simply wasn't the type to kill somebody. Not in cold blood."

Ray saw Frank cringe.

"Was it 'in cold blood'?" Carter asked Ray.

"Self-defense. I don't know how 'cold' my blood was. But my brain was functioning perfectly adequately, thank you very much. The man told me—and he believed it, and I believed him implicitly—that he would see to it that my lover and I would be killed. Period."

He shrugged. "Did I know what I was doing?

"I did. I weighed the value of our lives—of the lives of innocent people—against the life of the man who was going to take them away from us. For me it was the same as if he had been pointing a loaded gun at us.

"I made a choice that our lives were more valuable."

"Would you say," Carter asked, "that this was a conscious and considered choice on your part?"

"It was informed, conscious, and considered. And, given the same circumstance, I would probably make exactly the same decision."

Ray saw Frank cringing again.

"Your wife tells a very different story," Schneider said.

Ray smiled thinly and without humor. "I can imagine. Has she at least admitted that it was McTierney who had Ron Hadlow killed?"

"Not in as many words."

"So, I'm still a suspect for that killing as well?"

Carter leaned forward and steepled his fingers, bringing their tips to his mouth. "Officially, yes," he admitted. "However, there's little doubt in my mind that you will be cleared of that charge."

"What Debbie's version of how it happened?"

"That's not..." Schneider began, but Carter cut him off.

"According to her," he said, "there were no threats. You executed McTierney in cold blood."

Schneider looked at his superior with an expression of surprise. Carter ignored him.

"We just want the truth, Mr. Shannon. Whatever you think about us; that *is* our ultimate goal."

Ray shrugged. "Sure—but meanwhile you locking me up, right?"

Carter nodded. "Sorry."

Schneider made no effort to conceal his incomprehension of Carter's kid-glove treatment of Ray.

"The arraignment's at ten," Frank told Ray. "We'll ask for bail."

"I'll be talking to the Assistant DA later," Carter said. "I doubt she'll oppose it. I certainly won't recommend it."

Schneider grimaced like he was sucking on a lemon.

Frank asked for a few moments alone with his client. The officers departed.

"How's Lys?" Ray asked the lawyer.

"She's fine. She's free."

Ray exhaled sharply. "Good."

"She sends her...love."

The way Frank hesitated made Ray look up.

Frank gave him a wry grin. He shook his head. "You're one lucky s.o.b. you know that? Have you got any idea what some guys would give to hear her say that?"

"Maybe I do."

12.

They stuck him into a cell at the central station, together with a couple of youthful gang-members, a spaced-out drug addict, and a pimp, who tried to hawk his whores to Ray even in the cell.

Fortunately, the pimp was the worst of the lot. When he enquired what they had him in for, Ray shrugged and said "murder".

"First or second degree?" the creep wanted to know.

"Haven't made up their mind yet."

One of the youths looked up. "That sucks," he said.

Ray eyed him, wondering what he meant. Did it 'suck' that he was in here for murder? That he had committed it? Or that they hadn't made up their minds?

He decided to forego probing the matter further for fear of what he might find.

Evening came. They were served an adequate meal by an officer with a beer-gut and arms the size of Ray's quads. The styrofoam tablets were slipped into the cell through an horizontal frame welded into the vertical bars. Airline food, Ray decided. Or the closest thing to it. Slightly better possibly. He found it a bit off-putting to eat in a cell the rear of which featured a lidless stainless-steel toilet and hand-basin, but decided to be stoic about it. If nothing, it was a novel experience. One he could have done without, to be sure, but there it was.

Because of some stupid regulation he did not get to see Lys, and that bothered him. He bit down on his disappointment and got on with the business of dealing with his situation. The lack of sleep on the previous night helped. After dinner he lay down on his cot and went out like a light.

We woke up with the sound of footsteps. The cell-door slid aside. Through the haze of sleep Ray saw the fat prison guard and Lieutenant Carter.

Carter stopped and looked down on him. "Wanna leave?"

The last vestiges of sleep blew away. Ray jerked up and swung his legs off the cot.

"Well?" Carter asked.

"I can *go*?"

Carter nodded. "You're a free man. Courtesy of one very sleepy police lieutenant and one equally tired Assistant DA."

He reached out, took Ray's arm, and pulled him up. Ray, mute with surprise, gaped at him.

"I'll tell you about it in my office," Carter said.

Ray retrieved his belongings and signed for them. The barred doors clonked shut behind him. Carter took him up to his office. He pointed at a chair. "Have a seat."

Ray did; still dazed. "What happened?" he asked. "Does Lys know?"

Carter shook his head. "No. Just you. I haven't even called your lawyer." He grinned broadly. Ray was amazed at how relaxed Carter was.

What had happened?

"I wish I could claim that I haven't called Frank because I don't want to disturb his sleep. But it ain't so. Truth is, I just wanted to tell you myself. One of the small pleasures of the job."

He leaned his arms on the desk and looked at Ray. "I want you to listen to something." He retrieved a small cassette player from a drawer and placed in on the table. "Understand: this is heavily processed sound. The original was nowhere as clear. In fact it was virtually unintelligible. But we have a very good forensic lab."

Despite the enhancements Ray had to lean forward to understand the words. Then he knew what it was. There was him, telling McTierney that the rats had left the ship—followed by the man's threats. He heard himself say 'no' three times. Then the shot. A pause, followed by his exchange with Debbie. Then—silence.

"How..."

Carter grinned like a Cheshire cat. "You left your cellphone active, so we could locate you—remember?" He stopped the tape. "Confronted with this recording, your wife decided to change her version of the story. As a bonus she also admitted to being aware of a plan to kill Ron Hadlow—a plan in which she played a peripheral role. Just how peripheral I'm probably going to spend some time trying to figure out. I fancy that, when all is known, it's going to be sordid, cupid, and sickeningly familiar."

Ray shook his head. "I don't want to know, thanks."

Carter took a deep breath.

"Wise man! Anyway, prompted by my urgings and Mr. Nuovo's behind-the-scenes machinations, the Assistant DA listened to the recording. Mind you, she wasn't pleased when I phoned her at an intimate dinner with the current beau— but what the hell...

"Despite her displeasure, however, she decided that there was no point in pursuing the matter. Her superiors chose to agree. A wise move if you ask me. Fact is in that there isn't a jury that would *dream* of convicting you for what you've done. On the contrary. With the current mood in this town, and a murder rate of over one per *hour* in Atlanta alone, they'll probably ask for your autograph. They're almost certain to dismiss the state's argument that your killing McTierney was not self-defense. In the strict term of the law it wasn't—but the law is an ass, and prosecuting you would be a waste of effort, money and time. We've got our hands full with too many shit-serious cases. Frank Nuovo could—and probably would—use the media to blow this up into a major political embarrassment for the prosecutor's office. To find a jury that wasn't biased in your favor would be virtually impossible."

He leaned back. "So—case closed. You're a free man. There's some paperwork, but Frank can take care of that tomorrow. As for you, however, there's no point in keeping you here any longer."

He smiled thinly and shook his head. "You know, I'm glad."

"Thanks."

"You're one lucky s.o.b."

"You're the second person to tell me that today."

"Well, you are. For the record, I think what you did—when you went after your... friend...that was stupid. Capital letters. Stupid and irresponsible."

"I know. I knew it then."

"So—why did you do it?"

Ray considered Carter for a few moments.

"Lieutenant, when have you last been in love?"

Carter nodded, as if he'd just seen a suspicion confirmed.

"Off the record, Shannon..."

"Ray."

"Ray. Off the record... I *do* think that what you did was stupid. A part of me also tells me that you *murdered* McTierney."

He pulled a face.

"Self-defense? It's a strange, nebulous thing. What makes it justifiable? Who knows? Who dares to draw the line and say 'this is where it begins', or what it is that constitutes 'immediacy'?"

He sighed. "Another part of me wants to pat you on the back and say 'well done'. I am a cop, so I can't let that part get too strong—because otherwise I won't be able to function anymore. Still, that other parts admires you. You did what you had to. The old thing: protecting your mate, no matter the consequences. Primal stuff. Beyond the mere confines of the laws of an orderly society." He grinned ruefully. "Truth is, I'd be one of those people wanting the autograph."

He shrugged and stood up. "And now go home." He stretched out his hand and Ray shook it.

"Thanks for looking for the truth, Lieutenant."

Carter smiled. "We aim to please."

Ray turned to leave.

"Give Ms. Weaver my regards," Carter said to his retreating back. "Tell her she's a very lucky woman."

13.

The cab dropped him outside Lys's apartment. He hesitated, wondering if he should ask the cabbie to wait. But then he paid the fare and a generous tip and sent the man on his way. If he had to, he could take Lys's car.

The apartment block was quiet. A mild breeze wafted across from the north. Ray stood still for a moment, closing his eyes and savoring the simple pleasure of being a free man.

When he opened them again he was still a free man. So, he guessed, he wasn't dreaming.

He walked up the steps to Lys's and Susan's apartment and pressed the bell-knob beside the door. He could hear a faint chime somewhere inside. Then, after a few breaths or so, he imagined furtive footsteps. An eye on the other side of the peephole. And then—and this time he wasn't imagining! a small, excited exclamation. A rattle as a security chain was unhooked.

The door opened. She stood there, barefooted, in a knee-long white T-shirt, gaping at him. He noticed distantly that the ankle-brace was gone.

"Ray?" she whispered. She made a small, inarticulate sound and took a limping step in his direction. He caught her and hugged her to him, immersing himself in the scent and the feel of her, and still not quite believing it—though he knew it was true…and that they were indeed two very lucky people.

Then the whole, long, arduous day faded into insignificance in the face of the overwhelming reality of the present.

Friday

1.

When she woke, the memories of the previous day seemed unreal. The whole ordeal was like something from a time long ago. The night had put such a distance between it and her that, though she remembered everything, the events were simply were unable to reach her emotionally. The only part of it that remained real and present was what happened last night, when she'd opened that door, fearing that she was just dreaming.

Alyssa jerked. For one dreadful instant she wasn't sure…

Then she sensed his presence in the bed beside her and relaxed. She levered herself up on one arm and looked down at Ray's sleeping face. The day-old stubble along his cheeks and jaw-line; the depilated scalp, where tiny tips of hair were beginning to emerge from their roots again. Not a lot, to be sure, and there never would be. But it was coming back.

His breath came evenly and softly, and Alyssa fought the urge to wake him—plus doing a whole host of other things with and to him. After what he'd been through he needed the rest. So she just smiled to herself and slowly slipped off the bed and picked up her T-shirt from the floor, where it lay amid the tangle of Ray's clothes; which had been discarded there last night when they'd tumbled onto the bed and pretty much forgot about just about everything else.

She slipped the T-shirt over herself and quietly eased out of the room. At the kitchen table she found Susan, dressed to go to work, finishing a bowl of cereal.

"Good morning," Susan said and gave her a crooked smile. "Had a good night?"

Alyssa tried to keep a straight face but she just couldn't help herself.

"Yeah," she said and sat down on the chair opposite Susan.

"I guess that means he's in the clear, huh?"

"Completely."

Susan grinned. "And you're not coming to work today…"

"No way."

"Are you ever gonna come back?"

Alyssa sighed. "I don't think so. Something…."

She shrugged helplessly.

Susan snorted. "I'd say!"

"Do you understand what I mean?"

Susan shook her head. "'Understand'? No. 'Respect'? Yes. You've been through a lot of shit in the last week. I guess that just changes some people. I didn't think anything would faze *you*—and I certainly wouldn't have dreamt of some guy being the root cause of it all! but I guess I was wrong."

She twisted her mouth into a crooked smile. "Things happen, huh?"

"They're good things," Alyssa said. "At least this part is."

Susan stood up and took her dish to the sink where she rinsed it off before placing it into the dishwasher.

"What shall I tell Horrie?"
"Tell him to distribute my clients over the rest of the firm."
"He's going to shit himself."
"Do I look worried?"
Susan came over and gave her a hug. "You'll be fine?"
"Of course."
"Well, see you tonight. Or not—as the case may be. Just let me know what you're doing."

When Susan had gone Alyssa sat at the table for another few minutes, thinking. Her ruminations were interrupted by the beeping of her cellphone on the counter between kitchen and lounge. She jumped up hoping wanting to get it before it woke Ray. But she forgot about her ankle which twisted just enough to send a sharp pain up her leg. Biting her teeth together she hobbled to the phone and grabbed it.

"Ms. Weaver? It's Dr. Lopez."
Oh shit!
"Look, I'm so sorry," she said, supporting herself with one arm on the counter. "I know you were expecting us yesterday."
"Yes," he agreed dryly. "I suppose there's a good reason why you didn't show."
"There is, Dr. Lopez—believe you me. To say that we were 'indisposed" would be understating the case. I'm really sorry we didn't let you know, but it would have been… difficult."
"I daren't ask for fear of what you might tell me this time! Is everything all right?"
"It is now." She smiled to herself as she said that. It was good being able to say it—and for it to be true.
"I have a free slot just after lunch," Lopez told her.
"I'll ask Ray."
"Call me as soon as you can."

Alyssa put the phone down and limped back toward the bedroom. Ray stood in the door. When he saw her he took a quick step. She wrapped her arms around his neck. "Good morning, Mr. Shannon," she said archly.
"That it is," he agreed and kissed her. Despite the pain in her ankle, the kiss triggered off all sorts of things.
"Can you carry me?" she whispered in his ear.
He could. And the pain didn't seem to matter.

2.

Ray lounged around the apartment with a towel wrapped around his midriff as his clothes were washed and dried. The towel had a tendency to come undone. Which suited her just fine. It helped to pass the time.

They decided to take up Lopez on his offer.
"I've got to know," Ray told her.
"It's not going to make any difference," she said reasonably. "It's not as if we could do anything about the situation."
"I've still got to know."
"That's going to get you into trouble one day."

"Maybe," he said, and laughed silently. "But I've always thought that it's more likely going to get you *out* of it."

She took his clothes out of the drier and threw them in his direction. "We'd better get going."

3.

"Your prediction didn't come true." Lopez pointed at the graph. "The phase delay got shorter. In fact it's almost too small for the equipment to resolve."

The discovery disquieted Ray more than he dared to admit to himself. He glanced through the one-way glass at Alyssa, still stuck inside the surreal hood of Dr. Lopez' machine.

He took the graphs from Lopez held them next to the only comparison data they had. "We need a third reading. Two points aren't enough for anything but a linear theory—and I've never believed in linear theories."

Lopez nodded. "Neither have I. Certainly not in the life-sciences."

"Doesn't look like we're going to get another reading either," Ray said regretfully. "Unless you refine your experimental protocol."

"Sure—give us a few months," the tech said dryly.

Somehow Ray had the feeling that this was definitely more time than they had.

Time for what? What was he thinking anyway? Something was bothering him, but he didn't know what.

His theory had come crashing down. There was no positive correlation between the phase-shift and the time he spent in this merged time-line, or whatever it was.

Presently Lys's experiment came to an end. The hood retracted from her head and the nurse disconnected a battery of leads on various parts of her anatomy. The tech did his magic on the computer. Ray wasn't surprised to see that Lys's results were identical to his own. Whatever was happening, was happening to both of them.

"Any more suggestions?" Lopez asked him.

Ray shook his head. "Let's do another scan on Monday. Just to confirm that by that time there'll be nothing left."

Unless the phase shift passes through zero and becomes negative.

Now, why did that seem to be significant? Try as he might, he couldn't get his head around it.

Lopez agreed. "I suspect you're right." He looked at them over the top of his half-frame reading glasses. "But I still would like to continue our little project."

Ray looked at Alyssa. "For a while," she agreed.

Lopez nodded, as if he had expected the reply.

4.

"What's the matter?" Lys asked him when they walked to her car.

She was using him as a support and he liked it. It made him feel...whole.

Funny that. He didn't quite understand it, but there it was. Whatever this was, wherever it was going to lead to, he'd follow it.

"I don't know," he said truthfully.

"This really worries you, doesn't it?"

"Yes."

She tightened her arm around his shoulder. "You're obviously the obsessive-compulsive type."

"I just don't like it when things don't make sense."

She laughed softly. "The man's forty-something and he *still* hasn't figured it out!"

"I guess not…"

"What're we going to do now?" she asked.

"Haven't really thought that far. Start a new life, I suppose."

She stopped and looked at him. "Does that mean what I think it means?"

"Depends on what you're thinking."

"Us."

"So am I."

"Good."

He pulled her around so she faced him. "You and me, babe."

"That's the general idea."

He found himself smiling broadly. He just couldn't help it.

"You're turning me into a very reckless individual?"

"I've noticed," she said and kissed him. "A regular James Bond."

"OK then," he said. "Let's do it. But first we have to get my car from the airport."

"I'd forgotten about that."

"I haven't."

They drove south to the airport and Ray reclaimed his Toyota from the parking lot. A short time later they were heading north again along the interstate. Presently they came to the junction with 285 and continued north along it's eastern arc.

"Let's go to my place," Ray had said. "I'll fill up a suitcase with stuff. Debbie can have the rest. I don't want any memories."

Now he was following Lys's red convertible in the center lane. Her hair, unconfined, fluttered in the slipstream. Every now and then she turned her head to look in her mirror and gave him a wave. Ray waved back, thinking that they'd come a long way since…

…

And then he knew.

He looked at his watch—which once had shown the time of wherever he'd come from, but which he had reset to the world that now constituted his reality.

2:51 p.m.

One week minus two hours.

That's how it had started.

He considered the traffic on the freeway.

Treacle.

Not quite as bad as 'last' Friday, but close.

Him following Lys in the center lane…

About to pass…

…Ray glanced up to the right and saw the unmistakable outline of the glass-and-steel facade of the office complex in the center of Halcyon Business Park.

One week minus two hours…

A shiver ran through him, his heart started beating in his throat, and his stomach was a dark pit...

...because the on-ramp had *two* lanes.

Ray took a deep breath and forced himself to calm. He noticed distantly that Lys had picked up her cellphone and was holding it to her ear.

He honked at her and flashed his lights. She looked back in the mirror and shrugged. He honked again and put his hand together above the wheel, making a 'time-out' signal. He picked up his own phone from the passenger seat and waved it at her.

She make a signal of acquiescence. A short while later she took the phone away from her ear and pushed a button. A few seconds later his own phone beeped.

"Ray? What's the matter?"

What *was* the matter? Ray thought he knew but he couldn't be sure. And what he thought scared him.

Fighting back his despair and uncertainty he forced himself to calm.

"Who were you calling?"

"The office. I was just about to tell Horrie that I was going to be in first thing tomorrow to talk to him. About leaving the firm..."

Ray didn't really hear what she said. Just her voice at the other end of that phone was enough. For now.

"Lys, what did you say to me Tuesday morning after we woke up?"

"Ray, what..."

"*Please*!"

"I...I think...I told you that we'd have to do...you know...more often... Something like that."

Ray exhaled sharply.

"Lys, please listen to me now, OK? Don't ask questions because there isn't the time. Just do what I say!"

"What's wrong?" He could see her look at him in her mirror.

"Maybe nothing," he said. "Maybe everything.

"But I think we can make it right...if you do what I tell you now—OK? No more questions!"

"What do you want me to do?"

What *did* he want her to do? What could she do that would ensure that...

"Talk to me, Lys. Talk and don't stop talking until I tell you to."

"Just talk? What about?"

"About us. Everything you know about us. Everything you remember about the first time we met..."

There was a small exclamation at the other end. "Ray!"

She knew! At least a part of it. He could hear it in her voice.

"*Talk* to me, Lys. Tell me everything you remember. About the accident, the trip to the hospital, the evening at *El Gitano*, the next day. Everything that involves us meeting, and interacting, and talking. And please—*please*!—don't stop until I say so!"

"Now?"

"Now!"

In halting tones she began...

Ray didn't listen to what she said. It didn't really matter. He just wanted her to focus on their common experiences. Maintain the bond between them and hold onto what she knew of him.

As for himself, he just wanted to hear her voice. That was the connection. The cellphones were their life-line. Without them, they might just lose each other in...

...what?

What was it? A point of instability in the flow of parallel universes and time? A node where things could happen that couldn't happen anywhere or any*when* else?

Whatever, they had to keep that bond alive when they passed through that segment of time. The mind—whatever it was—*did* have something to do with it. It wasn't just physics. A week ago they had come together because they'd made a connection—and because, just at the right moment, their wishes and dreams complemented in a creative synergy. This time they would have to make sure that they would not be torn apart by the same forces that brought them together. Nothing else must be in heir minds but their awareness of who and what the other was and what they shared and what bonded them.

Her voice in his ear continued. Steadier and more fluid now, as she found her pace.

Now he had to do his part. Listen to her, at the same time as *he* remembered. Holding tightly onto his end of the connection between them.

But the situation was not complete. Because a week ago there had been another contingency...

Ray thought back.

The time...

He looked to his right and, through a gap between cars, saw a blue Ford two lanes to the right, trying to change into the lane next to him. The driver...

Shit!

The driver was of the card-players. And the passenger was his buddy from the farmhouse.

It's never over.

Jack McTierney's former subordinates had no intention of leaving any witnesses around to tell tales.

Lys's voice in his ear...

The meeting at *El Gitano*...

The blue Ford eased into the lane next to him.

Ray looked in his own mirror, trying to gauge the distance between himself and the cars behind.

"Lys! *Brake*! Now!"

At the same time he took his foot off the accelerator and hit the brake pedal.

There was a squeal of rubber, underneath and behind him. A blast from several horns. The surprised faces of the men in the Ford beside him drew ahead, carried along by the stream of traffic—reacting too late to do anything effective.

Lys's car skidded as she braked, but she controlled it.

"Follow me!" Ray floored the accelerator, veered recklessly into the lane beside him. More squealing tires and blaring horns. He pulled back into the center lane ahead of Lys.

The red convertible stayed close behind him..

At his ear was only static. Ray's heart sank. He looked into his mirror; saw her staring at in his direction.

"Lys?"
"Ray, what..."
"Keep talking!"
"About what?"
"Anything."

Ray, keeping an eye out for the blue Ford, forced himself to relax. The traffic had resumed its normal flow.

It would never be over.

Not unless...

Ray wondered if they were still in that critical stretch of time where things could... happen. If they were, then maybe if he...

Why not? It had worked before. Not that he'd known then, but it had worked anyway. What if, in these fleeting moments, he actually had *choices*?

Think!

Three wishes from the fairy.

No—make that...seven!

Lucky number. He could keep seven wishes in his head; circulating them, remembering, imagining them being more than just daydreams...

Lys's voice in his ear...

Telling him about the gallery...

I wish...

...

Lys's voice in his ear...

The kiss in the car...

A sign appeared overhead announcing an upcoming exit.

"Lys?"

She stopped talking.

"Let's get off here. And keep talking!"

He threaded the Toyota through the lanes, making sure that she was behind him every step of the way. They made it to the right lane just in time. As soon as they were off the interstate Ray pulled up on the grass strip on the side of the road. Even before Lys had stopped he was out of the car. By the time she'd pulled up he was at her door.

She took the phone off her ear and stared at him.

"Ray?"

He bent over, took her face in his hands, and kissed her.

"Lys, who was the first President of the United States?"

She looked at him strangely.

"Jackson."

"What's the name of Lieutenant Carter's creepy sidekick?"

"Schneider."

Tears of relief shot to his eyes. He just couldn't help it. It was all too much.

"Ray," she said softly and reached out to pull him down to her. He buried his face in her hair. He was so weak with the suddenly released tension that he thought his legs would buckle.

"Phew!" he said when he could talk again.

"It happened again, didn't it?" she asked tonelessly.

Ray opened the car-door and hunkered down on the ground beside her. He took her hand.

"It certainly did," he said.

"But we're all right, aren't we?" Her eyes were begging him for reassurance.

He smiled. "I think so."

She sighed. "What actually went on there?"

"I think we...caught up with ourselves," he said. "We passed through the same instant again. Or something very similar."

"And then?"

"I don't know," he said slowly. "Last time we were jerked...wherever. This time..."

He straightened. "I think I know. I *hope* I know." He looked at the cars streaming past. "Let's go home and find out."

"'Home?'"

"'Home'."

5.

What did he mean? But she could see that she wasn't going to get anything more out of him. There was a suppressed smile on his face, mixed with a bit of anxiety and uncertainty.

"Why all this stuff on the interstate?" she asked.

When he told her she went cold.

"Don't worry," he said and ran his fingers through her hair. The touch relaxed her.

"If I'm right," he said, "then we won't have to worry about these people anymore."

"Right about what?"

What was he talking about? These guys would *never* leave them alone.

He bent down and kissed her. "I promise—I'll tell you everything. But first, let's see if I got it right this time."

She yielded. Reluctantly.

He got back into his car and drove off. She followed closely on his heels.

Finally she figured out where he was heading: to his house...

'Home'?

Trust, Lys.

She sighed and tried to wind herself down from her hyper-tense state.

There's always something else. Only a couple of hours ago everything seemed to have fallen into place. And then this...

They pulled into a fairly new subdivision. Ray didn't seem to certain where to go. He drove slowly, checking the numbers on the letterboxes. At least he seemed to have found what he was looking for and stopped outside an expansive single-storey wooden house, which distinguished itself from those around it by being stained rather than painted.

Ray got out and, somewhat tentatively and, looking around with a slightly furtive air, walked over to the mailbox. He pulled a few letters out of the box and checked them. A broad smile spread over his face.

She opened the door of her car and heaved herself out of the seat. He came up quickly, placed the letters on the hood of her car, and helped her extricate her still-sore ankle from the car.

"Be careful."

"Fusspot," she said affectionately.

She looked at the letters on the hood. His gaze followed hers and she saw him grin. He picked up the letters and gave the top one to her.

"For you, I think," he said.

"For me?" She looked at the front of the envelope.

'Mrs. Alyssa Shannon, 3560 Huron Circle,...'

'Shannon?'

"Shannon?!"

He grinned like a little boy who'd just stolen some cookies and gotten away with it. Alyssa stared at him; then at the house; the street; and back at Ray.

He shrugged. "Sue me."

"We're *married*?"

Damn! She hadn't meant it to come out like that.

His face fell. "I hope you don't mind..."

Of course, I don't mind! But what did you do??

"I think it was an...instability," he said, as if answering her unasked question. "A point in time and space where everything hangs in the balance—and where, if you push the right way, you can do just about anything. A stretch in time where all your wishes can come true. Literally.

"Last time, when we reached that point—from wherever or whenever—we didn't know, and so we had no control. But this time..."

He shrugged and grimaced. "I'm sorry I couldn't explain...but it all went too fast— and I only figured it out in the last moment."

"We're *married*?" she repeated.

"Is that OK? If you don't want this we'll..."

Don't tease him so! He doesn't deserve this!

She pulled him to her and wrapped her arms around his neck. "More than OK, you idiot!" she whispered. "I'm just sorry I seemed to have missed our wedding."

The tight muscles in his shoulders relaxed. "Well," he muttered, "so did I."

Over his shoulder she looked at his—their!—house. "Can we go inside?" She still couldn't believe it. Probably wouldn't for a long time to come.

Or maybe she would. Maybe, with all the craziness of the last week, it wouldn't be so hard after all. It was amazing how the mind could adapt to even the most extraordinary circumstances.

He let her go, reached into her car, and withdrew the key from the ignition. He inspected the other keys on the key ring. "That one looks about right."

With one arm around his shoulder she limped to the house. Ray tried the key.

It worked.

Ray turned to her. "We may have missed our wedding, but I can still carry you over the threshold."

"I'd like that."

Our house...

He picked her up and took her inside. And, as she looked around, she saw that it *was* her house. It felt right. It had the atmosphere of 'home'. And it had her things in it.

Like the drawing of the beach scene she'd done at high-school; and the rug that used to be (When? Where? Had it ever been? It was all so confusing!) in her bedroom in the apartment she shared with Susan.

Susan!

"What about Susan?"

"What about her?"

"Is she still 'here'? Wherever that is…"

Ray frowned. "I don't know. I suppose so. I didn't really think about her when I…you know…when I made my wishes. There's no reason she shouldn't be. She works with you, right?"

Alyssa tightened her arms around his neck.

"What *did* you wish for?"

He grinned. "I wished that we were married—and that everything that had to do with Debbie had never happened. Meaning that Jack McTierney, if he exists somewhere in this world, has absolutely nothing to do with us. And Debbie, though she's probably around somewhere, may not even know I exist.

"And then…" He fell silent, looking around the house, as if seeing it for the first time. Which was probably the case.

"And then?" she asked.

He looked at her. "I also wished that we'd be the kind of people who would never lose sight of each other."

When she finished kissing him they were both very much out of breath.

"I better put you down," he said.

Carefully he lowered her to the ground. She sat down on a rustic-looking, very comfortable sofa and pulled him down beside her.

"What else?" she asked.

"What else what?" he said innocently. Too innocently. Teasing her.

"Ray!"

He shrugged. "Well, there were a few more tweaks and adjustments. Nothing world-shattering—because I don't think I could have believed or imagined it well enough. But it's stuff that would affect us. Our future. Our lives."

"Like?…"

"I don't even know if they worked."

"Tell me anyway."

"Do you really want to know?"

"You bet!"

"Now?"

"Why not?"

"You sure this can't wait?"

Of course it could.

Relax, girl!

She leaned against Ray and closed her eyes.

"Do we have kids?"

"Not yet."

"Good."

She wondered what other 'tweaks and adjustments' Ray had considered necessary and possible. He'd tell her, of course. And, if experience was anything to go by, they would be most interesting and imaginative.

Later.

"Let's have a look at the bedroom."

Saturday

1.23 a.m.

Ray awoke with a jerk. He found himself lying on his side, bathed in sweat. His heart was beating like after a major exertion or shock.

The dream…

The…thing…brushing him with its presence—only to be pulled away by the slipstream, flailing and spinning…

Gone into oblivion now, but not without leaving behind an abject fear.

Disorientation!

Where, of the many places he could be, was he truly? How much was dream?

Ray rolled onto his back. Turning his head to one side he could see the gray rectangle of a large window, patterned by the folds of the curtain, highlighted by a light outside. The moon? Something about the sharp shadows cast by the fabric's folds told him that it was.

Analysis. Even in moments like this it behooved one to ensure that the world made sense; that everything hung together.

A movement on the bed beside him. A softness touched his left arm. A warm, sticky body, its scent of perspiration and love mingling with his own, slipped over his. A head covered in a rich layer of thick hair came to rest on his chest. A few strands of it tickled his face.

"Lys?"

"Hmmm?"

He let out a sigh of utter relief.

"Ray?" she asked sleepily. A hand slid along his chest and around one side of his head.

He put his arms around her and stroked her back.

"I'm here."

She wriggled, fitting herself closer to him. "Hmmm."

He closed his eyes—and immediately snapped them open again.

He remembered… And if he was wrong about *that*—

"Lys?"

"Hmmm?"

"I have to get up for a moment."

"What's the matter?"

"I just want got check something."

"Don't be long."

"I won't," he promised. She stretched and brushed a kiss on his lips; then slipped off him. Ray rolled out of the bed and padded out into the short hallway, which opened into the lounge—surprised that he didn't bump into anything on the way.

He crossed the lounge without mishap, and went into his study where he drew the curtains and turned on the lights and the desktop computer.

His watch. Where was it?

He went back across the lounge and tiptoed into the bathroom where he'd taken it off earlier in the evening. He felt around in the darkness until he found it, not daring to turn on the light here for fear of disturbing Lys. With a pounding heart he returned to the study where the computer had finished the startup cycle.

Here goes our future.

He positioned the cursor above the time display and clicked twice.

The date…

He compared it with that displayed on his watch.

Weak with relief he sat down. It would *not* happen again! They had caught up with themselves and gone on into the future…

Lys had come up behind him, quiet as a mouse. She leaned over and wrapped her arms around him.

"Everything all right?"

"It is now."

THE END